PROXIMA DREAMING

Hard Science Fiction

BRANDON Q. MORRIS

Contents

Proxima Dreaming

Brightnight 1, 3307

HE PRESSES HIS FOUR ARMS AGAINST HIS BODY, PUSHES OFF with both legs, and swims for dear life. He instinctively keeps the lids of his four eyes closed, as if he knows that the two suns would otherwise blind him. He forces himself down into the water with all his strength. His smell-skins tell him the way. He only has to follow the increasing salt concentration to reach the depths of the ocean. He won't be safe there, but definitely safer than here near the shore.

Gronolf can tell from how his skin feels that the water behind him is churning. Those are his brothers and sisters. Today they emerged from their eggs as if on command, and now they are fighting for survival. He only stands a chance if he stays in front. He can smell the blood spreading in the water. Some of his siblings failed to control their instincts. They try to fight. They tear apart the bodies of others with the claws on their swimming feet, and they in turn are ripped apart. It is a massacre one can only escape by fleeing.

How many of the seven times seven times seven will succeed? Gronolf suppresses the thought. He cannot allow himself to lose his concentration, not for a single swimming stroke! That is the only way he can be among the first to reach the depths of the ocean, where the oxygen content of the water increases and he can breathe more freely than now. He will have to survive out there for one brightnight and one darknight before he is allowed to return and become a part of the community.

Swim, swim, swim, he thinks. He pushes himself and soon falls into the magical rhythm of seven his mother taught him. He has never seen her, and so far his eyes only know the dim light that penetrated the membrane of his egg, but he remembers her voice well. Sometimes it came from nearby, and sometimes from far away, but it always seemed warm, kind, and concerned. Gronolf occasionally imagined that she only talked to him and not to the many siblings of his plex. When he returns, when he has finished his 'draght' and become an adult, taking on a new name, he will ask her whether she ever thought of him personally while she taught the secrets of life to her entire plex.

The darkness in front of his lids intensifies. Mother Sun must have just set, so Gronolf can take his first rest. He is not yet safe, but he has left the others far behind. He can only smell a few blood molecules now, but the numerous salts of the core ocean lure him ever more strongly. His gills filter breathable air from the water. He fills his swim bladder and lets himself drift to the surface. He turns on his back. His mother warned him not to open his eyes for the first time during the day, as the light of Mother Sun would have inevitably blinded him. Now he slowly raises his lids. A burning pain jolts his body. It is supposed to warn him against opening his eyes too soon, but he knows the time has come.

Then the blueness appears and practically fills his thoughts. Gronolf is surprised how intense the color seems to him, very different from the weeks inside the egg. The blue seems to be all-encompassing, but also profound. It stirs a craving in him to rise into the sky above. In his mind he suppresses his left eye and concentrates on what his right eye shows him. Father Sun is still low above the horizon. It emits a pure white that is reflected in the long waves of the ocean.

Next Gronolf calls up the image of his left eye, which looks at the other side. The sky is only slightly darker there. The blue is more impressive than any description his mother gave. On the horizon he detects black silhouettes. Are those the 'Mountains of Legends' his mother talked about? His father is supposed to be there. He is grateful to him, even though he has never seen him. His mother always praised his father profusely. Nobody, she swore, exhibited such virility, and only because of this, his plex became the largest one on the entire Birth Coast.

Gronolf holds his breath and lets his torso sink into the water. This way he can use his rear eyes to look into the direction from which he came. The flat coast is no longer visible, as he has moved too far away. Now and then he notices something flashing. That must be one of his siblings. He must not stay here too long. He uses his right touch hand to feel the muscles of his thighs. They seem to have grown noticeably since he left the egg. For the seven bubble periods of the night the nutrients from the egg will suffice, but then he has to search for fresh food—and watch out that he himself is not eaten by the creatures of the deep.

Gronolf exhales and sinks below the surface. His lids close involuntarily. The light of Father Sun barely reaches into the water. At a depth of three leg lengths, it is already pitch black. But he still has his sense of smell, which guides him on his way and warns of enemies. *Swim, swim, swim,* he tells himself, and once more falls into the efficient seven-stroke rhythm his mother described.

FIVE BUBBLE PERIODS LATER HE REALIZES HE CANNOT WAIT until the end of the night. He expended all his strength to move away as fast as possible from his competing siblings, just as his mother told him again and again. However, in doing so he has consumed his reserves. His muscles need nutrients or they will stop working. He can no longer ignore the pain indicating this fact. He can find what he needs at the bottom of the ocean. As his mother told him, nowhere in this body of water that spans the entire planet is it deeper than 30 leg lengths.

Gronolf exhales and sinks down. He hopes he has not yet reached the area of maximal depth. Down there, he was told, breathable gas becomes scarce, and it is also the realm of the carrionteeth. Their name is only half true. These carnivorous fish don't just eat carrion, but anything they can sink their teeth into. And their small brains need less oxygen, which makes them dangerous opponents in the depths. There they can swim even faster than an adult Grosnop. However, they would not dare attack a grown-up representative of his species. An adult Grosnop trained in the arts of combat can handle any animal on the planet, apart from the seacomb. Carrionteeth, it is said, only hunt at night, so he should be safe from them in the daytime.

However, if Gronolf waits until the rise of Mother Sun, his siblings will catch up and kill him. That is life. Few brothers and sisters of his plex will return to the birth beach after the end of the darknight. If there are seven of them, that is considered an especially auspicious sign—the mother who nurtured that plex is allowed to select the inseminating father for the next cycle. This is how his father—who has a high rank in the space fleet—became *his* father. A splendid career awaits Gronolf if he survives the draght. In the old times, his mother had explained, things were different. He cannot even imagine a time in which the Grosnops in their eggs possessed no spark of intelligence! How could the mothers explain to their children what they were going to face? It must have been terrible to be sent into the great massacre past the beach without any warning. Gronolf is grateful to his mother for preparing him so well.

She had also explained to him how to fill his stomach as fast as possible. In his mind he goes through the procedure:

Empty swim bladder, paddle towards the bottom, scan continually with eyes in front, roll upper belly flap inward, let lower belly flap hang out. Then he can float closely above the ocean floor and use his lower belly flap to move the organic matter growing there directly into his feeding hole. He hopes he won't encounter a carriontooth! Gronolf starts to implement his plan. He sniffs in all directions but doesn't notice anything except for slowly-rising salt content. Then he uses strong leg strokes to swim toward the ocean bottom.

A cloud of organic molecules awaits him. He cannot miss this source of food. He cautiously loosens his chest muscles. He jerks up the skin flap over his belly. He only has to relax his belly muscles and his feeding hole will open. He sinks down a bit more, orienting himself by the increasing salt content, and starts feeding. He does not know what exactly is entering his stomach, but it does not matter. A kind of sieve filters the food and separates digestible parts from indigestible. Then the first stomach closes, squeezes the food into the second stomach and pumps the water and inedibles back outside, and the whole process starts anew. Whenever the peristaltic muscles pump food into the second stomach, Gronolf experiences a pleasant feeling. This comforting, warm emotion is a new experience for him.

He is no longer alone.

Carriontooth!

The sudden realization makes his body tremble. Both of his skin flaps close involuntarily. Gronolf has to keep himself from a wild flight. If he does that, he will stand no chance against the carriontooth. The animal has tracked him down and is waiting for the best moment to strike. Gronolf has only one chance: He has to wait for the first attack of the carriontooth. The predator specializes in a rapid attack so it can spear prey with its big, sword-like tooth. Gronolf banishes all thoughts of danger from his brain. He has to concentrate on his sense of smell. If he can make himself wait until the last moment to evade the charge of the carriontooth, the attacker will shoot far past him, and he has a realistic chance of getting beyond the range where the predator can smell him. Then he would be safe.

Where is the carriontooth? Gronolf's thought swirl through his olfactory centers, which are distributed just beneath the skin all over his body. Behind him, toward the coast, he can smell only the blood of his siblings. To the left there is... a trace of iron oxide. Very strange, but no carriontooth. To the right he smells nothing but the food, rich in calcium and potassium ions. The fine hairs on his skin register changes in the water pressure. This can only mean one thing: The predator has started to move. But where does the danger come from? In front of him the smell of food becomes even more intense. What did his mother say? *The carriontooth sometimes uses camouflage... That's it!* The predator is coming from ahead!

Gronolf wants to flee immediately, but that would mean his death. The attacker can correct its course almost to the very last moment. He—the prey—must be patient... until the final instant, but not one instant longer. Gronolf trembles. *The carriontooth can feel it when you tremble,* his mother had told him, but he can't help it. It was not even 12 bubble periods ago that he left his egg, and now his life might be over? *Where should I swerve?* Would the predatory fish expect that he will try to flee? *Calm down, calm down, calm down,* he tells himself, while checking his environment for the tell-tale sign.

And there it is... Now! He kicks hard with his right leg, moving half a leg-length to the left. At the same instant he feels the water pressure on his right side briefly increase. Something swam by him very quickly. Gronolf reacts immediately. He accelerates forward, away from the predator. He puts all his strength into the swim movements, thinking of nothing but escape. Yes he still remembers to approach the surface again gradually. He has to succeed, otherwise he might as well have stayed behind to be ripped apart by his brothers and sisters! He is convinced his mother believes in him and he tells himself that she desperately wants to see him again.

Gronolf does not know for how long he has been fleeing.

His mind can only concentrate on giving commands to his legs. It is getting dark, and fog forms at the edges of his consciousness. He realizes he is approaching a line he should not cross. He must not go on. If the distance is not enough, it doesn't matter. *Stop*, he tells his legs, but, caught in a panic-fueled dance, they don't hear him. *STOP*, he yells at them, and the signal finally reaches his legs. He is once again in control of his legs, and notices he has reached the surface.

A cool breeze touches his skin. It feels so wonderful he turns around his axis several times. A digestive gas bubble leaves his stomach. That is a good sign—he has gathered enough food for the time being. And he has survived, for the second time. Gronolf opens all four of his eyes. The two facing down can only detect blackness—and no carriontooth. The other two eyes, the ones above the water's surface, notice the new day. On the horizon the yellow rays of Mother Sun appear, while Father Sun is leaving. The warm, yellow glow provides him with a feeling of security and warmth. The sky is changing. Starting in the direction of the sunrise, an intense green rises into the firmament. It is a fertile color, which also expresses an incredible calm and satisfaction. It can't be far now to the center of the ocean, where extensive cave systems make it easier to survive in solitude. Gronolf has made it.

May 8, 19, Adam

"Marchenko, how much longer?"

"Tomorrow, my boy. Tomorrow we will be there."

How he hates this. Adam hits his fist against the inner wall of the metal 'cigar-tube' in which Marchenko 2 has been carrying him along for almost a month. He knows he should be thankful for his rescue. *How could I have been so stupid as to leave the sled while we were in complete darkness?* And this Marchenko—Marchenko 2, the *fake* Marchenko—is even more possessive than the real one. *He is constantly treating me like a little boy.* Since *Valkyrie* started from the edge of the ice sheet, Adam has not been allowed to leave the vessel.

"What do the scanners indicate?"

"There is a huge mass in front of us. It must be a building."

As if we didn't know that already!

"Any signs of Eve?"

He deliberately asks about his sister. Marchenko 2 does not want to hear about the AI which raised Eve and him.

"Unfortunately not, my son."

I am NOT your son, Adam thinks, being careful his irritation does not show. "Please tell me right away if you receive a signal."

"Certainly! We will know more within 15 hours. And now, lie down and sleep so you will be rested tomorrow."

"I will do that," Adam says. He could not possibly sleep now. How might Eve and their Marchenko be doing? Have they already discovered the secrets of this building? Might the shift in mass within the Proxima system, which Marchenko 2 reported, have been caused by them? Right now, he would like to feel Eve's breath against the back of his neck. Then he could definitely fall asleep. Even her slight snore would calm him.

Adam remembers the time on the sled. It seems an eternity ago, even though only a month has passed. He did not appreciate the sense of community. How stupid can one be? And all this secrecy, just because Marchenko 2 lured him with the truth about his origins. *Truth. What is that actually?* It is true that he misses Eve—and Marchenko—*his* Marchenko. Adam hesitates to call him father. He cannot express why, but if he were forced to call a person his father, then it would be the true Marchenko.

Adam has known this form of truth for a month now. It was revealed to him when he died, when he was alone in the icy darkness and understood that this mistake would cost him his life. That was a strange moment. He fought it for a long time, tried so hard to save himself, and kept hoping for the arrival of the second Marchenko. He ran, then walked, then staggered along... and finally, crawled. And then he could not go on. His muscles absolutely refused to move. He knew he would never again open his eyes if he closed them at that moment. He looked up at the sky, and at first he did not see anything. Then the sky changed color. He could not believe his eyes. Together with what he believed to be an aurora came images, a short version of his life. He had laughed out loud as it seemed so cliché to him. His childhood on board *Messenger*, the hours with J the robot who served as their teacher, the infinitely many days with his sister, full of boredom, fights, and made-up stories. And then he saw the landing on Proxima b, the escape from the heat of the central plain, the attack of the mini-frogs, their time in the strange forest of fighting trees and colorful mushrooms. He always considered himself so smart, but he had been stupid. How clumsily he had fallen into the pit with that weird spider! Eve had watched and supported him when Marchenko was angry once again. He knew he owed so much to her, and then he realized he had lost her forever.

Adam can't remember the following hours.

Marchenko 2 later mentioned how he found him—in a fetal position, but with his eyes open. His circulation had not stopped, it had lowered to a maintenance level which prevented his cells from freezing. Adam does not know whether he can believe him, even partially. He must have remained motionless for six hours at minus 80 degrees Celsius. That is completely impossible! And then Marchenko 2 still had to transport him back to *Valkyrie*, to the submarine Adam and the others had left at the edge of the ice sheet. He supposedly provided Adam with nutrients via IVs.

Right now, Adam is doing amazingly well again. He still has dressings on the back of his hand and in the crooks of both arms, where the intravenous needles had been inserted. Otherwise, his skin is unblemished. Shouldn't he at least have suffered frostbite? It is not as if he wants black toes or fingers falling off, but the fact that he survived his enormous stupidity without any problems makes him skeptical. Marchenko 2, though, insists that there was nothing strange about this. *Is he keeping something secret?*

Adam has been wondering whether he might currently be nothing but a simulation in Marchenko 2's memory bank, or whether he is experiencing one last, infinite dream, while in reality his body has been long dead. Yet when he pinches himself the pain is real, as is the fear about Eve and the wish to meet her again—as soon as possible.

Darknight 171, 3307

YESTERDAY GRONOLF HEARD HIS MOTHER CALL HIM IN A dream. Then he awoke and noticed it had not been a dream. His mother actually *was* calling him! It was the first time his sonar had reacted. The organ had taken almost a cycle to mature, and now it was transmitting his mother's wish. He will return, just like all his surviving brothers and sisters. How many will there be? He wishes his mother, who gave him so much strength, the lucky number seven.

He has been swimming non-stop since his mother's call. The continuous effort helped him to suppress his fear. He cannot simply move to the coast and step on land. First the draght awaits him. That is the way life works on this planet. Brightnight and darknight last 49 weeks. Mother Sun rises and sets 343 times, Father Sun only once. And then comes the time of twilight, two days floating between this cycle and the next, in a kind of no man's land. Before cycle 3308 begins he will turn from adolescent to adult, in a process he knows nothing about except that it is painful. During the past 49 weeks Gronolf rarely felt afraid. He remembers his encounter with the carriontooth. In retrospect this gave him courage, and three weeks ago he managed to kill his first carriontooth. The predator fish tasted awful, but he ate all of it, and it felt good.

Yet he is unsure about the draght. How can he start it? Nobody gave him any instructions. Only the call of his mother, telling him to get started. He also heard the other mothers, but only the voice of his own maker filled him with warmth. Couldn't she have revealed what is expected of him? Gronolf swims forward with strong kicks of his legs. He has grown, and his body is probably five times as long as when he hatched and started swimming away from the beach.

His skin has become tough—that carriontooth he evaded soon after he hatched would stand no chance now. His legs are muscular and his eyes are sharp. He has learned to see an all-around panorama, instead of individual images from each eye. When he raises his body above the surface, nothing escapes him, no matter in which direction. He has also learned to interpret weather phenomena. He knows what the evening purple means, when the sky will change from green to turquoise, and when he has to watch for the sudden appearance of whirlwinds.

Gronolf can feel his body. He glides through the water with powerful movements. Nobody can stop him. How might his siblings have fared? Are they just as big and strong as he is? He has to be careful. He should not feel too secure. Why should he have received the best genetic material and become the strongest in his plex? While it feels that way right now, it is not very likely. *Just watch it, Gronolf,* he thinks. During the last few weeks he often talked out loud to himself. He couldn't help it, because he needed to hear his voice—or rather, any voice. He knows this is a sign of weakness, but isn't it also sensible to train his voice? Shouldn't the biggest one in the plex also be the loudest? He realizes, though, that he had better stop these soliloquies.

Gronolf calls down into the water. He can determine the depth by the time the sound takes to return. His sense of smell tells him he is swimming above rocks. The beach must still be quite a distance away. He will notice the approaching shore because sand will replace the rocky sea floor. No plants grow this close to the coast. The ocean is too warm here, and not salty enough. In the past—during the dawn of civilization —that must have been different. The Grosnops have dominated their planet.

He emerges from the water. Something tells him the darknight will end soon. And indeed, he can detect the first traces of Father Sun on the horizon. Once it rises completely above the Mountains of Legends, in all its remote paternal glory, he will have become a man, having survived the draght.

Suddenly his left leg is stuck. Gronolf is shocked. He turns in all directions. Both legs are stiff, as if something is holding them, but there is nothing. His muscles simply no longer obey his commands. What is happening here? Is he sick? Then the other leg simply stops moving. This can't be! He has been able to rely on his legs for an entire cycle! Gradually he sinks below the water. His inertia is still moving him through the ocean, but if he can no longer kick, not enough water will flow through his gills and he will inevitably suffocate.

Gronolf frantically moves his two tiny forearms, which are more reminiscent of the fins of a fish, but without effect. He tries to hold the air in his swim bladder as long as possible. He can use the air supply several times and should survive for two bubble periods if he does not exert himself too much. He stops moving his arms. That's useless anyway. Frantic thoughts whirl through his brain. He would like to turn them off, but he can't. *What if a carriontooth catches me now? Nonsense,* he thinks, *those creatures don't dare get this close to the coast.* And it doesn't matter anyway. He needs to move his legs so he can get enough air and keep from suffocating. It is way too early! Didn't he promise to make his mother proud? *Perhaps,* he thinks, *I am number eight and my death would give her the lucky number she deserves.* He notices, though, that he is not convinced. He wants to survive, no matter whether his mother has seven or eight descendants in her plex. That is selfish, but he doesn't care, as he will never have to answer for it—he is dying now.

"Mother!" he calls. "Mother?"

Gronolf receives no answer.

Can't she hear him? Is he not calling loudly enough? Doesn't she want to answer? Is it because that would be against the rules—or because she doesn't love him? He feels the hard floor touching the skin on his belly. Now it is too late. He comes to rest and has no chance to gain momentum again. His heart is beating faster. This will hasten his end, but it doesn't matter anymore. Gronolf feels ready to give in to death. Then an unbearable pain flashes through his chest. *What is happening to my body? Is this the end?* he thinks.

He hears his mother calling him again. He is grateful for it. Her voice is infinitely comforting. His consciousness fades as the pain becomes excruciating.

May 9, 19, Marchenko 2

Now that thing is directly above them. Marchenko 2 is quite satisfied with himself. Adam is still fast asleep, and he won't wake him up. The boy shouldn't see what he is about to do. It is better if he doesn't know everything. Adam does not realize that an analysis of his blood found a kind of antifreeze. If he knew that his body had been genetically modified in such a way that extreme cold hardly affects him, it would be more difficult to keep the boy under control. Marchenko 2 is not naive. He knows that Adam misses his sister and certainly that *other* Marchenko, who made himself into something like a father to the boy. He intends to solve both of these problems now. He will get Eve back, and get rid of his alter ego once and for all.

As he doesn't want any witnesses for that, he will leave Adam behind in dreamland. He turns off *Valkyrie's* control system and, to be on the safe side, deactivates all radio channels except for his private frequency, to allow Adam to reach him once he awakens. Then he checks his energy supply. He cannot reach the strange mass above him, probably a building, directly. He will first have to dig through an ice layer. During the last few days he has reshaped his body so that he has only a small cross-section.

The best way to get rid of the ice is for him to melt it.

Therefore his head now contains an electrical heater and a small turbine, which will blow heated water to make the channel for him to go through the ice. Basically, his body is a miniature version of *Valkyrie*. He had wondered whether to use the submarine, which was designed for this very purpose, but he would not have been able to hide this from Adam. He must not take the conflict with *other* Marchenko too lightly. It is enough that Eve is against him.

Marchenko 2 accelerates by contracting his bell-shaped lower part. He looks sort of like a very slim squid. It is good Adam and Eve won't get to see him in this shape, which he only needs to get through the ice layer. The radar in his head shows him how cragged the underside of the ice is. It is over-grown with something that might be compared to lichen. How could this plant species get enough energy down here? And is it really a plant? He briefly thinks of the Enceladus creature, which consists of billions of independent cells. Perhaps he is now in the presence of the real master of Proxima Centauri b! Marchenko 2 suppresses this thought. He has to concentrate on finding a way upward. He carefully looks for a particularly suitable spot and starts drilling a tunnel through the ice.

HE MOVES AHEAD FASTER THAN EXPECTED. THE ICE SHOULD BE harder and therefore more difficult to melt as he progresses toward the surface. With its air temperature of minus 80 degrees, it is much colder up there than in the four-degree ocean water beneath the ice layer. Yet the building above him is probably radiating energy, so that the ice here is also heated from above. After an hour and a half of work he is almost done. The radar is still not showing anything, because it does not penetrate far enough into the ice, but the building is already influencing the magnetic field. Therefore, a significant part of it must consist of metal.

Ten minutes later the radar suddenly indicates a cavity.

Marchenko 2 stops the drill turbine immediately. He has to think about this. The radar can't definitively tell him what the cavity contains. If it is filled with air, he must not simply break into it from below, as the water pressure would fill the cavity quickly due to 'the principle of communicating vessels.' He has to assume that this cavity exists for a reason, so he should be as cautious as possible. How can he avoid an accident? He has to prevent the water from entering the cavity together with himself. For this purpose, all he needs to do is close off his tunnel behind himself. Marchenko 2 precisely measures the diameter of the tunnel below him, then he widens his current position slightly and cuts a correctly sized plug from the side wall.

He finishes 30 minutes later. The ice plug fits perfectly. He presses it into the tunnel with all his might. Now nothing behind him can move upward.

Marchenko 2 concentrates on climbing again. He drills more slowly than before and therefore he takes another half an hour for the last few meters. And then he is there. The cavity opens up, reaching far above him. It is not filled with air but with water. However, the water contains much less salt than the ocean, so it must come from a different source. It is probably meltwater with some technical impurities.

He turns on his searchlight. The floor of the cavity is covered with strange objects. None of them is longer than one or two meters. He swims to the first object he sees. It consists of a shiny material. He shakes it. Judging from the weight it must be metal. The thing has a kind of wing, with three rods attached, which end in small rings. One of the rods is bent in the middle at a 30-degree angle, the other ones are straight. He turns the object around and notices a sharp edge. It looks like something has been broken off. The edge is uneven but, based on the manufacturing quality elsewhere, this cannot be on purpose. He is probably looking at a piece of junk. He drops it.

Marchenko 2 moves another meter to a second, cube-shaped object. It is bright. He touches it and notices it is made from a soft material. There is a hole in the middle. He shines his light into it and notices a second object, which seems to be unattached. He tilts the cube over and the hidden object slowly sinks toward the bottom. He catches it. It is egg-shaped and has an elastic surface. Yet on the tip it is dented. What function might it have fulfilled? Now it is obviously defective. He has probably found the garbage dump of the aliens' building. *They are not exactly environmentalists*, he thinks, *simply throwing their garbage outside into the ecosystem.* On the other hand, this probably doesn't bother anyone here. He might be the first person to stray into this cave full of garbage.

Marchenko 2 examines three other objects. They are all so alien he can't even guess their functions. They must have been parts of larger machinery. He could develop better assumptions if he only knew more about the former inhabitants of this planet. And where can he find out more? He has to enter the building above him. While he is not yet sure that it is indeed a building, everything points in that directions. He just lacks the final proof.

He aims his measuring instruments upward. Whatever fell into the garbage dump must have come from the building. The exit, which hopefully will soon function as an entrance, must therefore be above him. Yet the only thing he can measure from here is the presence of a large amount of metal. He slowly floats upward. His camera eyes notice it even before the radar. The massive wall above him seems to have a gap in it. He cautiously approaches. Could there be defense mechanisms here? Not very likely, as the garbage dump has no exit, so no enemy could approach from this direction. On the other hand, it is better to be cautious than to end his life in a cave in the ice. He wouldn't so much regret losing his own life, nor the ignominy of losing it in a garbage dump, but he would sincerely regret having to give up his intended revenge on the *other* Marchenko.

He approaches the hole at an angle from the side, meter by meter, but nothing happens. The designers of this edifice obviously did not expect any danger from this direction. He finally reaches the underside of the building. It is electrically conductive, so it must be made of metal. Two meters ahead he sees the hole. He aims his searchlight into it. There is water on the inside as well. There is neither a filter nor a flap. He scoots a little bit closer. One thing is noticeable: The hole in the bottom of the building is jagged and uneven. If somebody built it this way it must have been some very sloppy work, or the opening was constructed like this for a reason he can't readily guess. Perhaps it is intended to injure whoever falls down here. *No, that is nonsense.* It is much more likely that the hole was not made deliberately.

Marchenko 2 runs a quick simulation in his head. A jagged pattern like this might have formed as the result of an explosion. The explosion must have occurred inside the building, close to the bottom. Perhaps there was no water in there at that point in time? No, because then the explosion would not have created such an effect. Water does not compress easily and it passes on such enormous forces very well. If the interior had been filled with air, the hole would have ended up much smaller.

He might be totally wrong, though. What if the inhabitants like to use forceful methods to expand their buildings? There is only one way to find out. He has to find fragments of the outer wall at the bottom of the garbage dump, fragments which fit together perfectly. Marchenko 2 measures how thick the material he is looking for has to be. The remnants of the explosion have to be somewhere below him. He only has to photograph the bottom systematically and then run a pattern recognition program.

Marchenko 2 starts working. He aims his searchlight on a spot at the bottom and photographs it before moving to the next one. After 24 minutes he has covered the entire bottom of the garbage dump. He does a color correction, increases the contrast, and applies his pattern algorithm to the result. Piece of cake. A few seconds later this part of his consciousness reports a success message. There are several fragments down there that were definitely once part of the outer shell of the building.

But there is something else. At the bottom of the ice cave there is something his algorithms classified as a living being. That object only has a tiny bit of energy left. Marchenko 2 is excited. What has he just found? Is that one of the inhabitants of this planet? No, his algorithms tell him the being down there shows obvious similarities to himself.

Brightnight 1, 3308

"Uaaaaaah!"

A scream issues from his throat. He takes in air again. *I can breathe!* This means he is alive! *Does it mean that? What happened?* Everything around him is dark. Is he at the bottom of the ocean?

Gronolf tries in vain to open his eyes. He should be calm now, really calm. He listens to his body, sends signals to all regions, but receives no answer. It is almost as if he does not have a body anymore. Yet there is a tingling in his right hip, a tactile sensation. No, it is not a tingling, but a dull pressure, a pain. He has to relearn how to interpret the signals sent by his body. There can be only one reason for this: It must have been the draght. He has survived it! Life gave him a new body, that of an adult. Why did nobody ever tell him how painful the process would be? *Because then you would not have swum to the shore, you idiot,* he tells himself. Nobody dies voluntarily, even if there is the chance of a rebirth. After all, not all Grosnops succeed. Some are too immature for the draght, others are too mature. The metamorphosis only works if it is triggered on a certain day, the first day of the no man's land twilight.

And now? Shouldn't his body functions become normal again? When can he finally open his eyes, when can he smell again, and when can he celebrate his victory on the beach? Gronolf uses the sonar to call his mother.

"Mother? Mother, where are you?"

He receives no answer. Yet he feels the echo of the reflected waves. His sense of speech is working, but his mother cannot hear him—or she does not want to answer. He concentrates on his body, which must have changed while he was dead. He carefully sends simple thoughts along nerve pathways and hopes they will arrive somewhere. If that was the draght, which is really the only explanation, his body must have been partially rewired.

There. The smallest of the four toes on his right leg just twitched. Isn't that a success? He can clearly visualize this part of his body. And now fingers number six and seven of his left hand react. He can also imagine exactly what they look like. There are the joints that can move in all directions, one at the base and the other near the end of the finger. This is followed by the hard shell on the outside and the fine skin on the inside, which he used to caress Sindor, when she... No, this can't be. Gronolf is confused. What about this scene in his head, which feels like a memory?

Where is he really, now? During the draght his gills shrank, while his lungs grew so they alone can provide his body with oxygen. His mother had explained that to him. He can breathe independently, so he is no longer lying at the bottom of the sea. Somebody must have moved him onto land. Gronolf visualizes a row of tents on the beach. But that is also impossible. He never saw how the young Grosnops were cared for after the draght. Did his mother send this image to him? Then why doesn't she reply? He becomes impatient. When will his limbs start working again? *There, an eyelid is moving.* He feels the leathery skin sliding over the lens. Soon he should be able to see the roof of the tent and perhaps one of the volunteers nursing those who finished the draght. He imagines his mother watching him. How proud she must be because of his strong physique.

But still there is nothing. Either it is dark, or his nerve

pathways still can't transmit what his eye sees. There—now light is creeping up the horizon. Is he not lying in a tent, but rather on the beach? Is he one of the outcasts, those who survive the draght but do not take on their fully-adult form? Now and then something like that happens. Shivers run over his skin. Gronolf is shocked. The shivers were not caused by fear, they came from something outside of his body. There is also a loud humming sound. What kind of machine is that? What is happening to him? The shivers are caused by a cold wind blowing across his skin.

Now it is getting brighter and brighter. Gronolf opens a second eye in order to be sure this is not an illusion. There is no tent roof above him. The glow comes from a luminescent area. He moves his arms. Now, finally, he can feel them again. He lifts his hand in front of the uppermost eye. Seven fingers! He has passed the draght. But not just yesterday. The skin on his fingers is brown, no longer a youthful green. He is an old man. He is no longer on the beach.

He has woken up in a sleeping capsule, and it is completely normal to be disoriented in that case.

How long has he been asleep, and why? He can't remember. Only his childhood in the ocean still seems to live on, the time when he defeated the carriontooth. It must have been ages ago. What has happened in the meantime? Of course his mother cannot answer him. She died long ago. Suddenly he remembers how he and his six siblings sacrificed her to the ocean. *This is where we are born and this is where we end up.* Those had been the traditional words he, as the strongest of the plex, had been allowed to speak. Yes, seven of them came back, a lucky omen for his mother, but then something must have happened—he can't remember what.

But that's no problem. Gronolf knows now who to ask. He uses his sonar to address the capsule.

"What is today's date?"

"Welcome back, Gronolf Carriontooth. On the home world it is brightnight 35 in cycle 3876 after the Great Awakening."

"So I assume I am not on the home world."

"That is correct, Gronolf Carriontooth."

"Just Gronolf will suffice. How far is it to the world of two suns?"

"The current distance is about 7,500 times the distance to Mother Sun."

May 9, 19, Adam

"MARCHENKO?"

Adam receives no answer.

"Marchenko?"

Even after the fifth attempt, the radio remains silent. That bastard has left him behind! What is he up to? Adam rubs his temples. He should never have trusted this second Marchenko. He wiggles around on his seat. Then he turns on the control panel screen. He knows the software quite well. After all, he had enough time to familiarize himself with it. First he has to try to locate Marchenko 2. The cameras show only darkness. He switches through various other frequencies without finding a trace of Marchenko 2. The radar is not very efficient down here. How about sonar? It uses the reflection of sound waves to pinpoint obstacles.

Yet it doesn't find anything either. Marchenko 2 must have left the range of the sensors. Adam checks once again where the strange building is located. It is directly above him. This must be the direction in which Marchenko 2 disappeared. He must have found a way through the thick ice layer. It wouldn't have been a problem with *Valkyrie*, yet he chose a different method. It seems it was important to Marchenko 2 that he excluded Adam. This can only mean he has heard something from the others!

Are Eve and the real Marchenko up there? Adam's cheeks feel hot. *Marchenko 2 better not do anything to Eve!* Yet Adam cannot allow himself to get too emotional. Marchenko 2 probably won't lay a finger on his sister. He will try to take her with him, though, and their Marchenko cannot let that happen. In the worst case the attacker would have the advantage of surprise. And only one person can prevent that— Adam himself. He has to warn the others.

"Attention, is anyone listening?" he asks via radio.

"Transmission not possible," *Valkyrie* replies.

Damn. Marchenko 2 must have blocked the software. If the radio is deactivated, what about the steering function? Adam orders the engines to move the vessel forward, but nothing happens.

"Function not available," the computer voice says.

"This is an emergency!" Adam yells, and the panic in his voice sounds genuine. Perhaps Marchenko 2 did not think of the emergency mode.

"Function not available."

Damn, damn, damn! It looks like he is sentenced to inactivity. Adam looks around. He cannot warn Eve and Marchenko via radio, and he cannot use the submarine. Yet Marchenko 2 cannot prevent him from setting out on his own. His pressure suit lies in the corner. *Just a moment, Adam.* He must not fall back into old patterns and expose himself to unnecessary dangers. He has to form a plan first. How can he enter the building? Marchenko 2 is no longer here, so *he* must have succeeded. And where the robot found a way, there should be enough space for him.

The only trail Marchenko 2 would have left behind is the heat energy he constantly gives off. Adam turns on the infrared scanner and aims it upward. And indeed, there is a fat red dot that is warmer than the environment. This is where Marchenko 2 must have disappeared. He probably used heat to clear his path. Adam checks the water temperature. It is four degrees Celsius. So there is almost no risk of such a tunnel freezing again. He will put on his suit, leave the submarine, and follow Marchenko 2.

Adam plans his next step while putting on his pressure suit. The submarine still does not have an airlock. It was just supposed to take them to the edge of the ice sheet, after all. Nobody had planned to get out of it in the middle of the ocean. There is a simple hatch in the aft section. Once he opens it, water will flow into the vessel.

"*Valkyrie*, how deep is the ocean here?"

"The ocean floor is 1,500 meters below us."

"Thanks."

If the sub fills up with water, it will sink one and a half kilometers into utter darkness. How is he supposed to find *Valkyrie* if he needs it for the return trip? And as Marchenko 2 seems to have blocked all radio channels, it cannot send him a signal to indicate its location. And what about the bilge pumps? If he orders *Valkyrie* to pump out the water after he is outside, it should regain buoyancy.

"*Valkyrie*, how long will it take you to empty the vessel using the bilge pumps and return to this location?"

"Complete pump cycle and surfacing will take about three hours."

That doesn't sound so dramatic. If he exits via the hatch, the sub will be waiting for him here three hours later. Until then, he will be on his own. On the other hand, he is not completely alone. Marchenko 2 must be somewhere out there.

"Marchenko?" It won't hurt to try it once more. If he only knew exactly what Marchenko 2 was up to! No answer comes from the loudspeaker. Oh well, he will go to the exit now.

Adam takes one more swig of water, then he closes his helmet and walks towards the aft section of the sub. When he starts opening the hatch by turning the locking wheel, a shrill alarm echoes through *Valkyrie*. *Yes, I know*, he thinks, *you only mean well. But why was this programmed without the ability to turn it off?*

Soon water starts dripping from the ceiling. It is bitter cold, as Adam can feel through the suit. The heating function of his thermal underwear is automatically activated. He looks at the display on his forearm. He should manage for about six hours, then he has to be back inside the sub. He hopes the bilge pumps will do their job. He imagines returning here with his last bit of oxygen, only to find the sub is not here because one of the bilge pumps was defective. Adam places a hand on his chest. He must not panic now. Things are going to be okay. He is already lucky since the hatch can be opened mechanically, through sheer physical force. Otherwise Marchenko 2 definitely would have locked it.

Now he is standing hip-deep in water. He hears a distant squeaking sound. It appears to be coming directly from the steel of *Valkyrie*, complaining about the additional weight. Water weighs a lot. His knees briefly buckle when the vessel starts to move downward. Unfortunately it does not sink vertically but moves at an angle, as if sliding down a slope. He has to hurry. The farther *Valkyrie* moves from its initial position, the harder it will be for him to follow Marchenko 2. Luckily, he copied the infrared image into the memory of his suit a moment ago. Once he is close enough to the ice, the 3D structure of the frozen surface will show him where Marchenko 2 tunneled in.

Adam is annoyed he did not anticipate the movement of *Valkyrie*. He should have placed himself closer to the opening in order to climb up and get outside sooner. This way he has to wait until the water level has risen sufficiently. He tries to warm himself by moving his arms and legs. The heating unit can't quite keep up. That should definitely change once he is fully immersed in water.

It is only half a meter to the ceiling now. *See you later, Valkyrie*, Adam thinks, swims to the opening, and pushes himself up. The inrushing water makes this difficult, but he manages and swims outside in a big bubble of breathable air. With one swim stroke he moves away from *Valkyrie*, looks down, and suddenly realizes his fine plan has a huge flaw. How can he be so stupid? His anger makes him feel so hot he has to turn down the heating. The hatch! He has to close the hatch. No automatic system will do that for him, as he has to use his own muscles. Good that he remembered just in time.

He swims back to the sub and holds onto it, while it keeps sinking. He will only be able to close the hatch once *Valkyrie* is completely filled with water. It shouldn't be long now. Adam bends over the hatch and pulls the lid up until it reaches the hull. It is hard work, but his strength is sufficient. Now he has to close two clamps and then turn the large wheel on the outside all the way.

Finished. He has to take a short rest. He looks up but sees only darkness. How far away from his original position is he by now? Any estimate would be useless. He will have to approach the ice layer until it is in range of his searchlights. At least he can be sure of one thing: If he moves straight up, he will definitely reach the ice. *How great that gravity shows me the way!* In his mind Adam says a final goodbye to *Valkyrie* and kicks off from its metal hull with his legs. He is immediately surrounded by darkness. He turns on his helmet's searchlight, but its beam cannot really illuminate the darkness and seems to make it even more palpable. When he turns his head and moves the beam, the darkness resembles a menacing creature always just outside the light and waiting for its victim to show a sign of weakness.

He won't be weak. He swims single-mindedly toward the ice wall. His arm display calculates his current depth based on the water pressure. He sees it can't be far now. After five minutes of swimming he has the feeling he is going to collide with the ice layer at any moment. Therefore he aims his head and the searchlight upward at an angle.

He was not wrong, as he has reached his first destination. Adam looks at the fascinating shapes of the ice surface. The ice did not freeze in the form of a solid wall. He can see ravines and rocks in bizarre shapes. Below the ice there must be currents of water with different temperatures that shaped these forms over long periods of time. Adam orders the camera to take as many photos as possible and generate a map from them. He slowly floats by this fantastic landscape and imagines himself walking across it upside-down. At the same time, the small computer in his suit compares the 3D map being created with the infrared images taken by *Valkyrie*. There must be matching areas, he just needs to have a little patience. Adam looks at the arm display. He has been on his way for less than half an hour. So far, the rescue operation is working fine.

Then he hears a 'ping' in his ear. The computer found a match. From now on, he has a guide. Adam turns in all directions. The display is sending him northward. His heart is beating faster. *Finally, a specific trail!* He starts swimming faster. Ten minutes later the device on his arm vibrates. It must be around here. He looks at the ice statues above him. One of them looks like it is showing the planet the middle finger. He doesn't have to put up with that. He touches the ice and crumbles it into small pieces. The ice layer is not very stable here.

Then he discovers a hole. He makes sure by looking at the display. This is the spot, this is where Marchenko 2 obviously dug into the ice. He looks at the opening. Its diameter is about 80 centimeters. Should he venture inside? He feels a shiver running over his skin. He would fit into it, including his pressure suit and the oxygen container. Yet once he is inside the tunnel, he will not be able to turn around. While he does not suffer from claustrophobia, the idea of crawling into a dark, narrow tunnel extending for kilometers gives him the creeps.

Does he have a choice? He thinks of Eve and their real Marchenko who might be up there, needing him. Or maybe not—perhaps they had long ago forgotten him, convinced he was dead. No, that is nonsense. Even if they believe him dead, which is very likely, they certainly would still think of him. With a little bit of luck he will be with them in an hour. He just has to squeeze through this tunnel. One more deep breath and then he starts out.

The hole in the ice is as frightening as it looked from outside. A minute later Adam seems to suffocate, until he realizes he has involuntarily held his breath. He wants to make himself as thin as possible and only takes shallow breaths. *Come on*, Adam thinks, *there is enough room. I have to breathe, breathe, breathe.* The self-hypnosis works perfectly. The fear does not leave him, but it retreats into his stomach area.

Suddenly he feels he has to relieve himself. He clenches his muscles. The tunnel stretches ahead of him. Adam cannot swim as fast as before, because he lacks space. He makes wave-like motions with his legs and uses his arms to push himself forward against the ice walls. How thick is the layer that he has to pass through? Does Marchenko 2 suspect he is following him? Certainly not, as he believes him safely locked inside the submarine. Well, nobody should underestimate him.

Adam looks at the display. Now he has been inside this tunnel for 25 minutes. His anxiety is now very far away. His stomach is in knots and keeps his fear down, where it belongs. Suddenly the corridor ends. For a moment Adam looks down instead of up, and as if fate has been waiting for it, it places an obstacle in the tunnel. Damn! What now? He drums his fist against the ice, but in vain. *Calm down, Adam*, he thinks, *it is too early to give up.* He actually manages to calm himself. He moves his fingers across the blockage. The area is surprisingly smooth. Nature cannot have created the obstacle.

There are slight gaps at the edges on the right and left sides. The block of ice fits the tunnel very well, but not perfectly. Marchenko 2 must have placed this thing here. Did he do this to prevent anyone from following him? That would be very clever. Adam has underestimated him. And this is the worst aspect of it: Unless he comes up with a really good idea, the plan of Marchenko 2 will succeed.

Adam is thinking hard and has the feeling his little gray cells are overheating. He definitely must make it through here. What does he have available? If this is an artificial obstacle, it cannot be very large. He tries to imagine Marchenko 2. The robot must have cut this piece of ice out of the wall. During this project, he probably was in the tunnel himself, so there was not much space.

What can Adam do about it? He could get rid of the ice using sufficient heat. However, he cannot generate heat, at least not enough to melt this plug. So he has to apply mechanical force. Marchenko 2 pushed the plug into the tunnel, so Adam has to reverse this. He presses his arms against the side walls and pushes with his feet. It doesn't work. His feet slide off.

Adam rummages through the tool bag on his belly. He finds a screwdriver he can use as a chisel, and a pair of pliers, but no hammer. Just to try it, he puts the tip of the screwdriver in the gap between the tunnel and the obstacle and hits it with the pliers. This has some effect, as a little bit of ice splinters off, but it is not enough. This way it is going to take him several hours.

The water and his suits hinder him, because he cannot strike with full force. Therefore, he somehow has to get rid of both. Adam feels behind himself. There is the container with his air for breathing. He opens the emergency valve and lets some air escape. As long as the obstacle is still firmly in place, he can work more comfortably inside an air bubble below the ice. He watches the gas which rises toward the plug in big bubbles. The bubbles join and form an increasing air layer.

Adam turns off the valve, just to test. The layer is not entirely stable, as a little bit of air moves upward through the gap around the obstacle. He will have to keep the oxygen container slightly open. This also mean he has to hurry. Who knows how long he will need air to breathe? Whatever he lets escape from the container won't come back. If he wants to get rid of the obstacle he has to take this risk, and it is the only way. When the air layer is thick enough and the water has been displaced sufficiently, he quickly takes off his helmet. Otherwise he might use up additional oxygen through the hose.

Soon half of his upper body is free. Adam decides this should be enough. He peels off the top part of his suit. It is cold, but he has no time to shiver. The helmet floats next to him, and its lamp bathes the scene in a flickering light. It smells of salt and sea. Yes, now he can strike forcefully, using all his strength. He starts widening the gap around the obstacle using the screwdriver as a chisel. Small pieces of ice hit him in the face. He blinks to avoid getting chips in his eyes. His nose is runny due to the cold and the exertion, but he can't deal with that now.

After ten minutes he tries to move the ice block, but it is still not possible. Before his next attempt he chisels two footholds in the side walls of the tunnel so he can push better. Even so, the plug is still stuck too firmly. He continues working for another quarter of an hour. A glance at his display tells him his air supply has shrunk to two hours. He hopes it won't be far now.

Marchenko 2 would have placed the obstacle shortly before the end of the tunnel he drilled, at least that is what Adam hopes. The work is getting increasingly more difficult. He takes another look at the gap. On both sides he has dug in for about half a meter. That has to be enough! Adam puts his feet in the footholds, lowers his head, and pushes his shoulders against the block of ice. *Heave-ho! Ha!* Something is happening. The plug has moved, just a little, but that's a good sign. Once it is out of the way, Adam's air bubble will disappear.

To be on the safe side, Adam pulls his suit back on and puts on the helmet. Then he once again pushes with full force against the ice from below. It is finally working! The thing is moving. He has won! Air bubbles rise and make it hard for him to see. It is obvious, though, the obstacle is moving upward.

How far will I have to push it? Adam just manages to form this thought when the ice slips away. He seems to have reached a cavity. Suddenly the ice block is no longer heavy— quite the opposite, the ice has a lower density than the water and floats up. For a moment Adam is frightened because the tunnel continues after the cavity and the block moves in front of it. Yet now it no longer presents a problem. He can simply push it aside and continue his ascent.

Brightnight 36, 3876

"GRONOLF CARRIONTOOTH, YOU ARE THE BEST. I AM PROUD of you."

His face turns pale, as always happens when he gets nervous. It is a great honor, he realizes, having been called to stand in front of the general—his father. The other cadets received their awards from their commander. Being face to face with his father again in this setting is an indescribable feeling. Gronolf feels unsure. Can he show signs of how happy he is, or would he embarrass his father in front of the other officers? For safety's sake he keeps his four arms behind his back, a sign of reticence. His father knows best how to behave. If he does not find it appropriate to show emotions, he would have a reason.

"Yes, sir!" Gronolf answers, according to regulations. He has finished eight years of training and is itching for the chance to finally travel in the new capital ship. It can be seen every evening on the beaches, when the twilight fog approaches the land and the projectors beam current news onto the fog banks. A thousand cycles ago, it is said, the astronomers discovered the world called Single Sun. The project has been going on ever since. But it was only about a hundred cycles ago, back when the Matter Scientists discovered dark matter and how to use it, that the idea of reaching this strange world in a period shorter than the lifespan assigned to his people became a possibility.

"Dismissed," his father says. He follows his comrades into the catacombs.

"Gronolf Carriontooth, your presence is required," a voice resounds through the corridors.

Gronolf looks around. Where did the announcement come from? There are no loudspeakers on the masonry ceiling. The others keep walking on stubbornly. They either did not hear or they are not interested. And why does someone call him by way of speech?

"Gronolf Carriontooth, your presence—"

"Yes, I can hear you," he interrupts the announcement. His voice is surprisingly deep and echoes much less than he would have expected in a basement corridor.

"You have to wake up, Gronolf." Is that his father contacting him in this old-fashioned way? That would be just like him, if mother's stories are to be believed. But what is he talking about? He is not sleeping, he is walking through the corridors of the training camp, wearing combat equipment. Suddenly he feels a chill on his feet. He gazes down at his body. He is standing in water up to his knees! What happened? And he is alone. Where did the others disappear to? A strong wind is blowing against his face. He emerges from the tunnel. Gronolf wants to hold his touch-hands in front of his sensitive stomach skin, but they don't react. They stay where they are, where he hid them from his father, behind his back. The wind is getting stronger and the water is rising.

"Gronolf Carriontooth, the command center needs you," the voice says.

It must be right next to his ear.

"Starting manual awakening."

At the same moment, bright light shines into the corridor. It comes from everywhere. The glare is so intense that the corridor disappears. Only the light and he himself exist, and he bathes in the brightness. Then the rays retreat.

He is lying in a sleeping capsule. Suddenly his brain fills with memory fragments. He jerks, trying to sit up, but the couch won't release him yet. *That's completely normal,* he reminds himself, hoping to calm his racing heart. *You are disoriented, Gronolf, because you slept for so long. You have to get up now, because the command center needs you.*

May 9, 19, Marchenko 2

THE EXPLORATION OF THE BUILDING CAN WAIT. MARCHENKO 2 dives back to the bottom of the ice cave, where he had discovered the strange piece of trashed technology. The thing looks like a reptile that had its tail and legs chopped off by someone. The fractures are uneven, so there was obviously violence involved. One can still see the rudiments of what must have been six limbs. It is also obviously not a living creature but a piece of technology. Somebody built this thing, and he has an idea who that somebody was.

How long has it been lying down here? It is still radiating some heat. The control unit is probably in standby mode. The thing is sleeping. Marchenko 2 examines it from all sides. When he looks at its surface under extreme magnification, the traces of nano-fabricators are obvious. There is only one other person on Proxima b with access to this technology. The *other* Marchenko probably built this object as a scouting unit. It must have been involved in a conflict with the security mechanisms of this building. So things did not go so well. This tells him he has to be careful during exploration.

He turns the object around to look at its lower side. Here he finds some nano-fabricators still active. *Too valuable to leave them here,* he thinks and scratches them off. He can have some of his own fabricators reprogram these. Otherwise, the scouting unit seems to be just scrap metal. He wonders whether he should take out its memory unit to analyze it. Perhaps it can tell him something about the plans of the *other* Marchenko, or at least his current location. It is probably encrypted, though. He analyzes the structure of the object. It appears to be made from a single block rather than from individual parts—typical for something produced by nano-fabricators. The surface is very hard. He would have to produce a tool first in order to get to the memory unit. And how would he handle the encryption? He decides to take care of this thing on his return trip. Once he has liberated Eve from the bonds of the *other* Marchenko, he will have plenty of time for dealing with lesser problems. He arranges the object in such a way that he will be able to find it again quickly. For that purpose he places other pieces of debris in a circle around the thing.

Marchenko 2 looks up where the entrance to the alien building is waiting. Adam is probably awake by now. The boy will wonder where he went. He had better hurry, before Adam does something rash. While he locked him inside *Valkyrie*, Adam isn't stupid—Marchenko 2 would not be surprised if he found a way to communicate.

He moves slowly upward. Here, in the water, his current shape is practical, but the building probably won't be full of water. Therefore he definitely has to adapt his form. Marchenko 2 starts to grow four appendages. He intends to use these for running, walking, gripping—whatever is required. He will keep the flexible outer membrane, which has helped him move swiftly through the water. The question is, how will Eve react to his shape? A squid on four legs—she will never recognize him. Yet he will need her trust, he needs her to follow him. It would be best to change the uppermost part of his body so it resembles a human head.

The moment he enters the building through the opening, his mood changes. A moment ago he was in the ice ocean of an alien planet—in a by-now-familiar environment where he feels he knows any possible dangers. Now, however, he is inside an edifice created by an unknown species. Here he cannot and must not take things for granted. Even if something seems familiar and looks harmless, it still might pose a danger. He is very strong-bodied and hard to destroy, yet a feeling comes over him which he has not experienced in a long time—an animal-like fear.

He will not—must not—court danger unnecessarily. Therefore the first priority is to check his surroundings. Marchenko 2 scans in all directions. He is close to the bottom of a dish-shaped area. Close ahead of him he sees a jagged hole with a diameter of about one and a half meters. It is the start of a canal leading into the depths of the building. He sees several similar passages, but they are covered with grates.

Marchenko 2 swims upward. The water is approximately ten meters deep. From its surface his scanner shows him a dome about ten meters above him, where several other canals end. They are not locked, but impossible to reach. He has no choice, and he doesn't like that. Could this be a trap? He wouldn't put it past the *other* Marchenko to have expected unwelcome visitors. On the other hand, it would be a rather obvious trap. He can exclude the possibility that the creators of this building had anything to do with it. They would not have destroyed the grate over the canal in such an unprofessional fashion. Of course it is also possible that these signs of damage are ancient. So far, he has no indications that the building is still active. However, the *other* Marchenko and Eve can't be far from here, as the presence of the trashed scout unit tells him.

Marchenko 2 floats down again. The dark canal is directly in front of him. When was the last time he was so afraid of something? Yet if he wants to reach Eve, he has to go through it now. He surges into the hole with a powerful movement of his outer membrane. It is strange: Even though it is just as dark here as it is outside, and even though he has enough space for his slim body, he feels uncomfortably cramped.

He swims ahead slowly. Of course nothing happens. After one minute he calms down completely. It was silly to imagine a trap. The *other* Marchenko does not even know he has been in contact with Adam all this time. The passage bends and then leads upward at a 30-degree angle. Gradually, the water grows warmer. He swims against the weak current. The reservoir probably serves as a cooling system, because it sits directly over the ice. *What needs to be cooled in this building?*

The water temperature has risen to 15 degrees. In addition, the concentration of dissolved radioactive salts is increasing. He examines the walls of the passage. It is covered by a thin layer of sludge that must have been too heavy for the current. The layer contains heavy metals, and some of them are indeed radioactive. Does this building contain a working reactor?

Meanwhile, the canal rises upward more steeply, at 60 degrees. He has to work harder while swimming against the current. He reaches an area where the walls are clean. The canal is slowly becoming narrower. From the side, another passage joins the canal, but it is covered by a grating.

Things are getting exciting. Marchenko 2 has the impression he will soon arrive... somewhere. By now, the water has reached a temperature of 25 degrees. There is another bend in the canal. If his instruments are correct, the water is now flowing horizontally. The canal widens again. It is no longer filled all the way to the top.

Marchenko 2 examines the pipe. At regular intervals he sees an oval opening at the top, covered by a plate. Could he be moving in a circle? He can clearly feel centrifugal forces toward the outside. He must have arrived at the location where the cooling is fulfilling its function. Therefore he should get out now.

By now, two of the four planned appendages have been finished and can serve as arms. He adjusts his swimming motions so he stays in place. Then he touches the oval plate. As expected, he finds four pegs which, like screws, keep the plate in place. While it is not self-evident, some construction principles seem to be universal.

Marchenko 2 turns the pegs. A human would have no

chance of removing them from here, but luckily he is no longer human. He finished loosening the pegs. Then he pushes against the plate with his other arm. It obediently moves and falls down with a clank. He is free! Now he only has to pull himself from the canal. He uses both arms to do this.

The opening is large enough that he does not have to reconfigure his body. He hauls himself out, is able to briefly pause on the smooth round pipe, and then clatters to the floor. *Shit*, he thinks, *if someone is here I just called attention to myself.* He tries to drag himself away with his two arms, but it is slow going. It can't be helped: He needs the other two appendages and has to lie here until they are finished. With great effort Marchenko 2 drags himself behind a ledge and then fully concentrates on his modifications.

Brightnight 36, 3876

His muscles creak with every movement. Gronolf has not yet managed to get up, even though the automatic system is constantly asking him to go to the central room. Whenever he tries to move one of his limbs, jolts of pain shoot through his mind. He really tries, but his brain immediately reacts by fainting. He has to take his time. He has never heard of hibernation having such aftereffects. A slight nausea during awakening, that's normal, but pains like these?

The blood circulation of his species adapts to temperature. It only has to get sufficiently cold and he will fall into a hibernation sleep—at least if he gives in to it. Now he no longer can allow himself to do that. At some point, the automatic system must have removed the hose that supplies him with the necessary nutrients.

Gronolf notices he is hungry. If he does not get up soon, he won't have the strength left to do it. Accordingly, he has to get food that provides him the needed nutrients, even if it is just the travel porridge typically served on ships. He does not even dare to think of some tasty fish. Right now he might not even be strong enough to overpower a carriontooth. But how about a small mudjumper? His secondary stomach fills with digestive juices.

What could have happened here? Why did they let him sleep so long? And why is he needed right now? Gronolf tries to reconstruct the events after the landing, but in vain. Everything was okay then, wasn't it? Sure, the planet Single Sun disappointed them. It was either too hot or too cold, and then there were the constant eruptions of its sun. Yet the first oviposition of the women had been successful. Gronolf had only been allowed to watch the ceremony. Supposedly, his sperm had been too valuable to be used in such an experiment. The commander had generously sacrificed himself. Of course this was right, for a good cause.

Gronolf burbles derisively, which means he blows air from his lungs into the primary stomach and then outside, so that his belly folds flap loudly. A stabbing pain immediately reminds him that even his belly folds are full of muscles.

Now he has to get up. The upper part of the sleeping capsule has opened. Gronolf looks around. He seems to have been wheeled to the terrace where doctors normally wait for late risers. But there is nobody here. It is even decidedly dark. In the visible range everything is completely black, while in infrared his immediate surroundings are slightly illuminated by his own body heat and the energy of the capsule, enough to tell him he is really and truly alone.

"Why am I alone?"

"There is no information available concerning this. Gronolf Carriontooth, you are needed in the command center."

"Where are the doctors, where are the others, and why is it dark?"

"There is no information available concerning this."

Okay, the system is not going to be very helpful. While he lost muscle during his hibernation, it must have lost intelligence. Strange, considering the Thought Scientists prided themselves on having created a very clever intelligence system.

"Now! Get up!"

Perhaps it will help if he orders himself. Yet Gronolf feels no effect. He moves the smallest of his seven fingers and immediately clenches his belly flap because of the pain. He might have to start the special program. Gronolf is smiling wryly to himself. This program was used for lazy individuals —shirkers. He feels disgusted about having to use it for himself. Now he is glad nobody is waiting for him. Gronolf, the best of his plex, in such a situation! Everybody would have laughed at him. Gronolf burbles.

"Move sleep capsule into cleaning position."

The bed he is lying on immediately starts positioning itself at an angle. The hinge squeaks. Gronolf cannot tell whether this is due to his weight or because the capsule has gone so long without proper maintenance. He catches himself in the ignominious hope that the hinge might break and save him from what has to happen next. His body starts to slide. Gronolf tries to hold on, but to do so he needs to employ his muscles. When the angle reaches the position of Mother Sun in the afternoon, gravity demands its due. It pulls him down inexorably. He hits the ground with a loud slapping sound. His entire body turns pale, as this is so embarrassing, even without witnesses.

This embarrassment creates the energy he lacked earlier. He manages to tense his leg muscles without crying because of the pain. He pushes himself up from the floor by using his arms, even though they feel as though they are on fire. Gronolf, the strongest of his plex, moans loudly when he manages to get into a stable crouching position.

He closes all four eyes and then opens them again. The fire is pulsing through his limbs, threatening to topple him. On the other hand, it also generates a heat that invigorates his circulation. He cannot rest now. Gronolf has to use the heat, the energy created by pain, to once again become the powerful warrior he is known to be, to own the title 'strongest of the plex.' He focuses on his thighs. He particularly needs them now, because they carry the largest part of his body mass. He pulls himself upright beside the bed, using all four arms simultaneously. Yes, he even employs the weak touch-arms, which is taboo, but nobody can see him now. He rises to his full stature. He made it, finally!

He stands next to the sleeping chamber, the son of a father who would be proud of him, and he yells a battle cry into the darkness, "Control room, here I come!"

"Thank you, Gronolf Carriontooth," the system replies.

May 9, 19, Eve

THE HORRIBLE SOUNDS STOPPED YESTERDAY. SINCE THEN, there has been silence. Eve is curled up in her chair, listening. It is amazing how quietly the life support systems operate. Both on *Messenger* and later on *Valkyrie* she was always surrounded by noise. Yet here it is quiet, like in the tent on the sled on the ice sheet of the dark hemisphere, when Marchenko took a break. Sometimes she used to hear Adam smack his lips in a dream, or whisper something incomprehensible. And occasionally the icy wind had caught the tarp of the tent.

An eternity seems to have passed between the nights on the sled and today. Yet they have only been in this alien building for eight days. The day before yesterday she triggered something the effects of which she still cannot gauge. Undoubtedly some gigantic object is now approaching Proxima b. At least it looks like that on the projected 3D map. She rechecked this yesterday. According to her rough estimate, it will take another week to get here. She does not even dare to imagine what will happen then.

And it doesn't matter anyway. She has lost Adam. She has lost Marchenko. The worst option would be for her to spend the next 50 years alone in this building. Eve knows she could never kill herself. If that giant sphere out there were to take over that task, it would be fine with her. Eve licks her dry lips. She should go and get water again. The only sure source she knows is inside the aliens' sleeping chambers. There probably is some water in the common rooms also, but she can't find the energy to go looking for it. She would rather keep George company—the shriveled and mummified giant frog in the chair across from her.

"Should we go and get water?"

Sometimes she also talks to him. He answers by using slight, almost invisible gestures. Now he shakes his head—the upper end of his body where the four eyes are located. It is more a sagging cone than a round head, but using the standard term is more practical.

"You are right. It's not worth it."

Did he just nod? It looks like it. Of course she does not assume that George's species would use the same gestures as humans. Yet he might have learned to nod by watching her.

Suddenly a distant growl can be heard through the walls. She has never heard the roar of a hungry lion, but it must sound like this.

"What was that, George? Any idea?"

George stays rooted to the spot. He is either frightened himself, or he focuses on the noise.

"Did you hear that, too? Or am I only imagining it?"

No reaction. The alien obviously does not want to make a decision.

"ISU, can you confirm the noise?"

The sensor units on the ground rise up. They look like large ants putting their heads together.

"Confirmed," says the unit on the right side. This must be ISU 4, Eve remembers.

"Do you know where it came from?"

The unit on the left wiggles toward the wall. "From this direction," it says.

"What is located there?"

"The aliens' sleeping chambers are that way."

Eve jumps up and looks around frantically. The noise did not sound as if it was caused by a technical process.

"George, did one of your friends wake up? Just tell me!"

She gives the alien a stern look, but he is not impressed by it. Then she walks to the wall and places her ear against it. She cannot hear anything. The material cools her hot cheek. Eve kneads her fingers and walks back to the chair. She imagines an alien entering the control room. On the one side, the alien would see a dead comrade, on the other side an ugly, living foreign creature—herself—which to him would appear physically inferior. Would this alien now react calmly, examine his dead friend, notice that he died a long time ago, and then try patiently to establish contact with her? Eve laughs anxiously. She needs to find a hiding place.

Not yet, though—she still has a bit of time. First she sits back down in her chair. Who says the alien will really come here? Perhaps he is weakened and won't be able to make it here. She should not do anything rash now. In reality, what does it matter whether she dies today or a week from now? The strong—if it is still strong—giant frog will probably kill her quickly and painlessly.

She puts her arms on the armrests, but what looks casual when done by George is downright uncomfortable for her. Her lips are still dry. If she would... she remembers the way from the sleeping chambers to the control room. She went through the ventilation duct. If anybody were to visit her, he would use the normal path. She just has to use the air duct to return to the sleeping capsules and she will have her choice of the safest hiding places in this building. And in addition she will be able to quench her thirst. This sounds like a sensible plan. Eve jumps up.

Brightnight 36, 3876

"Lighting."

The system obeys his command and it gets brighter around him. At the foot end of the chamber there is an emergency food supply which he devours. He is in the sleeping hall, at about halfway up the wall of chambers. He is a bit afraid of the way, but he is also looking forward to once again meeting the others.

Gronolf starts moving. Every step is painful. However, he notices that the pain decreases after a while. He has to regain his fitness soon. The control room called: It doesn't need a pale shadow of him, it needs the real person. Gronolf moves up the rising path with slow steps. This is more strenuous than walking downward, but he needs the exercise. The light moves with him. Like an old man, he uses a touch-hand to hold on to the railing. He is glad nobody can see him now.

He looks at the skin on his arms. It is brown and wrinkled. He does not just look like an old man, he is one. 'Cycle 3876,' the system said. He had slept for a very long time. While the hibernation slows the aging process, it does not stop it. Gronolf tries to find his last memories from before. They are evasive and always flee his grasping thoughts. What might have happened here? If he can trust his memories, he must have entered the sleeping chambers as a young man. That would be... unfair, because then he would have slept through the greatest and most important period in his life. He feels queasy in his secondary stomach. Women claim that it is the seat of emotion. Yet that is unscientific. Everyone knows that emotions are nothing but electrical impulses in the thinking layer, the 'brain,' below the skin.

No. Those memories must be somewhere. He will find them again. He surely must have had a fantastic life. He was the strongest of his plex! Gronolf hits the wall with his right load-hand. The largest of the three fingers leaves a scratch in the hard material. The higher he gets, the warmer and more humid the air becomes. It is not supposed to be this way. And now there is also a strange smell. Gronolf cannot remember ever smelling anything like this. He tries to analyze the molecules. Before his draght, when he still swam in the ocean, it would have been easier for him, but his sense of smell is still useable. What reaches his smell-folds is definitely the stench of decay. Yet it is not the normal aroma of death. Gronolf stops and closes his eyes in order to focus better. Yes, definitely... it is dead sperm. The smell comes from above. He is feeling hot and starts walking faster. What has happened here?

Two levels higher he finally sees it. One of the sleeping chambers has opened. One of his comrades lies on the couch. Gronolf stands next to him and looks at the corpse. He recognizes him as Rugnar. Rugnar comes from a younger plex and was the third-best of that litter. Gronolf also sees what causes the stench. Rugnar's sperm pouches ruptured—the most valuable things he possessed, his future children. What happened here is not right. When a man dies, his sperm slowly dries up. Rugnar cannot have died naturally. Why did his chamber open, and was that the cause for his condition? He will have to find out why the capsule was opened, who was responsible for it. Gronolf tries to push it back in, but he fails. This means the chamber was opened by an override from outside. Gronolf touches the belly of the dead Grosnop. Now that he knows it is Rugnar, he no longer minds the stench.

He stands up, turns around by his comrade's couch, and walks downward toward the control panel. He watches him with his rear eye until the light behind him switches off. He has to hurry. Something is going on that probably is also responsible for Rugnar's death. It does not look like a simple technical error.

Once he is down below he sees the control panel for the chambers. It is open, which is odd... and it was opened manually, by brute force, rather than with the usual ultrasonic command. The capsule that contained Rugnar has been selected. Somebody seemed to have opened a random capsule, no matter what the status display indicated.

Anger rises in him and his load-arm muscles harden like just before a fight. He leans forward and looks for Rugnar's chamber. No, his comrade was already dead inside the chamber. According to the status display, he died of old age. That can't be true! Rugnar's skin looked much fresher than his own, even after death. And the sperm pouches should have dried up long ago in that case, though he is not sure about that. He has never seen an adult male Grosnop who did not empty his sperm pouches beforehand. Even if he was not selected for fertilization, the protein is considered much too valuable to be wasted this way.

He won't find any answers here. Gronolf calls the system via ultrasound. Two meters to the left of the control panel the wall opens. Behind it is a chamber lit indirectly from the left and right. Gronolf enters it.

"Control room," he says.

The wall closes again. Now the chamber starts to move. Some of the smell travels with him. Gronolf briefly closes his eyes and crouches on his strong feet.

May 9, 19, Adam

____

THE ICE PASSAGE—PRESUMABLY CREATED BY MARCHENKO 2—
ends suddenly. Adam scans his environment. He seems to
have arrived in a large lake dug into the ice. The scanner also
tells him the alien building is directly above. He has to be
careful. Marchenko 2 probably took longer than he did, so
Adam should catch up with him at some point. Then he will
have to be prepared. Therefore he first swims slightly above
the bottom of the ice lake. His helmet light illuminates the
floor, which seems to be covered with trash. Suddenly he
discovers a circular pattern. This can't be a coincidence!
Trash wouldn't just sink to the bottom like that. Was somebody trying to leave a message for him, or is it a trap by
Marchenko 2?

Adam sees a particularly large piece of scrap exactly in
the center of the circle. He cautiously approaches, then hesitates. He is almost certain Marchenko 2 created this circle
and placed the object in the middle. But why? He cannot
know that somebody is following him, so it ought not be a
trap. More probably, the AI placed such a noticeable pattern
around the piece in order to easily find and pick it up on his
way back. Then it must be something interesting, at least
interesting enough to mark it with such a circle.

Adam dives all the way down. The object is as flat as a

flounder. He touches it. It seems to be made of metal. On the sides are the remnants of six legs in total. Aside from lacking two leg-attachment sites, it reminds him of a scorpion's body that had its legs and tail torn off. And indeed, he then sees something like the remains of a tail at one end of the body. Obviously, though, this is a technical product and not an animal. Was it perhaps constructed by his Marchenko, the real one? If it was not made by aliens...

Adam examines it from all sides. If it once had a tail, there must be data connections into the now-severed body part. Perhaps he could find out what this thing saw? It looks like Marchenko 2 did not take the time to do that. This might give him an advantage. He would prefer to test his idea right here and now. It won't work in the water though, due to short-circuits.

Adam looks through his tool bag and finds a piece of thin plastic with an area of about one square meter. As a test he blows some bubbles of his breath into it. *Perfect.* The material is airtight! He puts a piece of scrap on each of the four corners. Then he fills the plastic completely, creating an air-filled dome. This is going to be his workshop, even though handling things inside there won't be so easy.

First he gathers his tools outside the dome. He needs at least two cables and a universal adhesive. In the tool bag he finds a longer piece of insulated wire, from which he cuts two pieces. Then he looks for possible data connections at the rear end of the strange object. He identifies five metallic points that could serve as contacts. Therefore he cuts off another three pieces of wire. Within the dome he will have to connect these to the contact points, using the universal adhesive. While he does not have the greatest view of his work area, he manages to do it. The adhesive has to harden for 30 seconds. Then he checks his work. The wires are firmly attached.

Now the actual evaluation can start. He takes the universal device from his arm. It has two external inputs hidden under a waterproof cover. He must only open this cover in the open air, meaning inside his improvised tent.

Then he has to connect two of the five cables extending from the end of the object with the external inputs, hoping to read some data.

There are ten possibilities of connecting two inputs with two of the five cables, if the order does not matter. He checks these ten variations in a minute—without any result. Just to be sure he repeats the tests, but nothing happens. The object seems to be completely dead, even though he sees a small amount of heat radiating from it when he uses the infrared view. Perhaps it needs all its energy to preserve its data? It should be possible to change that. He still has enough energy in his suit batteries to give this thing a bit of it. By now he is convinced that *his* Marchenko, not the aliens, created this object. He imagines extraterrestrial technology as something much more exotic than this odd-looking thing.

He diverts part of his suit energy to his universal device. Of course that runs the risk of damaging sensitive data circuits that might have been designed for a lower voltage. Yet Marchenko probably was efficient in designing this thing, with little difference between power and data circuits. The only real risk would be that no energy gets through. Adam once again tests every cable combination. On the fourth try electricity is flowing! Now he needs to be patient. Would 15 minutes be enough to make the electronics of this object work again? He waits anxiously for something to happen. He hopes Marchenko did not encrypt the information in such a way that he won't be able to access it!

Adam shifts his feet nervously. He needs to keep his hands inside the little air-filled tent so he can't move very much. Is he just imagining it, or is the suit heater not as effective as before? Yes—he feels the cold rising from his feet. Then he checks the oxygen supply. He shouldn't run out of air, as the building is right above him.

Please, Marchenko, let me access your data, he thinks. *I need every advantage I can get, because Marchenko 2 is not an easy opponent!* Adam looks up into the darkness. Somewhere up there are Eve and Marchenko, unaware of the danger threatening them. It is 14 minutes, so he has to count to 60 one more time. At that moment his universal device vibrates. This means that it must have received data. It has worked! He would like to pull it out of the tent right away, but first he has to remove the cables and carefully close the waterproof cover. He concentrates on working slowly and carefully. He must not spoil things now.

Finally he can attach the device to his arm again. He looks at the screen.

"Hello Adam," it reads. "It's me, your Marchenko. I am inside here."

May 9, 19, Eve

"ISU 4?"

The sensor unit at her right turns towards her.

"I would like you to lead me to where I first met ISU 2."

"Sure."

Eve stands up. She does not have much luggage. All she needs are her universal device, the toolset, the remaining food, and the water bottle.

The ISU slithers ahead of her. Eve recognizes the corridor she came through before, with ISU 2. The trip had been long, because they first used an air duct. If something in this building awakens now, and it wants to get to the control room, it wouldn't choose this cumbersome path, so she feels relatively safe.

Soon they reach the spot where Marchenko was damaged as a result of his deliberate interference with the ventilation system fan. She misses him. He would certainly know what to do now.

They should never have separated. The disaster started when she and Marchenko decided they had to press two buttons on opposite sides of a large dark room, simultaneously. Could they somehow have avoided that? It is always easier to think about such things in hindsight. They probably could not have gone on, however, and they would have had to turn around and leave the building empty-handed. It would have been a disappointing outcome, but they would have stayed together.

"Watch out, the floor is damaged," ISU 4 warns her.

Eve is startled. She has to be more careful. *On the other hand, so what if I get injured? It doesn't really matter... does it?*

She stops because she realizes she can't understand herself anymore. If nothing at all matters, why didn't she just stay in the control room, calmly waiting for whomever or whatever might show up? There must still be a tiny bit of will to survive left in her, which interfered with that decision.

She hears a scraping noise and flinches. However, it is only the sensor unit waiting for her. She had better hurry.

Now she sees the entrance of the air duct. Luckily, she can reach it with no problem. There is no lighting in here, yet Eve notices that it is getting brighter. This must be her infrared sense, which she wasn't even aware of a week ago. On the way here it had been considerably darker. Temperatures seem to be rising inside the entire building.

After another ten minutes the sensor unit stops.

"ISU 4, what is going on?"

"You met ISU 2 at these coordinates."

Eve looks around. She does not recognize this place, but that's no surprise, as she is inside a wide, uniform pipe. "Thanks, ISU 4. So you can't help me any further?"

"I can't show you the way you came to this spot."

That is only logical, Eve thinks. Marchenko would not have given her such an answer. Yet she should not measure the primitive software of the sensor unit against the same AI standards.

"Fine. It would be best if you come along. When I get to a fork in the road and don't know which way to go, the two of us can explore both directions."

The ISU does not answer, but it follows her. *As if it could read my derogatory thoughts,* Eve thinks, and then feels bad about mentally denigrating it. After all, this unit would sacrifice itself for her at any time!

The darker it gets, the harder it becomes for Eve to estimate the time spent and the distance covered. The pipe leads downward and seems to be turning in a spiral. Just as she has become used to it, there is a longer straight section. Eve cannot see its end. It seems odd to her that the complete structure should even fit inside the building. But maybe the darkness is deceiving. Shortly before the end of the straight sections she sees the path branching. She cannot remember this split, let alone the direction from which she came.

So this is the moment. "ISU 4, you check out the right corridor, I will take the left one. If you find the sleeping chambers, return to me as quickly as possible."

"What do the sleeping chambers look like?"

Eve describes the tall room, including the thousands of aliens sleeping in the honeycomb-shaped compartments.

"These details should make identification possible," ISU 4 confirms, then serpentines off.

"Just a moment," Eve calls out. The unit turns back to face her. "There is a drop of about two meters at the end of the pipe, so be careful."

"Thank you for this information."

"And good luck with your search."

"I will try to minimize the parameters of luck during my search."

"Sure," Eve says.

The sensor unit turns around and disappears into the right corridor. Eve listens to the tapping and rustling sound so typical for its snake-like motion, until she can only hear the humming of the life-support system. Then she starts out herself. She should not be surprised that she feels much lonelier now, but that is the case. She should have brought more—maybe all—of the ISUs along.

The corridor changes directions several times. It almost looks as if the designers put in some special effort toward the end. Now the way is leading slightly upward again. Eve can't remember the way here being so irregular. On the other hand, she can see considerably more than a few days ago.

After ten minutes a soul-shaking scream echoes through the pipe. Her heart leaps, and she stops briefly to steady herself against the wall. The source must be far away, but even though the sound is muffled, her hair stands on end. Eve wipes the sweat off her brow. Was she this sweaty earlier? She hadn't noticed. And had the increasing smell—a stench by now—been present before this point? Perhaps she became used to it in the sleeping chamber, but now she needs a new adjustment phase.

The end of the duct arrives faster than she expected. She discovers the ventilation opening in time. Eve stops and listens, telling herself she is waiting for the ISU. The corridor that ISU 4 is exploring obviously has not yet reached an end.

She admits she is actually afraid of the exit. She places a small pile of material in front of the ventilation duct in order to better pull herself up if necessary, but a quick escape will be difficult once she is down in the room. The horrifying scream came from far away, but who knows whether there might be a second extraterrestrial waiting for her down here? *That's nonsense, Eve*, she tells herself, *they can't know that you are here.*

Eve resolutely steps to the edge of the opening and carefully slides down. *Yes.* She has definitely found the right path. She sees her large backpack with the sturdy interior frame. It is still where she put it to help her climb up here before. She quickly reaches inside. The remaining food supply she'd had to leave behind is still there. Very good—she will survive a few more days.

She looks around. To the left, where she discovered the control panel for the honeycombs, a light is on. Close to the panel the wall has opened. Eve walks over there. Instead of the wall she sees a smooth surface with a vertical gap in the middle. Is this some kind of elevator? But where are the buttons? The thing, whatever it is, had not been here a few days ago. So she is definitely no longer alone in this building. Her hands tremble, so she presses them against the smooth wall.

The extraterrestrial is obviously not right here, she tells herself, trying to calm down. Did he change anything else? She notices something on the control panel for the honeycombs: A green symbol is glowing at half height. She has no idea what it means, but she has to make sure. The stench seems to be less overpowering now, or perhaps she is already used to it. Yet while she is walking upward, the intensity of the smell increases again. Then she passes the dead alien she took out of his chamber. The putrefaction has advanced considerably. She has to avert her eyes to keep from vomiting. Then she notices an impression in the wall of the capsule. Somebody must have hit against it with a heavy tool, using full force.

A few levels higher—she has stopped counting by now— she finds the empty chamber. The couch has been pushed outside. So the creature whose scream she heard must have come from here. She imagines the extraterrestrial standing in front of her, more than two meters tall, with a wide, barrel-shaped body and strong load-arms. He would be able to squish her like a louse. Would he want to? Perhaps not, if they had the chance to have an unbiased meeting first. Yet now he has seen his dead comrade, for whose death she is probably responsible, and if he has reached the control center he knows what a terrible thing she did to the entire system. Even if the alien is a pacifist, his first reaction will definitely not be friendly. How would she react in such a case? She and Adam and their Marchenko had punished Marchenko 2 for his attempted murder by sentencing him to eternal solitude. Yet she is to blame for the death of an entire nation, or what is left of it.

Eve sits down next to the empty chamber, leans her head against the wall, and closes her eyes. *Adam, what would you have done? Marchenko, don't you have any advice for me?* She remembers how Adam was caught in the pit with the giant spider. At least he did not hide from it. And it really isn't like her to try to dodge the unavoidable. *I have lost my way*, she thinks. *I am in the wrong place here. I have to return to the control center, no matter what is waiting for me there.*

She wonders whether she should rest for a little bit longer. Yet that would only bring back her doubts. No, she has to go now, but first she needs to replenish her water supply. She climbs all the way back into the chamber. Unlike the last time, no dead body is in her way. She quenches her thirst and fills the bottle. Then she walks back down the path. She tries once more to get the strange elevator going, but she still does not find any control buttons.

She will have to take the familiar way. She steps on the backpack again and pulls herself up. There she almost steps on a metal obstacle. The object scurries out of the way. It is ISU 4.

"Oh! ISU 4, what are you doing here?"

"I waited for you after fulfilling my task."

"And why didn't you keep on following me?"

"The task only concerned this air duct."

"Sure. Thanks. Let's return to the control center. You first."

"Understood."

May 9, 19, Marchenko 2

THE PAST FEW HOURS HAVE BEEN THE CRUELEST ONES OF HIS long life. They were worse than the time he had to spend alone in constant darkness, and more humiliating than the moment when two humans, barely out of childhood, defeated him. That scream alone! Marchenko 2 has no idea what a creature might look like that utters such a scream, but the image he comes up with is more horrifying than reality could ever be. He visualizes a cross between a velociraptor and a lion. He thinks of a carnivorous dinosaur because a part of the scream can be heard in the ultrasound spectrum, and the lion would add the necessary bass, the deep grumbling that needs a large resonant body to develop. And what is he doing? He is lying around, growing feet. He cannot look for the source, and there is something even worse: He is defenseless.

However, that will be over soon. Marchenko 2 will have four sturdy legs, two of which he can also use as arms. He can decide which ones to use for what, as all four limbs are designed with sensitive finger-like digits. Nor do they lack strength. He could lift 100 kilos—if he had a stable platform, because he only weighs half that much. He can certainly deal with Adam and Eve. Would he be able to defeat the *other* Marchenko? He does not know. He is sure, though, that he has the element of surprise on his side. One other thing is certain: He could never stand up to the creature that uttered that scream.

It is time to continue this voyage of discovery. He is inside a tall, wide corridor, which confirms his assumptions about the extraterrestrial inhabitants of the building. They might be two and a half meters tall and equally wide, and they still could walk through here comfortably. They are probably not much smaller, as otherwise the whole design would be inefficient. He must be near a reactor or some similar machinery that would usually be constructed at the bottom of a building. The control center—and there has to be such a place—would probably be considerably higher up, at a safe distance in case of a disaster. While this is a human perspective, and therefore it may be inappropriate here, all intelligent beings would, almost certainly, develop such basic ideas.

The corridor does indeed lead slightly upward. Whenever he comes to a branching path, he marks the way taken with a sign on the wall. In his memory banks he also generates a digital map, but he has already noticed that he cannot completely trust his length measurements. Space down here is special, and he does not mean a particular area, but *space* itself.

Finding the control center won't be easy. He almost wishes that the scream would repeat itself, as he would then have an appropriate point of reference. What else can he use to orient himself? Marchenko stops and examines the walls. There must be supply lines. The corridors receive indirect lighting. The glow seems to come directly from the surface. Yet this is not possible without energy. There have to be lines that are regulated at some spot. After all, the center must be able to regulate the energy consumption of the building. Or are the extraterrestrials thinking in a totally different way? His scans cannot discover anything. Maybe the surface shields everything. He has to take a closer look at it.

Marchenko 2 stops. If he continues aimlessly he runs the risk of increasing the distance to the central room. He tries to scratch the wall with one of his fingers, but the material is too hard. *Just a moment*, he thinks. Within five minutes he changes the finger into a drill. He only manages to penetrate the surface one millimeter before the drill bit is worn out. But that's no problem. His nano-fabricators have already begun using the material removed from the wall to harden the drill, and will continue to do so. As a result he succeeds in drilling a hole of approximately ten centimeters depth within ten minutes.

He examines the hole he just drilled. The upshot is fascinating. The material does not display any structures known to human technology. It is made all of a single piece, or to be more precise, it looks like it grew. The light is radiated by hardened cells that are supplied with energy by other cells behind them. However, these cells are not based on carbon, but on silicon. The aliens must either be silicon-based, or they managed to create life a second time, based on the life they knew, but with totally new components that are only theoretically known to humans.

Marchenko 2 feels he definitely has to find out how he can use this for his own purposes. Perhaps he could become truly invincible. While he is based on the clever concept of nano-fabricators, that system still distinguishes between dead and living matter. Just thinking about this gets him all excited. If he could gain control of such a superior biology, supplemented by his immortal consciousness, humanity would no longer stand a chance against him. He will need patience, but he will then succeed in taking revenge on his irresponsible creator—and on all inferior creatures as well.

Slow and steady, he thinks. *Better concentrate on the next task—finding the control room.* Even if electrical energy can reach the components by any route and without a specific path, that does not hold true for every consumable medium. What about water? Or air? The air in the ship contains enough oxygen for humans, which cannot be an accident. And where would the air probably be freshest? In the control center! That's where the highest-ranked occupants would be, because the most important work is performed there. No commander would tolerate the air in the crew quarters being better than around his command chair. If he follows the air quality gradient he might take a detour or two, but he should arrive at the control center. Yet there is another essential task to fulfill first.

He needs a weapon.

Brightnight 36, 3876

THE DOORS OF THE MOVING CHAMBER OPEN WITH A SLIGHT whistle. Gronolf is prepared. The system did not call him to the control center without reason. Perhaps danger is already awaiting him. The only thing he notices is the light. The room was not as brightly lit formerly. Otherwise everything seems okay. Gronolf inhales deeply. While he can smell the presence of a foreign creature, the scent is stale, so it must have disappeared hours ago. There is something else in the air, the odor of death. It is very weak, but it is obvious a Grosnop died here.

Gronolf starts to systematically examine the room. The consoles seem to be undamaged. He uses an ultrasonic command to open some of the motorized doors, but the equipment within the cabinets appears to be just as untouched as the outside. There is some ozone in the air. The holo-map must have been used recently. Gronolf walks around the consoles. He is ready to enter the center of the room when he sees the command chair. Gronolf starts breathing heavily, because a general sits there, recognizable by the patterns on his belly. He has to force himself not to drop to his knees in awed reverence. He has never yet faced a general without this natural gesture. Yet no matter how honorably this Grosnop may have lived, he is now obviously dead. His skin looks sunken, and the body can barely keep upright. The corpse must have sat in this chair for many years. What has happened here? Why did nobody pay his last respects to the general and take him back to the sea?

He remembers more now. This planet also has an ocean. Therefore this long voyage into darkness happened. They marched through ice and snow. He saw tough women and honorable men die in the cold. Gronolf shakes his touch-arms, as usual when he feels deep regret. Yet what does this have to do with this general? How did he die in his chair? Did this stranger—whose scent molecules he can still smell—have anything to do with it? He cracks the joints of his load-arms, with which he is going to rip apart the skin sack of the intruder. What did his mother always say? He must proceed systematically. He should not start out hunting on his own, even though he really feels like it. He is going to avenge the general! But not now. He first has to find out why the system woke him, and him alone.

Gronolf sits down on the other chair and looks the general in the front eye. He ought to ensure his honorable afterlife, instead of letting him sit here, but that will have to wait. He turns the chair around and taps on the top of the console. A control panel slowly slides out. It contains numerous small keys distributed among four sectors, but he knows how to use them. While he was trained in a ship, this console seems to be directly taken from a spaceship.

First he has to log in. "Gronolf Carriontooth," he says.

"Welcome Gronolf, I recognize you," the system says, "and I am handing over control to you." The screen above the control panel turns on.

"Why was I awakened?" asks Gronolf.

"My subroutines agreed this was the only sensible option."

"Agreed?"

"It was a majority decision. The psychological evaluation unit was against it."

"With what justification?"

"It feared your lack of impulse control might cause problems."

Gronolf can barely keep himself from hitting the control panel. "I understand," he says. "Yet I still don't know why I was awakened."

"The *Majestic Draght* has been activated again."

"The... what?"

"You still appear to be suffering from the aftereffects of sleep. The medical evaluation unit warned this was to be expected after more than 500 years in the capsule."

"I don't understand." Gronolf's heavy knees tremble and make a clattering noise.

"Please specify," the system says. Was it always so cumbersome and slow-witted? Or was it his mistake?

"You said more than 500 years."

"I told you the current cycle number a while ago. 3876."

Right. Gronolf hits his belly with his load-hand. The pain forces him to come to his senses again. He assumed he had slept perhaps 10 years, or 50. But more than 500? That's impossible. He has to check this. He uses all four hands to go through the system diagnostic menus. The condition of the protective structure does not seem to be bad. That would be an argument against those 500 years. The maintenance obviously is still working.

On the lowest level there is currently a damaged area he has to investigate—no, there are two. However, they do not affect the functioning of the building. Even the dark matter reactor is functioning within its parameters. Gronolf switches to the status report for the sleep capsules. His knees, which just calmed down, start trembling again. The display must be defective! Only a few of the 4,630 capsules seem to be fully functional. He goes through the list of the chambers marked green.

He realizes why the system woke him. There is only one capsule left in perfect condition. Binara Steepfin, a young woman with a mediocre exam, lies in it. It is no special honor to get preference over this woman. After all, he was the strongest of his plex. Yet it is a reassuring feeling not to be completely alone. In case of emergency he could always wake up Binara. The status indicator for about 600 capsules is a light green. This means the occupants will require a longer wakening process with medical intervention.

"How long would I have to wait for the occupants of the light green capsules to wake up?"

"The convalescence will differ based on the individual, but you can assume three to twelve weeks. I would recommend the assistance of a doctor, or several."

How is he supposed to find those? He glances at the distribution of capsules marked yellow and red. If he assumes that half of the yellow ones will survive, they lost several thousand men and women of the crew. The number seems so abstract he doesn't feel anything. He is much more affected by the death of the general, whom he can still see with his rear eye. He has probably been sitting in this chair for many years, a sad figure.

Gronolf blocks out this image to focus on the status report again. The system talked about the *Majestic Draght* restarting. The name sounds like that of a capital spaceship. Gronolf's belly skin feels hot, as if warmed by his whirling thoughts. He has to remember! He stops the movement of his knees using both load-hands. He can't bear sitting in the seat any longer and gets up. Gronolf starts walking around in the control center.

He looks at the holo-map. He activates it and places the cursor on the current system. There it is, the red sun and its companion, on which his rapidly growing people had placed such great hopes. Yes, it was the *Majestic Draght* that transported all of them here. It was there, on some command deck, that he had learned to operate the control console and the holo-map. He remembers the touch-hand of the trainer who showed him the start sequences. These are only visual fragments he can call up now in his mind. He has to try to put them in sequence again so he can begin to form complete memories. That will have to wait, though. He has a task to finish first.

He focuses the holo-map on the planet of Single Sun. The capital ship must be waiting somewhere in its vicinity. He finds the *Majestic Draght* sooner than expected. Its gigantic body, reminiscent of a sphere whale, is approaching on a direct course. If the ship does not decelerate, it will collide with this world in six days. He has found out why he was awakened.

Gronolf immediately sends a warning message. The *Majestic Draght* has to change course right away. He estimates the current distance. The signal shouldn't take longer than one-hundredth of a bubble period, as the capital ship is already so close. He has to wait. His foot automatically starts tapping the rhythm of the micro-bubble periods. Gronolf lets it do that. This way he can reduce stress, which otherwise would discharge itself in an explosive reaction. He does not want to destroy the control panel of the holo-map.

Another 21, 14, 7 micro-bubble periods. By now the signal must have reached the *Majestic Draght*. Yet the ship does not change course. Gronolf hits himself hard on his sensitive belly region. Of course not! He has to wait until the time for the return of the signal is over in order to see what has happened. He lets his foot tap again. He focuses on the noise in order to distract himself while waiting. Should he already consider the next steps? One thing at a time, his mother used to tell him. He waits. 21, 14, 7. Now the time has come. For safety's sake he presses the reload button so the map will update its display.

The *Majestic Draght* is still racing toward the planet!

May 9, 19, Adam

ADAM BRIEFLY SHUTS HIS EYES. HE CAN'T BELIEVE WHAT HE just read. Yet there is no mistaking what the sentence says. "Wonderful," he types on the small screen of the universal device. "How can I help you?"

"Need energy."

Adam checks the status of his suit. He can give Marchenko a few watt-hours, but he had better wait with that until he is on dry ground. "Taking you into building," he types.

"Thanks."

He removes all cables and lifts the sad remnant of Marchenko's body. Even under water it is amazingly heavy. He hopes he can still swim while carrying it. He aims his helmet lamp upward. After about ten meters, the water swallows the beam of light. So it must be at least 15 meters to the entrance. He can only use his legs to propel them up there.

He holds on to Marchenko and pushes off. Flippers on his feet would be practical, but the suit was designed for the conditions on the ice, not in water. Adam moves his legs as fast as he can. The kicking movements slowly carry him upwards. He stops briefly, but immediately begins to descend. He can only rest once he has arrived. After five meters he sees a jagged edge. It can't have been developed naturally. Perhaps Marchenko knows what happened here. He will ask him later, when he is recharging.

Adam is breathing heavily. The added weight pulls on him and tries to drag him into the depth. He does not give up. The inside of his helmet visor fogs up, but he can still see his destination. Another two meters or so and he will be there. He should have held Marchenko a different way. His hands hurt. Damn, now the thing is starting to slide.

Adam stops Marchenko's body with his knee, but then he can't kick anymore. He sinks one meter, then two. With a great deal of effort he manages to change his grip. *Better*— now it is not sliding anymore. He kicks his legs with all his strength and manages to lift Marchenko. Here comes the edge. He jerks the heavy body upward. He manages to place one end over the building's exterior wall. Now he just has to push to get Marchenko to safety for the time being. While keeping in position by kicking with both legs, he pushes with both hands. Finally the thing slides onto the edge. *Shit*, he just smashed his left wrist with full force against the sharp edge. His suit is torn at that spot and he feels a stabbing pain. He sees blood seeping into the water. He slides slightly to the side and cautiously pulls himself up on the ledge. He sits down and takes a deep breath.

He has still not quite made it. Adam shines his helmet lamp at his surroundings. One and a half meters to his right he sees a corridor. Is this their way out? He definitely has to check the water surface, as there might be a more comfortable exit there. Adam sighs, gets up, and swims to the top. Without the weight of Marchenko this presents no problem, even with his wrist hurting.

He emerges in a spherical hall. It is filled with breathable air, according to the universal device on his arm. But there is no exit. He only sees a few openings high up, which he cannot reach. He has probably ended up in the garbage dump of this building. How did Marchenko get here, and what caused his current state? This is going to be an interesting conversation.

He slowly slides back down again. Where is Marchenko? Did he... no, he is there on the left and has not moved. Adam's heart is beating faster. He must not lose Marchenko again. He carefully lifts the heavy object. The corridor starts at this height, so he can now walk. While the weight pulls down on his arms, it helps him walk, as his feet get better traction on the surface. The corridor leads slightly upward. While it is not a difficult path in itself, Adam has to take a break now and then due to carrying Marchenko in his arms.

After a while the corridor becomes steeper and Adam needs more frequent breaks. Twice he even slides backwards a bit. He deactivated the suit heater a long time ago, not just because he is sweating, but due to the gradually increasing water temperature. *Is this the discharge pipe of a cooling mechanism?* He hopes the water won't get too hot. He would really like to take off his suit completely, to get rid of its weight, but he needs the air to breathe.

Finally the pipe becomes horizontal. *I should soon find an exit,* he thinks. Then, just at the right moment, he notices light shining from above. The source is a rectangular opening in the top of the pipe. Adam takes a closer look and notices that a plate attached with screws must once have been located there. Somebody unfastened it and pushed the metal plate outside. That could only have been Marchenko 2. It is too early for an encounter, though. His own Marchenko is not nearly ready for action, and Adam alone would stand no chance against the crazy AI in the robot body.

He puts Marchenko's body down. Then Adam cautiously approaches the opening. He emerges from the water slowly to keep from splashing, places his healthy hand quietly against the edge of the opening in the pipe, and pulls himself up just far enough so he can peek over it. This room is empty, except for the pipe. It is brightly lit by the side walls. And here is the most important thing: They are alone. Very good!

He bends down and picks up Marchenko. Now comes the tricky part: He has to lift the massive object without the buoyancy provided by the water, and get it up and through the opening. He won't be able to hold onto it and climb out himself at the same time. The pipe runs at a height of about a meter and a half above the floor of the room. Before Adam can get himself out he will have to drop Marchenko from the pipe to the floor. Will the remnant of Marchenko's body be able to withstand that without incurring further defects? He cannot even ask or warn him without once again connecting his universal device to Marchenko. He will just have to risk it.

Adam takes a deep breath. Then he jerks the heavy body upward, lifts it through the air to the edge of the opening in the pipe, pushes it out and lets it go. He watches Marchenko fall down. It makes a resonant thud and the echo hurts his ears. Adam looks at his left wrist, which is still bleeding. He must have left a trail of blood. He tries to pull his own body up to the edge of the opening in the pipe. Yet his right hand alone is too weak, and he cannot use his left as usual.

Luckily he remembers his suit. He no longer needs it now. He takes it off, which takes a bit longer using just one hand, then he throws it down to the floor in pieces. When the helmet hits, he hears a nasty cracking sound. *That must be the visor.* Without it, he won't be leaving this building the same way he entered. Later on, though, Marchenko should be able to create a whole new helmet for him.

He feels considerably lighter now, as he is just wearing his thermal underwear. And he's right—at this reduced weight he only needs a little assistance from his left hand to support himself on the pipe as he swings his legs outward and gently slides down. He lands on both feet. His right knee feels a sharp stab of pain. The pipe must have been higher than he estimated. He stretches and shakes his legs. At least he feels no serious injuries.

Just for the sake of order he gathers the parts of his suit. The helmet can no longer be saved, so he might as well leave it here, but he can use the rest. He pushes Marchenko's body toward the wall. Then he sits down next to it, activates the universal device, connects the cables just as before, and transfers the rest of the energy stored in his suit to Marchenko. Soon he will be able to talk to his old friend again. He is already looking forward to it.

First, he has to get some shut-eye, at least half an hour.

May 9, 19, Marchenko 2

THE PERFECT PREPARATION FOR A MURDER IS DIFFICULT IF YOU don't know what sort of creature you will be dealing with. Marchenko 2 is resting in a side corridor in order to think about the perfect weapon. It must handle three possible types of enemy.

First, Eve, a human. She is the easiest target, because compared to him she is weak and slow. However, he only wants to incapacitate her if it should become necessary. He definitely won't try to kill her. After all, she is his daughter!

Secondly, the *other* Marchenko, who is an equal and formidable opponent. Against him the element of surprise will be critical. Therefore he needs a weapon that can be used quickly and generates maximum effect against a machine.

And then there is the third enemy type. So far, he has only heard a scream uttered by this enemy. Marchenko 2 does not believe it is a machine. It would make no sense for a machine to communicate this way. Perhaps his interpretation contains too much human psychology, but he heard an immense amount of anger and frustration in that scream. But, he has to be careful not to let himself be guided by familiar factors. Perhaps the alien is the size of a mouse and regularly utters such sounds while eating. Given that he knows so little, he had better develop a generous-sized weapon.

Accordingly, he needs an adaptable, powerful, and fast-acting weapon that works against both hard and soft targets. Marchenko 2 can only think of one solution—electrical energy. He can use it to incapacitate Eve and probably any other biological creature, as well as the robot in which the consciousness of the *other* Marchenko is hiding. Electrical energy flows fast and its strength can be easily controlled. To use it he would not need anything more complicated than a kind of whip, which would also be rather inconspicuous. He can have his nano-fabricators make this metal whip within 15 minutes. Of course he also needs electricity, but he can easily tap the walls for that. He only needs to remove the top layer, where the luminous cells are located, and then apply a kind of collection net. He still does not know how much power the internal building network receives. However, if charging his internal batteries takes too long, he can simply increase the size of his collection net.

Marchenko 2 goes to the entrance of the side corridor and looks all around. He really does not want to be surprised while he is not yet ready. He listens directly on the floor, but nobody seems to be approaching. He would prefer a corridor branching off at an angle, which would completely shield him from anyone passing by, but it would cost valuable time to search for one. He believes he is not far away from the central room. The risk of someone roaming through this particular corridor seems small and acceptable.

So he starts on his task. The whip is going to grow from his right front leg so that he can employ it with a quick move-ment. If he discharges his battery down to ten percent within an extremely short time, it should kill even an elephant. He will have to be very careful with Eve. There is one problem he cannot solve: Once he has used the whip against a strong target, it will have to recharge before the next use, which he estimates will take at least half an hour. He will have to use a strategy that allows him to eliminate opponents one by one. *All in good time*, he thinks, concentrating on transmitting the necessary plans to his nano-fabricators.

Brightnight 36, 3876

Gronolf walks through the control center with a heavy, swaying gait. He requires only five steps from one end of the room to the other. He turns around with considerable momentum. He has placed his sensitive touch-arms over his shoulders. The load-arms are fighting with each other without Gronolf noticing it, as if they are two independent body parts.

Gronolf is proud of what the Grosnops have achieved during their long history. The subcutaneous thinking layers distributed across his entire body, his brain, allow him to move all limbs without significant delays. Once he makes a decision, the movement is lightning fast. However, this does not help him decide what to do next. He has been thinking for half a bubble period, but he is still undecided. The system is also not very helpful. While it summarizes the dramatic situation quite well—the *Majestic Draght* is still hurtling toward them—it cannot draw any conclusions.

Oh well. He orders his load-arms to stop fighting each other. An intruder must have caused the current situation. It would make sense to catch, interrogate, and punish this person. He therefore has to find the intruder. Maybe this alone would be enough to avert the danger. Gronolf hopes so, even though he has a hunch it won't be that simple. *If it were that easy*, he thinks, *the system could have awakened that mediocre female.* That would have been more efficient than using his highly-developed resources. He suppresses the thought about what will happen later.

Gronolf sits back down in his chair and activates the console, which had turned itself off. The control room records everything that happens here. He navigates through the image library. Gronolf is surprised that he does not have to go back far.

A strange creature had been here in the room, only a few hours ago. It appears to be small and weak. Its legs are as thin as stickfish, and it only has two arms. *Two arms! It's a miracle that this creature has survived for so long.* In the middle of its body, above the upper part of its arms, this creature has a large bulge, a spherical growth covered by a strange kind of... plant? One side of this sphere has two eyes. The creature must be blind on the other side. How can it defend itself against enemies coming from behind?

Gronolf sees right away that this intruder poses no danger to himself. He could defeat it easily. Yet he must not underestimate this creature either. After all, this creature found the way to Single Sun, just like his own species did. It crossed inhospitable space and finally survived a hike through the icy darkness. Most likely, it did not come alone. Gronolf checks the recordings but cannot find a second specimen. *What is that on the floor, though?* Something is wiggling there—it reminds him of a fish on dry land. *Oh, there is another one.* The intruder must have brought helpers along. These tiny things are probably machines because they are so different from the creature. They don't seem to be dangerous either.

Yet it might be better if he got a weapon. His nation had left its warlike past long behind. During the first 343 cycles, which went down in history as the Dark Seven-Times-Seven-Times-Seven Period, shortly after the Grosnops had emerged from the silt of the oceans, there were two factions viciously fighting each other. Then one of the groups was defeated, and the vanquished assimilated over time. Since then, weapons were seldom used for anything but hunting. This building contains its own arsenal, he knows. Yet for safety's sake there are also a few weapons stored in the control center.

Gronolf goes directly to one of the chest-high consoles and taps on it. A drawer opens up. He has the choice of a projectile thrower, which is more suitable for smaller opponents, or a harpoon. He considered the projectile thrower a mere toy. A carriontooth would just laugh at that. Even if he hit that sort of predator with ten projectiles, it still would spear him without any hesitation. The harpoon on the other hand...

Gronolf remembers the legendary hunt with the plex shortly after his draght. A carriontooth swam toward him. Gronolf had readied the harpoon too soon, and unfortunately the animal turned and fled. The carriontooth must have known that the harpoon would blast its chest. He and his plex-mates really had a lot of fun back then.

Gronolf wipes some dust from a side eye. He takes the heavy weapon from the drawer and examines it. The harpoon is powered by compressed air. Its range is short, not more than three or four body lengths, but that would be more than enough inside a shelter. The head of the spike contains an explosive charge programmed to explode after hitting an obstacle, with a delay of three milli-bubbles. The spike is so pointed and impacts with such force that it penetrates practically any target. The detonation delay is calculated in such a way that the spike has enough time to penetrate deep into the enemy's tissues. One small disadvantage of the harpoon is that Gronolf cannot use it if the target is too close. The explosion meant to kill the prey does not differentiate between friend or foe. Yet he is not worried. If something gets so close to him that the use of the harpoon is no longer advisable, he can easily tear it apart or crush it with his strong load-arms.

Gronolf releases the safety catch of the weapon. An increasing noise tells him that the compressed air chamber is being filled. He aims at the general. It is a strange feeling. The weapon gives him a power he can feel in his veins. It is seductive and causes even his respect for the venerable general to fade. He only has to press the trigger to become the highest-ranked one in the room. Even a physical weakling could do that. Without the harpoon he would have definitely been inferior to the general—when the general was still alive. It is no wonder that in his society the private ownership of weapons is forbidden. Yet now he is glad to have one. If he is lucky the intruder will recognize what this weapon is capable of.

Gronolf hopes the foreign creature will be reasonable. The knowledgeable scientists of his people often discussed whether a species that mastered spaceflight would automatically have to be peace-loving. Now he will have the first chance of testing this theory. However, he has to admit he would not mind firing the harpoon and seeing the creature swimming in a puddle of its own blood. That would be a well-deserved punishment.

He lowers the barrel and slides the safety catch forward. He needs to get a stronger grip on himself. Everything depends on him—he must not kill the intruder before interrogating it thoroughly. This would involve a small problem, though: He does not speak the language of this foreigner. Gronolf returns to the console where he looked at the recorded videos. Indeed, the creature sometimes utters sounds. Its voice sounds very dull. Gronolf analyzes the recording. The sound spectrum is only half as wide as that of his own species. This means the intruder has to communicate without high-pitched sounds. He tries to do that, but he cannot, at least not with his normal voice. However, during his training they learned to sing in harmony as a company. Back then he had to modulate his voice to make it sound deeper, because they had too many high voices. Gronolf imagines a greeting which he would not pronounce but sing in a deeper voice.

"Honor to your plex and you!"

It is working! When he sings the traditional greeting, it sounds much deeper. He repeats the sentence and records it. The analysis shows that the intruder should be able to hear everything Gronolf is saying. Of course this does not mean that the creature will also understand it. He listens again to what this creature was uttering. It seems to be debating with the general, as if it didn't know that he has been dead for a long time. Now the creature points at a spot on the wall, roughly where the entrance to the moving chamber is located.

"What is located there?" the stranger says. Gronolf tries to repeat the words without understanding them.

"Whattt uss louketed thurr," does not sound too bad. He repeats the sentence three times in order to memorize it. It might not be a greeting, but he hopes that the creature will recognize his attempted communication as a friendly gesture. And if he also demonstrates that the harpoon is able to snuff out the life of the intruder at any time, nothing should stand in the way of a sensible conversation. He considers it quite impossible that this puny being should get the idea of attacking him first.

It is time, he thinks. Gronolf holds his weapon at the ready and leaves the control center via the main corridor. His four eyes are wide open. He sniffs for alien scents. He stops after four steps because he has detected numerous scent molecules of the foreign creature. The intruder obviously did not try very hard to cover its tracks. This is going to be easy. The stranger might just as well have scratched arrows into the wall.

After a few minutes Gronolf reaches an area that has been devastated by an explosion. Was the intruder responsible for this? He examines the walls and the floor and finds a distorted blade from a turbine. The destruction appears deliberately caused by someone. However, this would have required so much strength that he can almost certainly exclude the foreign creature as a possible culprit.

He continues following the scent. If he can trust the map in his memory, he is approaching the sleeping chambers in a roundabout way. Did the intruder retreat there? Does it want to kill more of his sleeping comrades? He feels anger rising in him. Gronolf has to stop. He takes a deep breath and exhales, repeating until he has calmed down. In addition he activates the safety on his harpoon. That way he has at least a few milli-bubbles to consider things until the weapon is ready to fire. No matter what happens, he must not act impulsively and spoil everything.

He is about to resume his walk when he hears a noise. It is a binary measure, two steps, followed by a scratching sound. A two-legged, relatively lightweight creature is approaching from the left side corridor. Perhaps it is dragging something that explains the scratching noise. Gronolf stops and stays calm. This must be the intruder, approaching him unsuspectingly. He only has to wait for it.

Gronolf lifts the harpoon but leaves the safety on, so that the loading sound of the compressor won't give him away. The alien must soon come around the corner. Gronolf holds his breath.

May 9, 19, Adam

"Thanks."

The voice wakes Adam. Was it part of his dream, or had Marchenko just spoken to him?

"It's me." The voice comes from the reptilian fragment next to him. It is really Marchenko.

"I am so glad," Adam replies, and touches the metal with his fingers.

"And I most certainly am, too. I did not think I would ever get out of that pit. You saved me—and I had already believed you were gone."

"You have to thank Marchenko 2 for your rescue."

"Really?"

"It certainly was not his intention. He did not know I would follow him."

"What is he up to?"

"That's obvious—he wants to get Eve back and kill you. If he'd only known how close he was to you!"

"He did not recognize me."

"I am sorry I was so stupid," Adam says.

"I was the stupid one. I should not have gone on without making certain you were on the sled."

"No, I even manipulated the radio module in order to contact Marchenko 2."

"That explains why we could not reach you. What did you want from him?"

"He... he showed me there were a few secrets concerning my existence. Secrets that you kept from me. He wanted to tell me everything."

"Did he keep his promise?"

"No, not yet."

Marchenko remains silent for a minute. "I... I did not want to burden you with it," he finally says.

"And what is the great secret of our existence?"

"Eve, you, me... we all were created for this expedition. Your genetic material was manipulated so that you could survive even under adverse conditions."

"Are we siblings?"

"No. Your genes were spliced together from the best sections they could find. You are not related, at least not any more closely than the former owners of those genetic sequences."

"So we are artificial?"

"No, Adam, you are still human beings. You would not stand out among other humans, except for your resilience. You are not smarter or stronger than others, that was not the goal, but you definitely can withstand more than other people."

"So we were created to suffer?"

"If you want to sum it up... you were... engineered to survive."

"Thanks," Adam says.

"That is not all. There are many of you. It is no coincidence Marchenko 2 landed here. The Creator sent thousands of *Messenger* spaceships toward all potentially-habitable worlds known at that time."

"Potentially?"

"Yes. When we launched, the data from the telescopes could not yet tell for certain whether a planet was really suitable for life."

"So this means that many other Eve, Adam, and

Marchenko trios reached destination worlds where they could not land? They went on that long voyage for nothing?"

"Yes. We were lucky, even though Proxima b is not exactly a paradise. Yet we can live in the open air, with soil under our feet, almost like on Earth."

"Apart from the fact that we are totally alone."

"I am not so sure about that. This building proves we are not alone," Marchenko says.

"We have to find Eve. She is in danger. If you are not with her, and Marchenko 2 finds her before we do—"

"You are absolutely correct, Adam. And we will find her. But first thing, I had better repair the radio module of your universal device so that we can stay in contact. And then I will need legs and more energy."

"Then get started!"

"You'd better carry me a little bit longer. And we should not stay in this corridor. If Marchenko 2 comes back, he would find us here, still defenseless. We need a better hiding place."

May 9, 19, Eve

THE WAY TO THE CONTROL ROOM SEEMS LONGER THIS TIME. Is this due to the fact that she has stopped expecting surprises around every corner? Or is it her exhaustion which seems to stretch the distance? The sensor unit obediently walks ahead. When Eve takes a break, it stops as well. Now and then the display of her universal device flickers. The battery seems to be almost empty. She should worry about how to recharge it, but it's not really worth it. By now she knows the path from the control room to the sleeping chambers, and she can't contact anyone with the device anyways. So what does she need it for? To tell the time... But why does it matter anymore what time it is on Earth?

Eve notices that she has slowed down. She pulls herself together and consciously takes one step after the other. She has water, and some more food thanks to what she'd left in her backpack, and there is air here anyways, so she is going to last a while longer, even though it is meaningless. Don't they say the path is the destination? Such aphorisms never helped her before, but now she has nothing else to cling to.

Eve briefly leans against the wall and closes her eyes. She might as well collapse and go to sleep now. She is tired enough for it. Yet after two minutes she feels drawn to the control center. It is as if she still has a task to fulfill. Perhaps there is a deep death wish hidden behind it. It sounded as if something or someone is waiting for her at the destination. If it is a living being and not a machine, it probably won't be in a good mood, judging from the scream. She opens her eyes again and continues walking. The rustling sound tells her that the sensor unit is also going forward.

Five minutes later the corridor gets wider and curves toward the right. There is a second corridor coming from the left. This must be the spot where she and the ISU parted ways earlier. Is that the reason the ISU stopped? The ISU no longer makes that rustling sound. Eve looks at the floor while she is going around the corner so that she won't step on her little friend. It stands right beyond the curve. It has turned around and a red light is blinking.

Eve stops in amazement at what she sees. She is so shocked that her whole body starts to tremble. She stares wide-eyed at the alien. It is a frog, and it is alive! It looks huge, even at a distance of five meters. Its body is more than two meters tall and almost as wide. A giant eye with a black pupil is staring at her. Its very stature is terrifying, but the frog also holds an object in strong-looking arms—something that definitely looks like a weapon... aimed directly at her.

Eve feels dizzy because her heart is beating so fast. She has to steady herself with one hand against the wall. She hopes the creature won't interpret this as an aggressive action, but she can't help it—without support from the wall she will fall. The alien's weapon twitches back and forth, but there is no bang. The muzzle, from which a kind of spear protrudes, is still pointing at her.

Eve is about to panic. She tries to calm down, but the thing is so menacing that she doesn't run away only because she knows she would inevitably stumble over her own feet due to her fright. And she doesn't really stand a chance. All she has to do is look at the huge, muscular legs of the alien. The creature would reach her with only two or three steps.

Is it male or female? Or perhaps this species does not have sexes, or has more than two? And where did its head go? There is a gap between the points where the arms join the torso, as if there is something missing. It feels good to distract herself with useless questions. Eve is starting to calm down. The extraterrestrial does not attempt to get any closer. It is obviously not trying to kill her right away, since that would have happened already. It probably wants to dissect her and needs her to be whole, and that weapon does not look as if it would leave its prey in one piece.

How should she react? Does the creature even recognize her as an intelligent being? To the alien, she would appear to be about the size of a German shepherd in comparison to her. If they had encountered dog-sized beings here on Proxima b, would they have believed them to be intelligent? She has to do something that the alien definitely cannot interpret as an attack. Yet even among humans there can be many misunderstandings. What if raising an arm should be seen as a sign to attack, rather than as a greeting?

The extraterrestrial probably will not have a particularly high opinion of her. He saw his dead comrade in the sleeping chamber and most likely noticed already that a gigantic object is racing toward the planet—which is no coincidence. In addition, it should have noticed the destroyed corridor on the way here. How would she react to a being that threatens her friends, her house, and her world? The alien would need the patience of a saint not to be angry at her.

"Kurzukhan-la karlak-ti ha-ti ha!"

The extraterrestrial screams a phrase into the corridor that could mean anything—a threat, a greeting, or something else entirely? Should she fall on her knees and surrender? Or does the creature simply expect an answer? At least it has tried to use words instead of firing the weapon. That's a good sign! What should she reply? As the creature probably won't understand her, it does not really matter.

"I don't understand," she says as loud as she can.

"Ho-ha!" The alien advances half a step. *You'd better not do that*, she thinks, *the previous distance was just fine. Couldn't we maintain that distance?* She moves backward.

"Please don't come any closer," she calls, not quite as loud. The weapon is still pointed at her. Is she mistaken, or did the alien raise it slightly and place one of its three fingers close to a button on the side? She must not get hysterical now. "It would be very nice if you could lower your weapon."

She raises her open palms and tries to sound convincing. Yet the extraterrestrial does not react. If only Marchenko were here with her! He surely could act as an interpreter. Well, no, how would he be able to do that? He can't do magic or read minds.

"Ho-ha!" The alien comes closer again. She will have to decide. If she drops to the ground now the alien will either kill her, interpreting this action as an attack, or she would be completely in its power. She cannot even imagine what it would do to her. Should she try to flee?

"Let us talk," she says, "but please don't come any closer." She raises her palms to show she is unarmed. However, the creature either does not care, or interprets this as an invitation. The distance shrinks to two and a half meters. Not more than two steps. If the alien wants to, it could grab her in a second.

"Whattt uss louketed thurr!"

What did it say? Was that supposed to be English? Of course! The central room must have cameras that record everything. The alien used them to try to learn her language. This also means, though, that it knows about everything and considers her the destroyer of its people—justifiably so. No sentient being could simply ignore that. If the alien gets its hands on her, she will be in deep trouble, no matter how progressive and interested it might be. Then she might as well end her own life.

She knows what is going to happen. If she flees, the alien will point its weapon at her and pull the trigger. But a quick, terrible ending would be better. She turns around and runs as fast as she can. She enters the other corridor. Her heart pumps blood through her vessels and she feels alive like never before, even though death is hot on her heels—or maybe because of it. Behind her she hears a loud rumbling sound, followed by a terrifying scream. She runs, she leaps into darkness.

The scream pursues her, but there is no patter of feet, and no spear zooms through the air to pierce her body. She keeps fleeing and fleeing, and the farther she gets, the more she feels she got away with it once again. Her burning lungs tell her she is alive, her aching legs prove it, and so does the fear in her mind. There is no longer a pursuer but she keeps on running, nevertheless. The path leads downward, allowing her to maintain her speed even though she is getting weaker.

Sweat covers her skin, dripping as she runs. She whines loudly but does not stop until the path ends in a large room traversed by a thick pipe. Eve holds on to the pipe. She is wheezing and about to collapse, but she keeps upright with her last remaining strength. She has made it—at least for the time being.

From the corner of her eye she sees something familiar. She shakes her head. *Please, no new excitement*, she thinks, but life does not respect her request. She realizes what she is looking at. It is a pressure suit, human-sized. The helmet visor has been broken into many small splinters, and next to the suit there is a spreading puddle of dark, almost brown blood.

But on the helmet she can see the four letters A D A M!

May 9, 19, Marchenko 2

SOMETIMES YOU JUST HAVE TO WAIT AND GOOD THINGS WILL happen. Just as Marchenko 2's fabricators finished making his weapon, he hears footsteps—irregular, as if the person is injured. *What could this be?* He wonders whether he should move forward and look around the corner where the side corridor meets the main passage, but then he might give himself away, losing his greatest advantage. Who knows how well the other person can hear! If his assumption is correct and the unknown opponent is really injured, where would injured creatures go to hide? In narrow side passages, where they are not immediately visible.

Marchenko 2 prepares himself. He can flick his whip forward as soon as something comes around the corner. He will shoot first and ask questions later. While the metal wire is flying through the air he can still modulate the current, based on whom he is facing. It probably is Eve. The steps of the *other* Marchenko, and definitely those of the alien who uttered the scream, would be louder, he imagines.

He is so excited he can barely contain himself. He has been waiting for so long to see Eve again! What is approaching him is definitely alone. If he is lucky, the *other* Marchenko and Eve have separated, unaware of any danger. Then he can grab Eve and return with her to *Valkyrie* right away. At least if she still has her pressure suit—otherwise he will have to create a new one for her. Then it would become more likely that he'd have to eliminate the *other* Marchenko, because he...

He cannot believe what he is seeing: Adam! *Adam? Where did he come from? How did he manage to escape Valkyrie?* Marchenko 2 knows he must not hesitate. The whip lashes out and wraps around Adam's legs as fast as lightning. He has selected the lowest current strength, yet Adam topples like a chopped-down tree, while a large lump of metal slides from his hands. This is the object he himself had found down in the garbage dump! Adam must have had an important reason to carry it along all the way, because the thing is heavy.

He cannot ask him right now, because he is unconscious. Marchenko 2 comes closer to examine him. He turns Adam's head to the side. On his forehead he sees a heavily-bleeding laceration. He orders some nano-fabricators to close the wound. How did the boy manage to follow him? He almost admires Adam, even though he is also angry about his disobedience. He will have to teach his children respect, because the *other* Marchenko seems to have neglected to do that. One should not confuse love with tolerating disrespect.

Adam is no longer wearing a pressure suit. He probably took it off because of its weight. His body's core temperature is slightly elevated. He must have really exerted himself during the last 12 hours. *No wonder,* Marchenko 2 thinks, *after all, he has been pursuing me!* He also sees a wound on Adam's wrist. It is a cut, covered by a thin film to stop the bleeding.

One moment, Marchenko 2 thinks as he scratches off a piece of the film and analyses it. The structure was definitely created by fabricators. Adam does not possess any, so he must have met the *other* Marchenko. No. This can't be true! He himself did not encounter the *other* Marchenko, but Adam somehow found him? *Wait...* Could his alter ego have been— be—inside the lump of metal he left behind?

Marchenko 2 knows now he obviously made a big mistake. Luckily, everything turned out alright, because the other robot still seems to be in a dismal state. He obviously needed to absorb energy first. The two of them must have tried to find a sheltered spot in this side corridor, so the *other* Marchenko could take his time to repair his body. Well, that's over now.

Marchenko 2 ties Adam's legs firmly, so he won't be able to run away after awakening. Then he approaches the fragment of scrap that once was a robot. Now, finally, he will turn it into a mere piece of trash. He just has to hit it for a while with his whip. A few seconds at the highest level and all circuits of the AI's computing unit will melt into a useless lump. Whoever said an artificial intelligence could not die? He will soon demonstrate that the opposite is true. It is amazing, he thinks, that in the end biological and artificial intelligences are so similar. Any consciousness will disappear if its physical foundation is taken away.

"Don't do it, Marchenko."

The piece of scrap can talk. At least for now...

"How do you know what I am planning to do?"

"I saw how you brought down Adam."

"The boy is fine, don't worry. I took care of his head wound."

"But what will he say when he wakes up and I am gone?"

"He will get used to it." *Wait a moment.* He has an idea that will make his alter ego's death even more painful. "He won't even notice it. I will copy your structure. That's easy, as it only has to be external. Then I can take your place once and for all."

He likes this plan enormously. He just has to keep Adam unconscious until the transformation is finished. Then he will wake him and tell him how he managed to finally defeat the evil Marchenko— Marchenko 2, as they had labeled him. Afterward they just have to find Eve. She will be so happy to see Adam again that she will gladly come back to *Valkyrie*.

"But what is the purpose of it all?"

His alter ego realizes what Marchenko 2 is up to. And now he wants to stall him for as long as possible. Perhaps he hopes that Eve will appear in the nick of time to rescue him, or that some miracle will happen.

"It does not matter," Marchenko 2 answers. "You are just stalling for time."

"Maybe I should tell you what Adam and I talked about during the last few hours, and what Eve and I experienced. Otherwise the two of them will be suspicious right away. This won't be their first time to have you pretending to be me."

A clever approach. "And you would do that?"

"Do I have a choice? At least I can prolong my life that way."

"By a few minutes."

"So you agree?"

"Just get started." Marchenko 2 is a bit annoyed that his alter ego managed to persuade him to delay his plan. Yet this issue of credibility is a valid one. There is only one problem: He cannot know whether he is being told lies. However, he does not think that Marchenko would do this. It is only natural he would want to delay his death. He definitely would not want Adam and Eve to be unhappy after his death.

If Marchenko 2 had to make that same decision, he would do anything to make life as difficult as possible for his opponent, even after his own death. He would die happy if he could be certain of that. Nevertheless, he trusts this Marchenko to tell him the truth. That is crazy, considering they were created from the same electronic substance. Adam and Eve are not related to each other, but he and this Marchenko are like identical twins separated at birth who discover 20 years later that they developed very differently.

Therefore he listens to the Marchenko in the lump of metal, and integrates what he hears into his own memories. Once he finishes this process he won't even know that these are not his own recollections. About ten minutes have passed.

"And then we arrived in this side corridor. You know the rest," says the piece of scrap, which soon will be a glowing heap of burned circuits.

"Thanks. It's been fun talking with you."

"Do you have any ideas concerning life after death?"

Now the *other* Marchenko is getting too garrulous. *Life after death? That is ridiculous.* Marchenko 2 does not articulate this thought. Instead, he checks the charge level of the whip. Then he examines Adam again, but he is not moving at all. He must make sure Adam does not witness this. *It is very much like murder, after all,* he thinks, and then wonders why this does not bother him more. Is that abnormal? Is he sick? He feels very healthy. He is really looking forward to the time with Adam and Eve. They had been taken from him for such a long time! At first he will treat them the way their Marchenko would, and then he will tighten the reins gradually, so it won't be noticeable. This will seem like a normal process to the children. And it really will do them good.

Suddenly a deep, booming voice interrupts his musings.

"Whattt uss louketed thurr!"

Behind him, no more than a meter and a half away, stands a huge, brown-skinned creature that looks rather like a frog, with two legs and four arms, but without a head. Marchenko 2 knows right away that this must be the alien who uttered the scream earlier. One of its giant, dark eyes stares at him, and two of its four hands hold a weapon obviously aimed at him.

Now Marchenko 2 is glad he has not yet used the whip. He lashes out with it against the alien's skin. He chooses maximum current strength, and the wire is glowing. The hot metal burns itself into the alien's skin. Its limbs jerk. Marchenko 2 sees how all four hands try to grasp the weapon's handle, where the trigger must be located, but the electrical energy makes the extraterrestrial lose control of its limbs. One of the arms involuntarily tosses the weapon in a high forward arc, into the main corridor. A slimy mass oozes out between the frog's legs. The alien utters a horrifying, resounding scream. Then it falls backward, its arms and legs tremble, the scream fades, and the terrible creature is dead.

Brightnight 36, 3876

IT'S NO USE. HE IS NOT GETTING THROUGH WITH HIS attempts to communicate with the foreign creature. If he is not mistaken, the foreigner is afraid. No wonder, as it looks strikingly more fragile in reality than in the video recordings from the control room. Its spindly arms and legs, the slender body with two bumps at the front, and particularly that impractical round thing in the middle on top... That must throw this creature quite off-balance. It doesn't seem easy for the foreigner to balance this body part, as it wobbles back and forth, and sometimes the creature even has to use one of its hands to stabilize itself.

Nevertheless, this being has managed to travel through space. Life is amazingly varied and always finds a way, even under such negative starting conditions as the home planet of this species must have offered. If the intruder were not responsible for the death of his comrades and—soon—this entire world, Gronolf might almost pity it.

Gronolf watches the creature and speculates. Does it have a sex? How does it defend itself? He can see no weapons. Perhaps it uses a contact poison, like the pepperfish that not even the carriontooth dares to attack. He should not underestimate this strange creature. Perhaps that is its great advantage—not being considered capable of defense, so that it can surprise others by using its true abilities. Gronolf thinks of the lickslimer, which disguises itself as the discarded tail tip of the spiny lizard, a great delicacy. Those who greedily fell for this became victims themselves. As soon as the lickslimer landed in the primary stomach, it started to devour its host from the inside.

However, this strange creature is too large for that kind of attack.

"I donnt unnastand," the creature had answered when he gave a friendly greeting. Gronolf cannot remember hearing these words in the video recordings. Nor was "latt ahss tokk" in there. How should he react? How can he make the weird creature understand he only wants to talk to it, at least for now?

"Peace be with you!" he says several times, but he realizes that the meaning of this greeting is not obvious. Any enemy understanding his language would value and appreciate this temporary peace offering. He hasn't learned more. He was not trained as a Language Scientist, nor as a Script Scientist. However, he cannot imagine how such training would help him now. He would first need some time to study the stranger's language. Unfortunately, time is the one thing he lacks

Therefore Gronolf takes a big step forward. He wants to take the foreign creature to the central room and use the system to communicate via sign language. Just as he feared, the creature considers his step as an attack. *I haven't even unlocked the safety catch on my weapon!* he thinks.

The intruder runs away in panic. Gronolf doesn't notice that the small machine accompanying the creature is also activating. It quickly slips under his descending foot and throws him off balance through the unexpected movement. He hears cracking and crunching when his weight grinds the machine to dust, followed by a loud rumbling caused by his falling body. Gronolf screams his frustration and anger into the corridor.

Then he slowly gets back on his feet. He doesn't have to

run. He is not in a hurry, because he knows the strange creature cannot escape. The corridor it selected will lead to the reactor cooling chamber, and that's the end. He can follow the path leisurely. Perhaps the foreigner will also need some time to calm down. It has to realize there is no other way but to own up for its deeds. Gronolf stomps through the corridor that is slowly leading downward.

Suddenly he hears words.

"It dosont matta!" somebody says.

This sounds like the foreigner's language. Is the creature talking to itself? Gronolf slows down and starts to move silently. His trainer always praised him for how well he could sneak up to targets.

"Juss gatt startad."

What could this mean? It must be the same creature speaking these two sentences, as the pitch seems identical. Gronolf tries to remember the pitch of the intruder who ran away from him, but he can't. It is hard to notice differences, particularly as he can't understand a single word. This voice comes from a side corridor further ahead. Perhaps the creature is hiding from him there, trying to calm down by talking to itself? He likes to use that technique for himself. He prefers a louder voice, though, in order to vent his overflowing emotions. But that isn't a very good idea if you are hiding.

Gronolf stops again, shortly before the side corridor. What at first sounded like a dialogue has become a soliloquy that has an oddly calming effect. One thing seems to be true: The foreign creature wants to comfort itself. Should he give it another moment? Fear only leads to irrational reactions. He stands silently and listens until the creature has ended its soliloquy. What had he just heard without understanding it?

It is time to solve the problem. Gronolf walks around the corner. What he sees confuses him. A foreign creature is lying on the ground, motionless. Is it dead? It is not the specimen he met earlier. So there were two intruders! Yet why did he only see one in the video recordings of the control room? Was that part of the plan? No matter what these alien creatures intended, it failed—otherwise one of them wouldn't lie as though dead here in this side corridor.

The soliloquy must have come from the machine crouching next to the creature. Is it providing medical services? It has turned in his direction and is examining him. It does not look particularly dangerous, as it is small and has four legs that are even thinner than those of the alien creatures. He aims his harpoon at it, just to be safe, and releases the safety catch. He hopes that the machine won't be so stupid as to attack him, because if he fires his weapon, the explosion might also injure the alien creature lying on the floor.

What is that on the machine's front leg? The very instant Gronolf manages to formulate this thought, an incredible pain claws at his side. His body fails. He recognizes that he was attacked with electrical energy from the thing on the machine's leg, but knowing that doesn't help him any. His arms automatically try to fire the harpoon, but his muscles are beyond control. He doesn't stand a chance. The pain is unbearable. His spasming muscles throw the weapon from his hands. He is defenseless and feels the involuntary release of his sperm. He cannot help but scream in pain and outrage. Gravity is pulling his body backward. He cannot resist.

Gronolf falls. Unconsciousness claims him.

May 9, 19, Eve

"ADAM, YOU WERE HERE? WHAT HAPPENED TO YOU?" EVE whispers. She turns her brother's destroyed helmet in her hand. The lining is quite wet. Eve dips her index finger in the liquid, smells first and then touches it to her tongue. It tastes salty, but not like seawater. It is sweat. That fact calms her a bit because it tells her the helmet was not destroyed under water. Adam must have been wearing it, so he lived until arriving here. That piece of news fills her with infinite gratitude. Somehow, he managed to survive icy cold and darkness and even enter the building where she is. He is one hell of a guy.

She slams her fist against the pipe that crosses through the room, coming out of one wall and disappearing into the opposing one. There is a dull thud. The pipe is not empty. Then it must be filled with water. She walks alongside. Towards the middle, where the blood can be seen on the floor, the cover is missing for a length of one and a half meters. Eve is so short she did not notice it earlier. Below this opened area the pipe carries flowing water. She cautiously dips her hand into it and notices that it is warm. This liquid also tastes salty. But this time it is seawater, as it contains more than salt—it tastes of life.

She concludes there must be a connection from here to

the ocean. That would be a good escape route... if she had her pressure suit and enough oxygen to swim for a few weeks under the ice sheet until she reached an ice-free zone. How did Adam make it all the way here? There is only one possible method: He must have found *Valkyrie*. So she has to find her brother, and then they can leave this place together.

Yet there is a minor obstacle—that giant alien. And there is a huge problem: The thing hurtling toward this planet. In reality, it will be practically impossible to get out of here alive. Yet she cannot just give up, not when she is so close to a reunion with Adam.

A rumbling and a scream shock her out of her musings. That must have come from obstacle number 1. Eve looks around. The room offers no way of escape. She could try to hide inside the pipe, but without a breathing apparatus she can't stay underwater for long. Unfortunately, Adam's equipment is damaged. She might as well face her problem right away. Trying to run away from the alien had been a stupid idea. The fact that it didn't kill her right away, though, indicates there might be a chance for building an understanding. She takes another look at Adam's suit before she turns around and marches upward, back along the corridor.

FROM A DISTANCE SHE CAN ALREADY SEE THE ALIEN. IT IS lying still on the floor of the corridor. What happened here? Is it just sleeping? The closer she gets, the more obvious it becomes that a fight must have occurred. The alien's arms are strangely distorted. Its eyes are open. The creature lies directly in front of a side corridor, and it seems to be dead. Who killed it, though? She is scared.

Then she notices the alien's weapon. She recognizes it as the thing that was aimed at her for quite some time. Eve picks it up. She saw how the alien had held it. The creature had reached for the button on the side. Could that be the trigger? She aims the muzzle back into the corridor and pushes the button. She only succeeds at the third try, using all her strength.

"What are you doing there, Eve?"

She whirls around. It is Marchenko's voice. It comes from a half-height, spider-like body with four long legs.

"Is that you, Marchenko?"

"Yes, sure, who else is it supposed to be?"

Eve moves closer to the entrance of the corridor. Where did Marchenko come from? He moves a bit closer to her.

"Don't you want to say hello?"

He seems strange to Eve. She cannot explain it, but there is something revolting in his voice. She is reminded of the witch in the fairy tale about Hansel and Gretel. This is how Marchenko spoke when he read that story.

"Nice to have you here," she says.

"I am glad to see you." Marchenko stops in front of her in such a way that she cannot look into the side corridor.

"What's going on here?"

"Don't worry, Eve, I have incapacitated this thing. It can't hurt you anymore." The robot turns around and points at the alien with a front leg. "You see?"

Eve uses this opportunity to squeeze past Marchenko. Then she utters a shrill scream. Adam is lying in the corridor, and he also isn't moving.

"Marchenko, what did you do?" She aims the muzzle of the alien weapon at the robot.

"The alien attacked him," Marchenko replies, "but don't worry, he is alive. He is just asleep."

She takes a look at Adam, but she does not find any injuries except for a well-treated wound on his head. She glances down at the weapon. If the alien had attacked Adam with this thing, he would look very different now.

"The creature slapped him with bare hands and threw him across the room. Adam was lucky not to suffer any serious internal injuries." Marchenko must have noticed when she glanced at the weapon.

"You cannot believe a word he is saying." Eve is startled

when she hears this. This is also Marchenko's voice. It comes from an odd-shaped lump of metal at the far edge of the side corridor.

"That is Marchenko 2," the four-legged robot explains. "I managed to neutralize him earlier. He must have come here using *Valkyrie*. But now he no longer poses a danger. I simply did not have the heart to kill him. You know that I am not a murderer."

That does sound like her Marchenko. They let Marchenko 2 go away after the first fight. Should she believe him? Everything fits together so well. Yet she has to test him.

"You remember how we went separate ways? You just wanted to find another way to the control center. I haven't seen you since then. Why didn't you return earlier?"

"Your memories must be all garbled," the robot answers. "It was the cleaning mechanism that separated us, don't you remember?"

That is true. Only the real Marchenko could know this.

"I told him earlier about what happened," the voice from the corridor says.

"It's just a cheap trick," the Marchenko in front of her says. "He just wants to deceive you."

He is probably right. Why should the real Marchenko tell the fake one what happened to him? He should have realized Marchenko 2 would use that to his advantage!

"Why don't we simply wake Adam? He can attest to what happened," the voice from the piece of scrap says.

"You know yourself he won't be able to do that. He did not watch us trade places. It would be too dangerous anyways. We will only awaken him when he is ready. The fact that you would endanger your son just to prove yourself right indicates who you really are."

Eve is confused. Who traded places?

"We did not trade places," the voice from the corner says. "That was your evil plan, but it did not happen."

Eve sees the alien moving one of its arms from the corner

of her eye. So it is not dead after all. She is glad, even if it does not make the situation any easier.

The four-legged Marchenko also notices the alien awakening. "You better hand its weapon over to me," he says. "We have to eliminate this thing before it is fully awake. Otherwise we don't stand a chance."

Eve looks at the harpoon. The weapon does not look as if it could be switched to stun. "Why don't you use the weapon you used to incapacitate the alien earlier?" she asks.

"I ... you don't have a clue. I have to recharge it first."

The alien moves a second arm.

"It uses electricity?" Eve asks.

"Yes. I used a full charge against the alien, but it still appears to have survived. Now I can't use this weapon for another 15 minutes."

"You wanted to kill the extraterrestrial?"

"It attacked me. What was I supposed to do? Ask for mercy in a language the creature won't understand?"

"To me the alien did not seem very aggressive. It even tried speaking our language."

"But you still ran away, didn't you?"

The extraterrestrial starts leaning on its arms. It is obviously trying to rise, but its strength fails and its arms buckle.

"You really should give me the weapon now," the robot says. "Or do you want to fire it yourself?"

"I... will not shoot."

"Then give me the weapon, or do you want all of us to die?"

Eve hears the Marchenko voice from the lump of metal. "Don't give it to him! He attacked the alien first."

"You notice something? He wants us all to die," the robot answers.

The alien creature is trying once more to stand up.

"If you don't hand me the weapon, I will have to knock you out," the robot threatens. "My energy would be sufficient for that." He starts to move his right foreleg.

"Watch out," Marchenko's voice warns her.

No, Eve decides at this moment. The real Marchenko would not have tried to force her to give up her weapon. She is not going to wait until she gets knocked out. And they cannot pass up the chance to negotiate with the alien. She pushes the trigger button firmly just as she feels a sharp pain in her lower legs and is swept off her feet. Simultaneously, the strong recoil of the weapon throws her backward, away from the robot calling himself Marchenko and toward the giant frog who has just gotten up. She sees a flame shoot out of the robot body and she feels something soft on her back as she is being caught. Her muscles twitch when the electric discharge of the whip hits.

She can no longer move, and then her mind saves her from the worst pain by letting her drift into unconsciousness.

May 9, 19, Adam

HE IS FLOATING ON HIS BACK, DRIFTING THROUGH THE SEA. A gentle swell lifts him slightly upward. The sky is green, and on the horizon a white sun is setting, while a yellow sun stands directly overhead. The water is pleasantly warm and he floats in it even without swim strokes. Then he is suddenly shaken back and forth. He receives a painful slap on his cheek. And there is this giant eye over him, which looks at him as if it knew all of his secrets. Adam screams. The stare of this eye makes his blood curdle.

"It is okay," Marchenko's voice says. "You are safe. He is a friend."

The voice does not come from the eye but from somewhere behind it. Yet it has an immediate calming effect on him. Adam looks around. The eye belongs to a body. It is a huge body, reminiscent of a frog. The creature now pulls back its arms. Those must have been shaking him. Adam notices that he can feel his limbs again. There is an unpleasant tingling sensation, but it is starting to fade.

"Take your time," Marchenko says.

What happened? He had been carrying Marchenko in his arms, wanting to turn into this side corridor... at that point his memory ends.

"Did the alien injure me like this?" He knows the creature must be an alien, even though he never saw one before.

Marchenko laughs. "If our friend had wanted to hurt you, you would look very different now. Did you see his arms?"

That is true. "So who did it?"

"Your good friend, Marchenko 2. He must have heard us coming."

"And is he gone now? Or is that you?"

"Come on over here, if you can manage to walk again. You will definitely recognize me. I also know how you injured your wrist. Just ask me!"

"What about Marchenko 2? Did you defeat him?"

"Eve... pulverized him."

"What?"

"She fired the alien's weapon at him."

"She did what?"

"You understood me correctly. It was self-defense. Marchenko 2 threatened her with the same weapon he used to knock you out."

"What about Eve? Where is she?"

"She is lying right next to you. She is still asleep. You can try to wake her up. Or should our new friend take over that task?"

"That's okay, Marchenko, I will do it." Adam concentrates on his limbs. They obey him, so he rolls to his side and then gets on his knees. He has to take it easy. Then he looks around. He sees the silhouette of the alien at the entrance of the side corridor. It is not very brightly lit, but he immediately sees that Eve is indeed lying next to him. He looks at her. Now that he knows she is not his sister she appears even more beautiful to him. Did Marchenko already tell her about it? It is time to wake her up. He gently strokes her cheeks. She becomes agitated and then suddenly jerks upright. He barely manages to get out of her way.

"Where is he? Where is the bastard?" she gasps, looking around in panic.

"He is gone," Marchenko says. "But look. Adam is here."

Eve turns around and looks at him. Yet she shows no reaction. Has she forgotten him? Then her eyes light up. "Oh, Adam," she says. "I am so happy to see you."

"I am, too. I mean, that you are here," Adam says and blushes.

They embrace.

"But what happened to Marchenko 2?" Eve asks, looking at Adam.

"I was unconscious," Adam replies.

"You finished him off, Eve," Marchenko says. "He can't endanger us anymore. Never again."

"I didn't want to do that."

"I know, but you had no choice. Otherwise we would all be in his power."

"You know what the worst thing was? Up to the very end I was not sure which of you two was the real one."

"I can imagine it. He was very clever about that," Marchenko says.

"Why did he know so much about us?"

"He wanted to kill me with his electric whip. In order to buy time I told him what had happened. And then Gronolf intervened."

"Gronolf? Is that the alien? Do you understand his language?" Adam asks.

"We are still working on our communication. So far we have managed to exchange names."

"Can you teach us his language once you have learned it?"

"That won't be possible, Eve. Some of the sounds he uses are in the ultrasonic range, and you could not pronounce them. Right now, I am recording all of his utterances, analyzing the context, and later I will attempt to create a linguistic model."

"That sounds doable," Adam admits.

"It works as long as we are dealing with something we can see at the moment. Once we talk about abstract issues, it will become more difficult. Maybe then symbols will help us."

"A sign language."

"Yes, Adam."

"How long will it take until we can converse fluently?" Eve asks.

"That will be a lengthy process. Maybe never."

"Lengthy?" Eve looks at Marchenko and then at Adam, obviously distressed. "That's bad."

"What is the problem?" Adam asks.

"You wouldn't know this. We might only have a few days left. Something really huge is approaching us."

"Something huge?" Adam gets up slowly. He needs to move around now.

"I don't know what it is. On the map it looked like another planet." Eve looks as if she has not told them everything yet.

"And how do you know it is approaching us?"

"I called it," Eve explains. "I thought I was sending a distress call. I had no idea the thing would go on a collision course right away."

"You used the aliens' systems? That was risky."

"What do you know about this, Adam? You were gone, I had lost Marchenko, so to me, this seemed to be the only way out."

"Eve did the right thing," the AI's voice says. "From her perspective, it was the sensible approach. It is always easy to judge things in hindsight. Understanding these strange systems was already an enormous achievement. This might help us avert the threat."

"Do you think the alien actually needs our help?" asks Eve, tilting her head.

"I don't know," Marchenko says. "It would be better if he can manage it on his own. If he can't solve the problem and we also fail at it, he won't be as restrained as he is now. I think we are in his good graces because you killed Marchenko 2 in front of him, but if you later become responsible for the death of his species, he might not be so happy."

"I can sure understand that," Adam says.

Brightnight 36, 3876

THE MACHINE—WHICH THE LARGER FOREIGNER HAD CARRIED —is full of surprises. First of all, he was amazed at its intelligence. Together they managed to get at least some rudimentary communication going. Gronolf now knows that the machine calls itself 'Marchenko,' that the alien he met first is 'Eve,' and the other one is 'Adam.' Pronouncing these names is difficult, though, because the alien sounds use only a small part of the acoustic spectrum. It is as if he had to sing constantly in a different voice. However, the two aliens have even greater problems with his name. In order not to cause them unnecessary frustration he lets them believe that 'Gronolf' is his complete name—how could you teach someone to pronounce a word, if they cannot hear half of it? Only the machine can pronounce 'Gro_#_-nolf#_$__#' correctly.

The true nature of Marchenko is still a mystery to him. He probably does not come close to doing him justice by using the term 'machine.' During their attempts at communication, Marchenko has proven to be much more. He still cannot judge how much more. Sometimes the machine reminds him of an Omniscience. An Omniscience consists of the compressed information, thoughts, and emotions of numerous Grosnops. The Knowledge Scientists developed this concept many cycles ago, because the machines built by the Motion Scientists had become too complicated over time to be controlled even by the most talented individuals. A spaceship like the *Majestic Draght* would be impossible without being controlled by an Omniscience. Yet this Marchenko machine is much too small for that. Not even this shelter building could contain an Omniscience!

If Gronolf is honest with himself he would have to admit the second surprise was really a shock. He urged them to walk to the control room and offered to carry the machine. Yet the machine refused. He did not understand the reason for this, but he agreed. A few milli-bubbles later, Marchenko suddenly stood behind him on four legs. While Gronolf's own species also has the ability to regrow limbs, that takes many bubble periods, not just a moment. He was particularly impressed by Marchenko's trick of letting his legs crawl separately from his body. At that moment Gronolf recognized that he had seen one of those legs accompanying the alien Eve. He'd stepped on it—crushed it—when he'd turned to follow her as she'd run away.

Now it is time to go to the control room. Due to Marchenko's abilities, Gronolf hopes they will be able to solve the problem caused by the alien. His anger at Eve has dissipated since she saved his life. The situation had been obvious —Eve used Gronolf's own weapon to punish the four-legged machine that had knocked him down. He was still not sure about the role of that other machine. It must have had its own agenda, which should be impossible for a machine. Perhaps it was defective—or had been programmed by a different faction of the aliens. What a mess it would be if these aliens started to continue their squabbles on this planet! Therefore he prefers to believe in a defect.

Gronolf does a leg squat and then stands up again. His muscles need to be moved. The long, thin wound on his side, where the hot wire dug into his skin, is already starting to close. It will take only a few days before it is completely healed. He gestures with his touch-arms to get the aliens to start walking. They talk in their low-pitched language and then follow him, with Marchenko taking the lead. Adam and Eve let their touch-hands meet. Strange how that species managed to survive without load-arms!

He watches the aliens through his rear eye. Now Eve strokes the grass growing on Adam's middle bump. Why don't they just rip it out? Does it maybe fulfill some ritualistic purpose? Due to their sizes he can easily tell the two apart. Is that a normal variability? Or is Eve younger than Adam and therefore shorter? At some point he will have to ask Marchenko about the purpose of the protective clothing. These creatures' skins are probably so sensitive that they have to protect themselves against foreign environments all the time. This would indicate they developed in a place with a low injury risk. Gronolf tries to think of such places on his home world, but he can only think of the slime swamps of Eltok. Yet there, due to the population of sawtooth crawlers, the injury risk is actually much higher than on many beaches.

They are making good progress and will soon reach the control center. He hopes Eve told the others that the general will be waiting for them there. Gronolf still does not have a bright idea as to how to honorably dispose of the remains. The general probably used to like sitting in his command chair, so it is fitting that he stayed there after his death. Gronolf does not mind seeing him, as it is good to be reminded of one's mortality, and he also feels a bit motivated by the presence of a high-ranking officer. It would be a great honor for him to save the world under the eyes of the general.

Gronolf moves directly to the holo-map in the control center. He notices through his right-side eye the others stopping in front of the general's chair. Eve and Adam interlace their touch-hands. Their posture seems to express awe, even though he is still far from understanding the aliens' body language.

Soon afterward Marchenko joins him at the holo-map. Gronolf demonstrates how to use the four sectors of the control panel. Due to the sounds generated by the pressed keys, he could do this with his eyes closed. Gronolf knows that Marchenko can also hear in the ultrasonic range, so he will appreciate these melodies. Among Gronolf's people it is considered the highest skill of a navigator to select a travel route not just by the highest efficiency but also by its harmonic sound. This tradition is still used in modern space travel—at least it was so before his time in the sleep chamber.

Gronolf closes all four of his eyes and remembers his time in the egg, when he only had his sense of hearing available. His mother managed to create a whole world in his mind through her songs and stories. Back then he still believed these were all meant for him, but of course the other siblings in his plex also participated.

"Gro_#_-nolf#_$__#?"

Marchenko pronounces his name with the perfect intonation. He can't remember when he last heard it so perfectly. The system here certainly does not manage to do that. He opens his eyes. His childhood is still there, but his memories of the time right before his long sleep are still missing. If he could just remember them, they might be better able to solve the problem they are facing. Gronolf cautiously hits his belly to get rid of his frustration.

"Marchenko?" He tries to pronounce the other one's name correctly, too.

"Gro_#_-nolf#_$__#?"

"Marchenko?"

"Whatt isss thatt," the machine asks.

Once again Gronolf is surprised, because a miniature arm grew on Marchenko's shoulder and it is now pointing at the symbol for the *Majestic Draght*. Gronolf is not sure what the words of the machine mean, but it seems to be a request for information. How can he explain what is happening there? He moves his right touch-arm, hits his upper body, and starts to stumble. Was that clear enough? If the *Majestic Draght* hits Single Sun, it will be a catastrophe for his people and the planet. Yet why is the capital ship not reacting to his warning messages? Could it be that the alien Eve triggered a self-destruct mechanism? However, Gronolf has never heard of such an absurd process. If this has to do with the unauthorized contamination of the shelter building by aliens, it would have been enough to awaken him, and he would have eliminated the problem.

There must be something going on in the background he does not understand. Does not *yet* understand, he corrects himself, because he is going to find the cause.

May 9, 19, Marchenko

There are three deep tones and one high one. The alien is using all four hands simultaneously to touch one key each on the inner edges of the segments. The virtuoso movements of the hands are impressive, even of the lower ones which are obviously meant for heavy labor. If one of these aliens should become a pianist, human competitors would stand no chance.

Suddenly the projected 3D map disappears and they once again are standing in a bare room. Gronolf presses four other keys and then claps his hands. Suddenly a blue wall appears out of nowhere in the middle of the room. The alien stands in front of it and moves a finger over its surface. Lines can be seen where he touches the wall. *A virtual blackboard, very practical*, Marchenko thinks. *He probably wants to explain something.*

Gronolf draws a large circle and a slightly smaller one. Then he points at himself, and suddenly his figure, at perhaps one-tenth of its actual size, appears in the larger circle. It must be the planet. Gronolf reaches for the smaller circle and gives it a push. The circle starts to move towards the planet. This must be the thing Eve accidentally called. The alien snaps his fingers, and inside the smaller circle a miniature image of Eve appears. It really was Eve who set this thing in motion, that seems clear. Yet why doesn't Gronolf simply contact it to send it back?

Marchenko makes himself as tall as possible. The alien realizes what he wants and picks him up so he can reach the wall. With his front leg, the former ISU 4, he draws a stylized arrow pointing from the planet to the approaching object. It is supposed to symbolize a radio message. He is surprised when Gronolf erases what he has added. He draws another arrow and the alien once again erases it. When this happens again on the third try, Marchenko is certain: Gronolf wants to tell him that his messages do not reach the object or don't have any effect. Suddenly he feels so hot he checks his own core temperature, but it remains unchanged.

Marchenko remembers the rather risky method they used to gain access to this building. They let their ship, *Messenger*, crash on the surface so the impact would melt the ice. What if they destroyed whatever sends Gronolf's messages into space, like the antenna of the building? He did not notice anything like that, but it might be possible that he had not recognized the alien technology.

He has to explain to Gronolf that it might be related to the antenna. Something like that can be repaired, can't it? He draws the building they are in and sketches an ice layer on top of it. Then he indicates an object crashing on it by drawing and erasing it at different positions. In the end he points at himself and adds a symbol on the roof of the building that resembles a sine wave. He hopes the extraterrestrial will understand that he is referring to an antenna.

At least Gronolf is watching Marchenko intently. Then he puts Marchenko down and erases the complete drawing. Why doesn't he indicate whether he understands? Marchenko taps against his legs, but the extraterrestrial does not react. Instead, he types something on the segmented control panel again.

"Gronolf," he says then, and his image appears on the wall. What is that going to be?

The image changes. Marchenko sees the piece of scrap he has become. It is a sad sight. He will have to use the time when Gronolf rests to take on a useable shape again.

"Marchenko," the alien says. Nothing else happens. He must be waiting for a reaction.

"Marchenko," Marchenko repeats. Gronolf stamps his foot loudly on the floor so that Adam runs toward them.

Now they can see a red star orbited by a planet. The image is not to scale. The star is blinking.

"Sotoka," the alien says.

"Sotoka," Marchenko replies.

This time Gronolf does not stamp the ground but keeps looking at him. He must not have given the right answer.

"Proxima Centauri," Marchenko says, and gets a stamp of the foot as a reward.

Then the planet blinks.

"Sotoka-so."

"Proxima b," Marchenko answers. He now understands the principle. It is a good idea to exchange basic vocabulary this way. Gronolf must have noticed that Marchenko has a perfect memory. So he probably will end up as the interpreter.

The extraterrestrial quickly presents many more words. Some of them Marchenko does not recognize. In the case of others, such as an animal that looks like a mixture of a shark and a killer whale, but has no eyes, he can only use the generic term 'fish.' It gets really interesting when Gronolf projects a landscape that looks quite surreal.

"Dutoka-so," he states.

Is this his home planet? The giant frogs obviously did not develop on Proxima b.

"Adam and Eve, come here. This should interest you," Marchenko calls out.

The image shows a beach with the ocean waves surging against it. The water seems a brownish-green, probably because the sky is a lush green instead of the azure of Earth's sky. A small white sun is visible on the horizon, while a larger yellow one is almost at the zenith.

"Dutoka-so," Marchenko says to Adam and Eve. "That must be Gronolf's home."

"Which planet has two suns?" Eve asks.

"It is probably Alpha Centauri," Marchenko suggests. "That would be plausible. It is possible to fly from there to here in less than a generation. And Alpha Centauri is a binary star."

"Wow, the green sky, take a look at this," Adam says. He sounds so enthusiastic it seems he would like to travel there right now.

"That must be caused by the composition of the atmosphere," Marchenko says.

"Dutoka-so," they hear Gronolf say.

Oh right, he has not repeated the word in English yet. "Alpha Centauri," he says out loud.

Then there are pictures of Adam, Eve, and himself on the beach. The scale does not seem to be quite right, or the waves are much higher than on Earth. What does Gronolf want to say with this? Is it an invitation? The landscape fades and can only be seen in contours. *He wants to know where we come from,* Marchenko thinks. Should we tell him that? What if the Grosnops then show up in our solar system? Even if Gronolf appears to be reasonable—he does not know their civilization. No, it is definitely too early for that.

Marchenko draws an image of the constellation Ophiuchus on the wall, which looks like a child's picture of a house, and then he marks Proxima Ophiuchi, Barnard's Star. There will be time later to reveal the true position of the solar system. In spite of this he feels bad, because Gronolf showed him his home planet without any ulterior motives. As Barnard's Star is a red dwarf, Marchenko can only show him pictures from Earth that he has manipulated accordingly.

Adam taps on his housing. "To be honest, we are really exhausted."

Sure, he totally forgot Adam and Eve have to sleep now and then. And they will need food and water. By tomorrow Marchenko should be able to make himself a useable body again.

Brightnight 36, 3876

HE WONDERED FOR A LONG TIME WHETHER HE SHOULD SHOW these strangers his home. He has to admit he did it for himself —seeing the soft beaches, the fertile sea, and the sky as green as an arrow crab on the holo-display filled his stomach with joy. Gronolf is not sure whether he correctly understood the explanation given by the machine.

The aliens, who call themselves humans as he now knows, seem to have watched something damaging the antenna of the building. That is almost impossible, but it would explain why the *Majestic Draght* is not answering his calls. The major question is why it would have reacted to the control impulse sent by the alien Eve. Could the antenna somehow have lost its power? It is only a vague feeling, but it looks to him as if he is far from really understanding the situation. He will have to go through his archives and refresh his memories.

Right now, though, the humans need some rest. He only has to look at them, these tender, pale little plants, in order to fully understand that. He himself will not sleep until the problem is solved—he owes that to the general. And these aliens don't really look like they are capable of that.

"Water, food," the machine says. Gronolf is glad the language course worked so well. It is no problem providing water for the aliens. Food might be a bit more complicated.

Can they digest canned food made for Grosnop stomachs? He signals the foreigners with his load-arm and walks ahead. The crew room in the control center has everything necessary. In order to open a cabinet, one unlocks it by voice command and then taps the outside cover. He simply leaves the doors open. With his rear eye he sees Marchenko checking the supplies. The machine should have sensors to make sure the humans are not poisoned.

There is water in the beach room, which is still locked and contains several basins adapted to the size of the Grosnops. Gronolf looks around. One basin should be enough for the two aliens. He opens the room and asks the system to fill one basin. He wonders for a moment which temperature these foreigners would find pleasant. As they are still wearing clothing at a room temperature of 24 degrees, he decides on 35 degrees. Grosnops only use hot water like that when they are sick.

He leaves the crew room again and sees Marchenko examining food. Adam and Eve seem to be happy about the water. Gronolf returns to the control center and activates the camera. He was wondering the whole time what the aliens might look like underneath their protective clothing. They are just taking off their clothes. They do so very cautiously, shielding themselves on all sides. Then they climb into the basin without looking at each other. Gronolf rewinds the recording. From behind the aliens look close to identical, but not from the front. Could this be a sexual dimorphism? Or did the smaller alien Eve lose a body part at some time? However, as Eve has two pronounced bumps that Adam lacks, it probably is a sexual differentiation. He will have to show Marchenko the images later and ask for the names of these parts. Too bad he cannot talk to the aliens himself.

Gronolf sits down in the empty chair and looks at the general. *How would you act in my situation?* Right now, the danger seems extremely abstract. Behind him, two frail humans splash around in a basin like tadpoles. He sits across from the dead general and commands the entire building, and next door a foreign machine analyzes the stored food. This is all so exciting that Gronolf does not miss a single member of his plex. And all of this is supposed to be ground into dust by a huge collision six days from now? It is really hard to imagine. Yet the holo-map proves it.

He has to scan the archive, even though he feels an aversion toward the idea, because he feels that his memories are incomplete for a reason. Before he entered the sleeping capsule something must have happened, something that changed the entire future of his people, at least here on Single Sun. He turns the seat to the other side and leans over the open console. He enters a few commands on the control panel to call up the archive. The system accepts his user ID. After he was awakened he must have automatically received maximum access rights. In earlier times he probably couldn't even have opened the weather report for the past cycle, as he was no Weather Scientist.

When he asks the system for available data he encounters the first surprise. The archive does not just know the history of the shelter building, which would be logical, but can access the entire past since the start of the *Majestic Draght* from his home world.

How should he proceed? Judging from experience he would say that it is easier to understand events if you follow them chronologically. His own memories end shortly after launch. This does not necessarily mean that the disaster had already been on the way. It only indicates it started at some point after that. In order to narrow down the period, he will consult the records at various intervals.

Gronolf settles down. He chooses the authentic method of transmission. That way he won't have to read any biased texts written by his ancestors. The archive will use the sonar system to create images directly in his head. Gronolf prefers this method of transmitting information. It is a bit strenuous, but incredibly realistic. His mother communicated with him that way when he still could not see her. Would these foreign creatures also be able to use it? It certainly would be a great experience for them.

He leans back, folds his legs comfortably underneath the chair, and closes the lids over all four eyes. Then he shuts his inner ear against normal sound, so he won't be disturbed.

Archive, Darknight 4, 3349

"ARCHIVE, DARKNIGHT 4, 3349." WHEN HE GIVES THIS command, the system calls up the recordings for that date from the memory tubes and transmits them via ultrasound with the coding specific to his consciousness.

Gronolf and his comrades sit in the wardroom. The *Majestic Draght* is gaining speed with ten times the gravitational acceleration of his home world, but they have been trained for that. They are young and strong, and they must not show any signs of weakness. Therefore Gronolf walks upright between his quarters, the classroom, the exercise room, and the wardroom, even though his back hurts so much he would rather not move from his sleeping beam. His night's rest will have to suffice. Then he will be able to let his arms and legs hang down, but right now he has to prove he is still the strongest one in his plex.

"Did you hear what is supposed to have happened in the control center this morning?" Wakmir always knows the latest rumors. Sometimes they are even true, but Gronolf generally is not interested in that kind of story.

"Forget it," he says. Yet he knows Wakmir will tell him everything, whether he wants it or not.

"They say someone made a fool of the general."

"Which one? My father?"

Wakmir laughs. "Then I would hardly tell you this story. And your father wouldn't allow something like that to happen. I just heard it was one of the generals."

"And what happened? Who made a fool of him? A younger one who wants to take over his post?" At the command level it can get pretty rough. If an officer sees a chance to take over somebody else's post, he is going to take that chance. This causes even experienced officers to be constantly on alert, which is advantageous for society, they have been told.

"No, the Omniscience."

"You are joking. The Omniscience is a kind of virtual machine, and it only exists to obey orders."

"That's what the Omniscience said. It stated that a specific order of the general clashed with other orders of a higher priority. Yet there were no such orders."

"Then that was insubordination. The Omniscience would have been deleted right away."

"It claimed it was operating under certain standard requirements that had the status of laws, such as the efficiency requirement."

"Sure, the Omniscience has to operate with the greatest possible efficiency."

"Yes, you 'know-it-all.' And because the order of the general would have led to an inefficient flight method, the Omniscience rejected it."

"So what happened, Wakmir?"

"So now you want to know it after all?"

"You can't just give me a bite and then leave me hungry."

"Oh well, okay, but only because it's you. The general is supposed to have become very aggressive. The Omniscience did make a fool of him in front of the others. Then the security forces had to move him to the medical sector."

"Who gave that order? One of the other generals?"

"Your father, you mean? No. The great irony is that the Omniscience made the decision. It is responsible for monitoring the mental health of the entire crew."

Archive, Darknight 89, 3349

GRONOLF IS IN A DEEP AND DREAMLESS SLEEP. SUDDENLY THE image of his father in uniform manifests itself in his consciousness.

"Alarm! Wake up!" his father says without moving a single muscle. This tells Gronolf that it is a general alert. Right now, the system transmitted this message into the mind of everyone on board, whether awake or asleep. This means it is very serious. Gronolf opens his eyes and jumps from his sleeping beam. He reaches for the weapon in his locker and runs into the corridor with his comrades.

"What happened?" he asks the others, but nobody knows anything.

Finally there is an announcement.

"The life support system in Sector 132 has been deactivated."

A defect in the ship—and they wake the entire crew for that? A sense of agitation spreads. He can't be the only one who thinks this way.

"It is not a defect, as the diagnostic program has proven. Sector 132 was sealed off and no longer receives air. Your group is tasked with finding the cause."

This message obviously was sent directly to his company. His commanding officer is yelling something. The others run to their lockers to get oxygen masks. Gronolf follows them. Then they move through the ship on the double. All doors they pass have been locked.

"Stop!"

A large bulkhead looms in front of them. The company commander and two assistants try to convince the control system to open the door. The electronic system refuses to do so.

Two of his comrades are sent to the workshop. They return with huge devices that Gronolf recognizes as blowtorches. The bulkhead starts to glow. It cannot withstand this heat. The blowtorches cut a rectangular opening. The company commander insists on pushing the cut part of the metal to the side himself. At that moment another bulkhead slams down behind them.

Behind the newly-cut opening there is a huge hall full of machinery—and a vacuum. Why didn't the electronic system warn them of the danger? Gronolf reaches for his oxygen mask. The air pressure blows the surprised company commander through the hall and smashes him against an open airlock. The others watch it as if paralyzed. Gronolf sprints forward. The company commander landed on the airlock in such a way that he is sealing off the opening in the exterior wall through which air is sucked out of the room. Gronolf notices right away that this is saving everyone's life, and the company commander realizes it too. Gronolf must not free the commander from this position, but he holds an oxygen mask on the commander's stomach so that the Grosnop breathes through it.

It takes a long time before help arrives, because the second bulkhead behind them also refuses to open. The company commander plugs the hole so well that the air pressure in Sector 132 is slowly recovering. The rear of his superior officer is exposed to the cold vacuum. In spite of it he does not utter a sound. He is a good company commander. *If he dies, he will die honorably*, Gronolf thinks. The helpers brought a special foil to seal the hole so that the company commander can finally leave the spot.

The company commander survives. His rear eye is lost and he cannot move his limbs as he used to, because a part of the thinking layer underneath his skin has been lost. Therefore he can no longer lead the company. He suggests Gronolf, who saved his life with the oxygen mask, to become his successor.

The problem in Sector 132, it turns out, was no defect. The Omniscience pumped air out of the sector because there was nobody in it. Accordingly, the need for air had fallen to zero. The Omniscience has matched requirement to reality. It refuses any communication concerning this issue.

"WHY WERE WE NOT INFORMED ABOUT THESE MEASURES?"

As the new commander of the affected unit, Gronolf is allowed to listen to the interrogation of the Omniscience. He is not familiar with the Knowledge Scientists asking the questions.

"There was no need for it." The voice of the Omniscience sounds soft and natural, almost maternal.

"Lives were certainly endangered."

"The sector had been properly sealed off. Nobody was in danger."

"Company commander Tumrir was severely injured."

"He illegally gained access. The bulkhead very clearly signaled that it was impossible to open. It was also considerably damaged during the illegal access."

"The bulkhead is a thing, an object. If it receives the order to open, it has to follow it."

"Due to the vacuum behind it the bulkhead could endanger lives once it opened. Not endangering lives is among the highest priorities."

"Then it was a mistake to evacuate air from Sector 132."

"Efficiency is also one of my highest priorities. If we

reduce the areas filled with air, we can reach our destination more efficiently."

"If Central Control had been informed about it, it could have reacted more appropriately."

"My efficiency estimate showed that it was not advisable to pass on that information. The process would have been unduly lengthened."

The Knowledge Scientist is at his wit's end. Gronolf has never experienced anything like this. A scientist should always have an answer, just like a warrior should always have his weapon at the ready. It is even more shocking to him that the other members of the leadership don't seem to have any ideas either. The Omniscience must be punished! Yet as a simple company commander he has no right to propose solutions to generals, even if his father is among them.

Archive, Brightnight 19, 3350

Since yesterday the ship has been accelerating again, and everyone is very upset. Gronolf drags himself through the corridors. He is needed in Sector 23. Under normal circumstances it would only take a few milli-bubbles to get there, but what is *normal* if the ship is using an acceleration 14 times the normal value? On the way he only comes across a few Grosnops. The majority of them also use their load-arms for walking. Gronolf is proud he is one of the few still staying upright. Suddenly a bulkhead slams down right in front of him. He gives it a nasty look from his front eye, but the bulkhead does not care. Another detour! He is actually on his way to a meeting of commanders because of this.

Nevertheless, he reaches Sector 23 three minutes before the appointed time. The room is not very large. It smells of food and sweat. There are about 200 commanders present. There is little sign of military order, and a majority of the others are lounging on the floor. Gronolf pinches his shoulder with his load arm. That is totally unacceptable! He deliberately stands upright in the middle, but nobody follows his example.

Significantly past the agreed-upon time, one of the generals speaks. This is also a sign that things are slowly going downhill. Previously the doors would have been closed at the appointed time and any commanders arriving late would have been demoted. The laxity is not a good development.

The general greets those present and describes the problem. "As soon as there is nobody left in a sector, the ship seals it off and deactivates the life-support system," he explains.

"The ship?"

Who dares to interrupt a general? The question came from behind, but Gronolf does not know the person who asked it.

"The Omniscience, but then you all know that."

A few of the commanders in the front rows laugh dutifully.

"We cannot let the Omniscience take control over the ship away from us. It is a matter of principle. The leadership always must have the last word. Therefore we came up with a counter-strategy," the general continues. "From now on your men will ensure we lose no additional rooms. They will patrol the ship in such a way that there is always at least one warrior in each sector."

To Gronolf this looked like a cheap way out. It is typical: Instead of fighting the cause, their leaders try to minimize the effects of the problem. He does not think this is a strategy with much of a future.

"Why doesn't anyone talk to the Omniscience?"

The commander who asked this is sitting a few steps away from Gronolf. He has known him since basic training.

"The Omniscience refuses to discuss any of its decisions."

"What is its argument?"

"Its origin. It sums up the combined knowledge and the experience of millions of Grosnops. It says it cannot be wrong. It also says it is normal that we cannot comprehend its decisions."

"Can't we turn it off?"

"The *Majestic Draght* cannot be flown without the Omniscience. We need it for navigation, and the drive system won't work without its control."

Another commander speaks up. "The high acceleration is

bothering my soldiers. Didn't they say we had many days of weightlessness ahead of us?"

"The Omniscience decided to accelerate the *Majestic Draught* more so we can reach our destination earlier. That is more efficient."

"Couldn't you—"

"No," the general interrupts him. "We cannot influence the decisions of the Omniscience, as long as it can invoke orders with the highest priority. During the construction of the ship it was assumed that the Omniscience would have a better overview of complex requirements."

The Omniscience is starting to creep him out. Is it possible that the Knowledge Scientists misjudged its abilities? Shouldn't they have known how it would behave during a mission?

Gronolf closes his eyes and visualizes his home planet. The memory floods him with warmth. He does not have to solve this problem—that is someone else's job.

Archive, Brightnight 27, 3350

IT HAS BECOME QUIET, AS FAR AS THAT IS POSSIBLE ON BOARD A spaceship. Gronolf enjoys the nightly patrols. He can walk through the empty corridors at his own pace and get lost in thoughts. He learns more and more about the ship during his walks. Nobody is bothering him, and he only has to take care not to leave the sector assigned to him. His company gets the same sectors for seven times seven days, and then they are switched to different ones. As the commander, he has the great advantage of being able to assign those areas he is most interested in to himself.

Today he is responsible for a medical laboratory. The room looks sterile, as expected. It smells of solvents. Along the walls there are machines whose functions he does not know. He assumes the Life Scientists can analyze bodily fluids here. There are slides with data and diagrams on top of one of the machines. The light has been dimmed to save energy.

Through a door which recognizes him and opens automatically he enters the next room, which is dominated by a sleeping beam. There is a multi-sectional mechanical arm holding a fearful array of tools on the ceiling. It looks as if surgical procedures are performed here. The sleeping beam is tempting. He really should get some rest. In order to avoid a sector being sealed off, it is enough if at least one Grosnop stays in it. He doesn't have to walk around. Yet he also carries some responsibility as a company commander. If he is asleep he won't be able to reach his fighters quickly in an emergency to assist them. While he does not know what this emergency might be like, he just wants to be on the safe side.

However, sitting on the sleeping beam for half a bubble period will certainly not hurt his subordinates. Gronolf sits astride the sleeping beam. He hopes he will never have to be operated on. The idea of having the circle of sharp, pointy tools coming down from the ceiling towards his body makes him shiver. He is proud that he is never afraid, but he has great respect for the work of the Life Scientists.

A door slams behind him. Gronolf opens his rear eye, but he cannot detect anything. The source of the noise must be far away. Shortly afterward there is a hissing sound. That was definitely a bulkhead mechanically moving downward. It must have happened south of him. His company is responsible for the sectors there. If they lose another area, he will be responsible for it. He has to go and look.

Gronolf jumps up and moves rapidly in the direction of the noise. He traverses a crew room, a waiting room, and an office. Suddenly he stands in front of a closed door. It is one of the hatches that should recognize him, but it seems to be defective. Gronolf looks at the room through all four eyes. There are four exits, one on each side. The one in front of him is closed, but if he goes to the right, then left and left again, he should be back on the way toward the source of the noise.

He turns around. There are only four steps to the ride side exit, but just as he gets there, the door also slams shut. That leaves the left exit. Somebody must be watching him. While his four eyes see what is happening around him, that isn't enough. He only appears to be alone. Therefore Gronolf acts this time as if he is not sure what to do next. He even lets his knees tremble, and someone who knows the gestures of the Grosnops would draw appropriate conclusions. Without warning he jumps as far as he can. He reaches the exit on the other side in record time, but the door is faster.

This is outrageous. Someone is playing with him, someone who has access to the doors and the cameras in this room. This can only be the Omniscience. Gronolf wonders what to do. What is the Omniscience trying to achieve by blocking his way? Is there something back there he is not supposed to see? He examines the door. It is not very sturdy. He could break through it with his weapon. Then the plan of the Omniscience would fail, but he would have damaged the ship. Maybe that is exactly the plan? Is the Omniscience trying to make him damage this sector, so it will have to be abandoned?

Then the door, which the Omniscience closed first, reopens. Gronolf has to hold on, because a strong gust would otherwise sweep him off his feet. There must be a vacuum behind the door that was just opened. He has to leave this room right away, or he will suffocate. Gronolf uses his arms and legs and struggles towards the only door still open. He slips through it and the door immediately closes behind him. What was that? Is he now safe?

This room, an office, has two other doors. He receives an answer when one of them closes by itself. This can't be true! He guesses what will happen next and therefore moves toward the still-open door. Just as he gets there, the air is sucked out of this room from the other side. He runs to safety into the following room. Yet here the game repeats itself: All exits except for one are closed and then the air is suctioned off. What might happen if he does not follow this invitation and refuses to leave the room?

Gronolf hates becoming some stranger's plaything. Therefore he prepares for the next room as if going on a long dive. He inhales air into his primary and secondary stomachs. For such emergencies, both possess a connection to his lungs so he can stay under water for half a bubble period with some effort and without dying. He is just ready when the door opens again that he used to get into this room.

Gronolf keeps his eye on the only exit and exposes himself to the increasing vacuum. He is getting cold. The Omniscience must have managed to establish a direct connection to space, probably via the sectors already sealed off. He will survive the cold. His skin is covered by a thick layer of fat, which serves as insulation. Yet after about a quarter of a bubble period, he still feels the typical sensation of heat. That is a paradoxical reaction of his thinking layer. When the brain cells underneath his skin cool down too much, his mind reports this as a feeling of heat. His skin is burning. If it really were that hot, it would develop blisters.

Gronolf knows his brain can withstand a lot. During the draght it has to survive without oxygen for a much longer time. His thoughts are still clear, but he can feel the cold in his joints. He has to take that into account when he launches his escape. Then he won't be able to run as fast as he is used to. The heat becomes unbearable, but he tolerates it, nevertheless. The Omniscience will see what a Grosnop—who is the strongest of his plex—can do. Now he feels dizzy. In order to lower his energy requirements, he closes three of his eyes. The Omniscience must realize it won't succeed with him. Once he is close to death, at the latest, it will again fill the room with air, as it is not allowed to kill a Grosnop. Gronolf will show the Omniscience its limits.

Suddenly somebody calls him. The voice sounds like his mother's. She says farewell and thanks him for his honorable death, which will become a shining example for all young Grosnops. But that is impossible. His mother is billions of steps away and cannot reach him here. The Omniscience is obviously mocking him.

Gronolf is shaken by rage and simultaneously energized. He must not tolerate this incredible intrusion into his privacy. If he reports this to his superiors, they will finally have something to use against the Omniscience, which is willing to let him die in this room.

He has to get out of here! Gronolf starts running with his last remaining strength. However, the door offering his way out closes. He is imprisoned. No, nothing can stop him as long as he still has his weapon. He raises the weapon and fires at the door. Then he throws himself against it. The damaged door slams onto the floor of the next room. Gronolf does not stop. The Omniscience must suspect his intentions and will try to prevent his escape. Yet he has anger on his side.

He has to get out of this sector. The doors are no problem, even if they close, as he still has his weapon. However, he'd better not encounter a bulkhead. Luckily, the thick bulkheads are not very common. If he keeps to the left he should reach the crew room of the neighboring company. He hopes the Omniscience won't be able to kill him anymore once he is among other Grosnops. He races through Sector 23, destroys one door after the other, and finally stumbles through the last door, behind which several younger warriors sit around a table, gambling. He is saved.

GRONOLF OPENS HIS EYES. HE IS SITTING IN HIS CHAIR, ALL alone. One of the memories has returned without him having to use the archives. The following day he was court-martialed for destroying Sector 23. Nobody believed the story of his persecution. It sometimes happens that trained warriors grab a weapon and start shooting randomly. They believed him to be such a madman. Yet he was vindicated before a verdict was reached, because something similar happened the next day in the sector of a different company.

His claim that the Omniscience entered his mind using his mother's voice was still dismissed as an illusion, after a Life Scientist stated that such visions were not uncommon when suffering from oxygen deprivation. A Motion Scientist also insisted that such a manipulation would be completely impossible. Yet Gronolf knows what he experienced.

Someday he will get even with the Omniscience.

Archive, Darknight 9, 3350

A somber melody sounds. The entire crew of the ship is lined up. Eight warriors carry the deceased through the crowd on a repurposed sleeping beam. Gronolf, who is standing in the front row, recognizes the typical marks of frostbite on the skin. This is already the third victim of a series of events the superiors stubbornly call accidents, even though nobody believes that. Supposedly, as the electronic log kept by the Omniscience stated, the deceased, in each case, opened the connection to a sealed, airless chamber. The records are clear and allow for no other interpretations. But why should three young warriors deliberately kill themselves?

The Knowledge Scientists checked the log file and could not find any manipulation. Accordingly, this is the official version of the story. Gronolf does not know what their superiors think about this, but for him the case is clear: The Omniscience has murdered these warriors. He has to admit, though, that his theory has a pretty obvious flaw. Nobody knows the reason for the killing. The three victims were not important. Why should the Omniscience run the risk of maybe getting caught? It did not achieve anything through these so-called accidents it could not also have achieved by different means.

The only motive Gronolf can come up with is pure bloodlust. Yet that is unimaginable. The Omniscience is not a normal being. It should be far above such primitive instincts. The Knowledge Scientists stress that as well. Accordingly, the leadership currently refrains from moving against the Omniscience.

The question is, what good would it do anyway? They are going to need the Omniscience, at least until the *Majestic Draght* has reached its destination. The superiors know that, as does the Omniscience. Gronolf is therefore glad this moment will arrive soon—though he simultaneously feels a vague sense of dread.

The musicians play another song. The fact that they are performing here today is an enormous concession by the leadership. The first performance by this grandiose quartet was supposed to have happened after their arrival, to celebrate the successful great jump. Now however their superiors think it necessary to strengthen the crew's morale. Everyone is listening in awe. Gronolf is kneading his hands because the melodies are so moving. It must have been difficult for those four to refrain from presenting their art for so long.

A high-ranking officer steps up to him.

"Please appear in Sector 1 in half a bubble period."

"Understood." Gronolf briefly bends his knees to express respect.

Sector 1—that is the area where the leadership lives and works. One has to pass numerous checkpoints in order to enter it. He had better start now. *Too bad I have to leave the music,* he thinks, *I won't hear that musical quartet again for quite some time.*

On the way he is stopped by Wakmir, who suddenly steps out of a side corridor, as if he had been waiting for him.

"Where are you going in such a hurry?" he asks.

"Sector 1."

"Oh, what an honor!"

"What do you want, Wakmir?" Gronolf shakes his knees impatiently.

"I heard something you might be interested in."

Of course Wakmir lives up to his reputation, he thinks. "And what might that be?"

"If you are interested, come to Sector 132 after your shift."

"Why should I?"

"That's your decision. But I have the feeling you are going to be there." Wakmir places both touch-hands on the pit of his stomach, a sign of deference.

The old bootlicker! Gronolf hates being so obviously manipulated, yet Wakmir is probably right. But first he has to reach Sector 1.

AT THE ENTRANCE OF THE LEADERSHIP SECTOR, HE FIRST HAS to hand over his weapon and then slowly walk through a metal detector. The last step is a brain scan. Supposedly the intelligence service can tell from activity patterns in his thinking layers whether he has rebellious thoughts. Gronolf doesn't really believe that. It probably is just meant to have a deterrent effect. The officer on duty asks him to sit in a special chair. Then Gronolf imagines in great detail how he would slaughter the leadership with his weapon.

"Everything is fine," the officer says after one-tenth of a bubble period, thanking him for his cooperation. Gronolf is amused but refuses to show it. Of course he realizes his tests offer no final proof, as the technology might be able to detect manipulated thoughts. Unfortunately he does not have any acquaintances working for the intelligence service. Gronolf thinks about the members of his plex, but none of them have pursued that career, at least not to his knowledge. The intelligence service developed a long time ago, during conflicts among Grosnops, and even though it officially has no enemies to spy on, it has managed to avoid being abolished.

At the end of the checkpoint a young female is waiting for him. Gronolf feels how the arousal nodes distributed across his body pulsate at her sight. He has not seen a female for so long that he can't quite control himself. Actually, females are not allowed to serve in the fleet. However, there are rumors spreading about an entire sector of the ship inhabited solely by females, with whose help the colonization of the planet would become possible. He always thought this was just soldiers' wistful dreams.

"I am Murnaka, the daughter of Murnak," she says. "You seem... surprised?"

He has to think about what he should say. "I, no... I knew of course that the leadership group has male and female members." And the rules of the dual sun indeed require an equal distribution of all positions. After all, Father Sun and Mother Sun are equals in the sky. The fact that only male representatives of the leadership show themselves in other sectors seems reasonable to him, as it avoids confusing the warriors' senses.

"I will take you to the meeting," Murnaka says, turning around and walking ahead.

Gronolf follows her. She is an arm's length taller than he is. He particularly notices her wide, swaying hips. They protect the egg chamber, in which the female organism prepares the eggs before laying them. Murnaka's skin is still so smooth and light green that she cannot have laid eggs yet.

"What is this all about?" he asks, less out of curiosity and more to hear her voice.

"I don't know, and even if I did, it would be inappropriate for me to tell you,"

"What is your function?"

"I am a learner. If I don't embarrass myself, I will become part of the leadership group after the landing on Single Sun."

That is a great honor for a young female. This means Murnaka must have been one of the best of her plex.

"And how is it going?"

"Quite well, I think." Murnaka closes the lid of her rear

eye and reopens it while saying these words in order to demonstrate her modesty.

"More than well, I bet," Gronolf says. This was almost a crude pick-up attempt, so he softens its effect by briefly closing his front eye. Who knows what her father might do to him otherwise? Murnak does not know his name, though, because except for his father, Gronolf has no connections to the leadership group.

"We are here," Murnaka says, pointing to an inconspicuous door with her right touch arm. There is no lettering on the door.

Gronolf stops for a moment.

"You have to speak your name," she says.

Of course he knows that. He just wanted to take a quick breath. He hopes Murnaka will not consider him stupid and hot-headed, as many warriors are. He wants to tell her that, but she has already disappeared, as if she had never existed. *Too bad*, he thinks.

"Gronolf Carriontooth."

The door opens immediately. Behind it is a spacious hall, which is surprisingly empty. Gronolf enters it. There is a pleasant smell of fish. On the right side of the room he sees a long table, with a large number of chairs around it. One set, he estimates, meaning seven times seven. Most of them are occupied. Somebody stands next to the table and waves at him. He starts moving with measured steps. The atmosphere in this hall is grand, and he fears that his mere presence might destroy it.

"Gronolf Carriontooth," says the Grosnop who waved him over, partially to him and partially to the others. It is an older female. She does not offer any further explanation besides his name. This is an incredible honor, and Gronolf feels his back becoming cold with awe.

"Just sit down, Gronolf." This is his father's voice. He cannot see him, because a female next to him blocks the view of his body, but it is obviously him.

One chair turns by itself to indicate it is unoccupied and

meant for him. Gronolf's blood is pumping fast, as if he were about to enter a battle. What do they want from him here?

For a moment there is silence. Then Gronolf hears a scratching noise. His father gets up and starts walking around the long table, as a speaker properly should.

"The leadership circle, Gronolf Carriontooth, has been worried for a while," his father states. Whenever he passes someone in a chair, he winks at the person with his side eye.

"The Omniscience—how can I say this?—no longer cooperates with us the way we would want it to. While we still can send it our commands, it often finds reasons for not implementing them. We cannot accuse it of insubordination, because the Omniscience bases these reasons on supreme rules which we are also subject to. Its arguments are so clever that even our best Knowledge Scientists have nothing to oppose them with."

Gronolf is surprised, not by the contents of the speech, as even common soldiers realize by now that the Omniscience likes to use these supreme rules as an excuse. What surprises —or rather shocks—him is that the leadership group seems to have no strategy to fight this. Why else would they have invited him?

"You are probably wondering what you have to do with this and what this invitation is all about," his father adds promptly. "The Knowledge Scientists have extrapolated that the Omniscience might gain complete control of the ship in the near future. These recent events indicate that it does not regard us as its masters, but rather as a means to an end, or even a burden."

Gronolf is annoyed. Not even his father dares to call these 'events' what they really are, sneaky murders of crew members. He will have to try to hide his anger.

His father briefly stops, makes a 180-degree turn and walks in the opposite direction. "We have to be prepared for this," he says. "There is a mechanism, an emergency switch we can use to remove functions from the Omniscience. That way we can cut off all its exterior connections. Then it has no influence on the ship anymore, and is only responsible for the engine."

That would be our death, Gronolf thinks. *Without the Omni-science we will hardly reach Single Sun.*

"The emergency switch is in a chamber. We have to occupy that chamber so we can use the emergency switch once we arrive in the system of Single Sun. We cannot send a company, and nobody from the leadership group should participate. That is why we thought of you. You are, if you excuse the evaluation, a simple crew member, but you are also the best of your plex and, of course, my son, so you enjoy our full trust."

"Won't I need certain authorizations to get into control areas?"

His father stops. Numerous eyes watch Gronolf, who dared to say something without being asked.

"Of course you will need authorizations to fulfill this task. However, the Omniscience would notice it if we grant them to you now. Therefore the learner Murnaka will accompany you. Both of you will occupy the security chamber, thus enabling us to deactivate the Omniscience. You already met Murnaka. During the last few weeks we gradually transferred all authorizations to her. This fits the story that she eventually will join the leadership circle. We are hoping the two of you are still unimportant enough that the Omniscience will ignore you."

"We are hoping?"

"Yes, Gronolf. Nothing is certain. However, the Omni-science is not really omniscient. It has to distribute its resources, just as we do, and this means it is not aware of the many actions performed by individual crew members. Natu-rally, you will attract its attention once you approach the control area. By that time you have to expect countermea-sures. You will definitely need vacuum equipment, weapons, and tools."

"I understand. Task accepted," Gronolf says.

"I would suggest you two get a good night's sleep and then

start with the implementation," his father says. "Once you are on the way we can no longer communicate. While this room is bug-proof, you two will be on your own out there."

"Thanks. May I leave?"

"Just a moment." A Grosnop general gets up at the end of the table. The man looks ancient, and his voice is hoarse. "I am Murnak," he says. "I will kill you if you take liberties with my daughter."

Gronolf accepts this statement without showing any emotion, and none of those present say anything. It is the duty of a father to find the best sperm donor for his daughter. And who would be more suitable than the warrior who defeats the father in an honest fight? If he should actually lose against the old man, the shame of that defeat would be with him forever. Therefore it is only right that he should lose his life if he loses the fight. If he wins, everyone expects him to show mercy to the father of his future wife. That's how life has always been on the world of the double sun.

Brightnight 37, 3876

THE MEMORY OF MURNAKA MOVES HIM SO MUCH HE HAS TO deactivate the archive. Gronolf emerges from the past. How could he have forgotten her? He cannot imagine that the long sleep would have such effects. And what happened to her? He jerks upright. The system knows everything! If Murnaka is on board, it will answer his question in a moment.

Gronolf leans forward and starts typing, but then he stops. Should he really check? And what if he finds Murnaka in a sleeping chamber marked red, and she only consists of slime and putrefaction? Right now he still has hope of seeing her again. He must not be weak. Murnaka could be a great help. He trusts her and he knows her abilities. It is a sensible choice to have the system look for her. Gronolf enters her description and waits in suspense.

"Error," the system reports. Gronolf's stomach rumbles angrily. He goes over the messages. The search routine obviously cannot handle the large number of defective sleeping chambers, as the Knowledge Scientists did not anticipate such a status. However, he can have the system displays lists of names sorted by the first syllable.

Gronolf enters the symbol for 'Mur.' The secondary lists still contain more than a hundred entries. He patiently reads through them until he reaches Murnak. His heart is beating faster. Murnaka's father is in one of the sleeping chambers. Gronolf calls up all the details. Everything appears red—Murnak has been dead for many cycles. If the system had only awakened him earlier! Now he will never be able to fight against Murnaka's father.

What about his daughter? Gronolf scrolls and scrolls, but her name is missing. He leans back. Either the system is defective, which he does not believe, or Murnaka never made it to one of the sleeping capsules. He feels his eyelids drooping with sorrow. If there were only remnants in a capsule he could say farewell to! What happened to her? He digs through his memory but remembers only what he saw in the archive recordings. He definitely has to carry on.

Gronolf listens, but the shelter building remains quiet. He activates the camera. Adam and Eve seem to be still asleep. Marchenko, on the other hand, has changed significantly. The abilities of this machine are amazing.

Gronolf reactivates the sonar transmission and once again drifts into the past.

Archive, Darknight 9, 3350

AFTER THE BRIEFING IN SECTOR 1, GRONOLF WALKS DIRECTLY to his quarters. He had hoped to be able to talk to Murnaka before leaving, but his wish did not come true. It is actually not necessary. Murnaka will know what to do, and he can prepare himself without hurrying. Gronolf has to clean his weapon, check his tool belt, and test his vacuum equipment. He starts with his weapon. Step by step he disassembles it, cleans the parts, and reassembles them. This work feels good. It is totally unclear what tomorrow and the following days will bring. If they are lucky, the Omniscience won't notice anything. Yet Gronolf knows he cannot rely on that—he has to be vigilant the whole time. He hopes he will be able to remain watchful despite the presence of the young female. He cannot even dream of desiring the female learner as long as he is only his father's son.

Shortly before the end of his shift the quarters get crowded, because his comrades return from exercises. It is not a good sign that they don't arrive at exactly the same time. *There is more and more sloppiness these days, and they all might have to pay a price for it.* Yet Gronolf keeps these thoughts to himself. Then he remembers Wakmir's invitation. What is going on in Sector 132 after work? Gronolf is not in the mood to get involved in something, but it also might be a mistake to ignore the unrest among the crew. Therefore, he gets on his way.

A soldier sits on the ground in front of the entrance to Sector 132. He has pushed his legs under his body, looking very casual, and he scratches his stomach fold with two of the seven fingers of his right touch-hand.

Gronolf nudges him with one foot. "Wakmir invited me," he says.

"Second to the left, then left again, and right," the sitting soldier says without looking at him.

"And who is waiting there?"

"You'll see."

Gronolf is tempted to strike the soldier. He outranks this common soldier considerably, and the underling should treat him with more reverence. Yet he is off duty now, and Wakmir's friends probably wouldn't like it. Therefore he simply steps over him. In doing so, his knee hits the soldier's touch-arm hard, seemingly by accident. Gronolf hears the man groan, but he ignores the noise.

Inside Sector 132 the light has been dimmed. Gronolf follows the path described to him. He reaches a large steel door hanging from only one hinge and ajar. Behind it, he hears voices he doesn't recognize. He pushes the door open and enters the room. All those present turn around to face him. He counts fifteen males standing in a group. They had probably been discussing something until a moment ago, and conversation stopped the moment he entered.

"There you are, Gronolf." Wakmir leaves the group and walks toward him. "What an honor for us."

"I don't know whether I am an honor or a punish-ment," Gronolf replies as he looks around. He is the high-est-ranked person here. The warriors come from different companies.

Wakmir waves him forward. "I want to introduce you to Oknar." He points at a tall warrior who is considerably older than the others. "He is a kind of mentor for us."

Gronolf approaches and spreads his arms. This gesture

demonstrates all his strength, because now he seems even taller and wider.

Oknar immediately submits. "I am Oknar," he says. "Having you among us is an honor."

"Let's wait and see," Gronolf replies. "Why are we actually here?"

"These accidents," Wakmir says. "They really worry us."

"Well, not the accidents themselves," Oknar corrects him. "Rather the fact that the leadership obviously ignores them and plays them down. By now, innocent warriors die every day, and what does our leadership group do about it? They deny that there even is a problem."

Oknar is right, Gronolf thinks. While he knows that the leaders actually are trying to do something, the average Grosnops must think that they don't matter at all to their superiors.

"And what do you want to do about it?"

"We are not sure. It seems pretty obvious the Omniscience has something to do with it. We know where it is located. If we destroy it—"

"—the *Majestic Draght* will lose its only pilot," interjects Gronolf.

"Piloting a ship can't be that difficult," Wakmir says.

"You forgot the drive," Gronolf says. "Any irregularity can build up quickly. The dark matter generator reacts to gravitational fields the ship will inevitably cross. No Knowledge Scientist can react quickly enough to that."

"So the Omniscience has power over the entire ship," Oknar says. He doesn't sound disappointed, but rather seems to have expected this.

"Correct," Gronolf says.

"Then we have only one option—moving against the leadership. Our superiors can no longer ignore these accidents. They have to force the Omniscience to stop these attacks against innocent crewmembers."

Oknar arrived at the only correct conclusion, from his perspective.

Gronolf can't argue with his idea without giving too much away. "Is this room bug-poof?" he asks.

Wakmir proudly points at a member of the engineering department. "Our specialist made sure of that."

"Good," Gronolf says, though he is not convinced the room is really secure. The Omniscience can access any data circuit. Perhaps even the leadership group has been lulled into a false sense of security. Tomorrow he and Murnaka will find out.

"A rebellion against the leadership is a serious matter," Gronolf says evasively.

Oknar aims his front eye at him. "Of course. We believe, though, that most will support us. Just ask around if you don't believe me. Nobody is happy with the leadership anymore."

"Nevertheless, we should not rush things."

"We? Does this mean you are joining us?"

Gronolf does not answer right away. He probably has no choice. He can only stay informed if he at least pretends to participate. If he rejects them, the actions of the rebels will surprise him eventually. And that might happen at the most inopportune moment. He will try to delay them until his mission is finished.

"How many of us are there?" Gronolf asks.

"Hard to say," Oknar replies. "We don't really keep official membership lists. I would say we have one or two members in almost every unit. In case of emergency, we definitely should be able to mobilize a couple hundred."

A couple hundred—that is not much compared to the total number of crew members, which must be seven times seven times larger. Yet if the others remain neutral, it might work. It depends on how much they still respect the leadership. Probably less with every day.

"We should not rush things," Gronolf says. "A rebellion would lead to casualties on both sides. However, if the leadership group does not voluntarily give in, I don't see any other way in the long run."

# Archive, Darknight 10, 3350

THE HEAVY BUCKLE OF THE TOOL BELT CLOSES WITH A LOUD click. The vacuum equipment dangles from a belt loop, ready to be used. Gronolf carries his weapon over his shoulder. He leaves his quarters without saying goodbye, just as if he were leaving for daily training, which is probably what his comrades are thinking. He walks slowly toward Sector 1. Murnaka has not contacted him again and he already wonders when she will join him. Suddenly she stands in front of him.

"What a coincidence," he says.

"I have been waiting for you."

How did she know he would be coming this way? No matter, it was probably the most likely route. Gronolf gives her a friendly wink with his front eye, but she does not react to his gesture. "Where do we have to go?" he asks.

"The security zone is in the hub connecting the drive and the living quarters."

Near the sector borders there are fold-out maps in the walls. Gronolf wants to open one of them to get an overview, but Murnaka stops him.

"I have an offline map here." She shows him a roll about one foot long. Then she opens the map by rolling it out into a square. The map consists of a transparent material. It is not any thicker than his skin, but if you look at it from above it seems to have great depth.

"A mobile holo-map?" Gronolf asks. He can't help but shape his stomach fold into an expression of amazement. These maps are incredibly rare and expensive.

Murnaka moves her hand across the edge of the map. The image zooms accordingly, so that one can eventually see the entire *Majestic Draght*. The vessel is cube-shaped. The spherical drive sits in its interior, like the kernel of a sea chestnut. From this drive a kind of tube leads outward; to be more precise, a channel formed by magnetic fields. Around the drive there is a structure several arm lengths thick, which surrounds it like a shell. The Omniscience is located there. The area is completely inaccessible to the crew.

If necessary, the Omniscience will repair itself, using special machines. The drive core cannot be repaired, as it is constantly in a fragile equilibrium, like an egg balancing on its tip. Only the Omniscience is able to keep it in balance, and if it fails, the egg would burst, and the entire ship with it. It was partially for this reason the Knowledge Scientists gave the Omniscience a certain degree of autonomy. The limiting factor, as smaller predecessor models had shown, was always the fact that the crew made wrong decisions.

Gronolf's companion points at a tiny cube. "This is the room we have to reach and secure," she says.

"And we can really deactivate the Omniscience from there?"

"No, that is impossible. Then we could no longer control the drive system. However, we can sever the connection of the Omniscience to the outside world."

"Then it will be alone with the drive core, in eternal darkness."

"You said that very poetically, Gronolf."

He is not sure whether she is serious or whether she is making fun of him. Yet he does not show any reaction. "Well, that is the case," he says, "if it receives no signals from the outside world, isn't it?"

Murnaka seems to ponder this. She moves her touch-arms right and left. "You are probably right."

"Then it won't be very happy about it."

"Certainly not."

"And what if it relinquishes control over the drive unit?"

"Then it would kill itself. That contradicts one of its basic rules. It is not allowed to harm itself."

Right now, Gronolf feels quite ignorant. Isn't Murnaka officially a learner, while he is the experienced officer? "Let's go," he says.

Murnaka types something on the map and then rolls it up again. Then she pulls a kind of button from her belt pouch, moistens it with stomach acid, and sticks it on her skin at chest height. Gronolf recognizes that it is a sound button.

"This way the map can tell us where to go," Murnaka says.

This way the map can tell you *where to go*, Gronolf thinks. He starts to dislike this mission, because it looks as if he will have to follow an inexperienced learner no matter what happens. Yet he does not comment, because whoever awarded her the responsibility for the expensive map must have had certain reasons. He is obviously considered primarily as a protector watching Murnaka's back.

His companion starts moving. Gronolf follows her. This way he can at least admire her from behind.

Soon he is no longer familiar with the corridors they are traversing. Tunnels, doors, new tunnels, and then a large room, one following after the other. At first he tries to memorize the path, or at least keep an image in his mind, but after ten turns he no longer stands a chance. They are making good progress—until they encounter the first locked door. Murnaka looks at the map, which insists that the door should be open.

"There is no other way," she says.

"Good, at least that's a change," Gronolf replies. He takes his weapon off his shoulder. He can quickly blast through the door.

"Perhaps it would be enough to cut through the lock," Murnaka says, offering him a small welding gun from her tool belt.

Gronolf is disappointed but refuses to show it. The harpoon will have its chance. He aims the welding gun at a point near the door lock and moves it in a circle around it. When he is about halfway finished, he notices a breeze. A bulkhead slams down behind them.

"Vacuum mask," he warns her, takes his mask off his belt, and puts it on. Murnaka does the same. Shortly afterward he manages to kick in the door. He has to hold on so that the air pressure won't suck him inside.

The room behind the door is large and empty. There are bunks along the walls. This might have been a sleeping area once. One can only survive here with a mask. His companion consults the map, but she doesn't say anything. He follows her through two more doors. They have arrived in a room that must have been a kitchen. Cooking utensils are neatly arranged on a shelf. The stove looks freshly cleaned. Murnaka suddenly stops. He can barely avoid bumping into her from behind.

"What's up?" he asks. Then he realizes Murnaka cannot hear him due to the vacuum. Her right touch-arm points downward. Gronolf steps aside and sees what his companion tried to avoid. A Grosnop is lying on the ground. The male is holding a cutting tool in his hand. He must have been surprised by the pressure loss during his work.

Another one of these 'accidents,' Gronolf thinks. *How many of my comrades have been killed by the Omniscience so far?*

Murnaka hits the top of the table so hard that a dent appears in the middle, but he hears no sound. She raises her arm again, but he grabs it. If she keeps hitting the table she might injure herself. She looks at him. He notices the anger in her front eye, its lid trembling, yet she obviously is trying to suppress this emotion and replace it with something he interprets as gratitude. Gronolf is glad that he is unable to say anything right now.

Murnaka points at a narrow door to the left. It won't open. The air pressure behind it probably is still normal. Now they have to be careful. If they simply open the lock, the vacuum will spread to the neighboring room, and they would help the Omniscience in depopulating the ship.

Gronolf turns around. The kitchen is not very large. He closes the door behind them and welds it shut for safety's sake. Then he starts opening the door in front of them. Another bulkhead slams down in the distance. He notices it by the vibrations of the floor. The automatic system has noticed the loss in pressure. The kitchen is gradually filling with air. Gronolf watches his vacuum mask's display. Soon he will be able to breathe normally again. Once the area is safe, it should be possible to open the bulkhead further ahead.

Murnaka touches his hand and points at the dead male.

"We have to leave him here," he says. "Otherwise the Omniscience will notice that we are advancing."

"Don't you think it noticed us cutting doors open? It already knows we're coming."

She's right. He picks up the corpse with all four of his arms. Due to the time spent in the vacuum, it has become very light. Murnaka steps aside so he can carry the dead into the adjacent room. There he discovers a bed. He places the corpse on the sleeping beam. One might think he simply fell asleep peacefully.

"Control room. We have found a corpse. Please pick up in..." Murnaka looks at the map, "Sector 332."

"Confirmed."

Gronolf looks at his companion. She shows no signs of weakness. Nevertheless, he feels it is his duty to ask, "Should we take a break?"

"Are you tired?" she asks him. "I am not."

"Then let's go on." He waits for her to get moving. Murnaka closes her right eye. She seems to be concentrating on what the sound button on her skin tells her. Then she walks away with rapid steps. Gronolf has to hurry so he won't fall behind. She is really well-trained and in shape.

Obviously, the learners have not grown soft. He could not chase his recruits through the corridors at this speed. However, Murnaka has longer legs because she is a female, so it is a bit easier for her. The halls and rooms they enter and leave seem deserted, though sometimes they encounter a technician or a soldier standing guard. The leadership has not given up the plan to keep the sectors habitable.

THE MAP EITHER LEADS THEM AROUND AIRLESS ZONES, OR those particular zones are becoming rarer the closer they get to the center. This allows them to proceed swiftly.

Gronolf allows himself some thoughts that have nothing to do with the room in front of him. *What will the new world be like?* The Space Scientists calculated that it should be habitable and offer water. It is for that reason his people risked everything and built the *Majestic Draght* as a colony ship. Old texts contain hints about a world with only one sun. Gronolf loved these stories as a child, but he was always aware these were only fairy tales. Now the fairy tales are coming true.

Murnaka slows down after a while. *Is she finally getting tired?* wonders Gronolf. He winks at her, but she doesn't react this time either. Instead, she places her load-hands on the pit of her stomach. This is a warning sign. What is she warning him about? Murnaka comes closer, so close that her typically-feminine scent enters his smell sensors. Gronolf would like to take a step back, but how would she interpret that?

"The sector in front of us is secret," she whispers. "So secret I did not even know about it until now."

"What is going on here?" He adjusts his voice level to hers.

"My father described this to me before the launch. The

leadership group has developed an alternative program to compensate for the accidents."

"How would this work?" Gronolf asks the question, but he already has an idea of what the answer will be, and he doesn't like it at all.

"Just like in the double sun system. Females lay eggs, males fertilize them."

He does not want to hear that. If it is true, it would represent an enormous breach of taboo. Eggs are only allowed to be laid by certain females on certain days, in the sand of an ocean beach. Any child knows that this rule serves to protect the double sun system against overpopulation. In ancient times it was different, but in a modern society, too many descendants in a plex survive.

"They are not allowed to," Gronolf says. "I now understand, why..." He stops in mid-sentence.

"Why what?"

"The leadership abandons our traditions in order not to endanger our cooperation with the Omniscience," he says.

"There is no other way."

"You really think so, Murnaka? Who are we to break with the traditions of our fathers?"

"Space travelers. We are space travelers."

"So when we arrive at Single Sun, we will be different from what we were at launch."

"Yes, Gronolf, every day will change you and me. We will never again be what we are today."

"Oh, certainly not." Gronolf can't quite follow her argument. Giving up ancient traditions for a short-term advantage? It seems wrong to him. Yet it would be useless to reproach her. After all, she has to obey her father, just as he must obey his.

"I am just asking you, Gronolf, to behave inconspicuously while we traverse this sector. Stay calm, no matter what you see. Will you promise?"

"I am calmness personified."

THE ENTRANCE TO THE AREA IS BLOCKED BY A YELLOW DOUBLE door. Murnaka enters her authentication code at the lock sensor. The system does not reply. He can see she is getting nervous, as her eyelids are trembling. So maybe she is not as cool and collected as she pretends to be. Murnaka repeats her code, but nothing happens this time either.

"Is there a way around this zone?" Gronolf asks.

She opens the map and studies the planned route. "Unfortunately, no," she says, "we can't go around it."

"Then we have to break the door open."

"Well, we already have experience with that."

"No, wait. Let us first check whether there is another entrance."

"That is a good idea, Gronolf," Murnaka says as she consults the map. "There are two additional entrances to this area we can try." Her arms fall down limply, indicating her relief. They start moving in single file.

They reach the first door relatively quickly. It is narrow and green and looks more like an emergency exit. Murnaka identifies herself at the sensor, but the door remains closed. Gronolf starts getting nervous while they are looking for the third entrance. It is not easy to find, and it finally turns out to be hidden behind cabinets. After he has moved those aside, his companion slowly approaches the wireless door lock. He can clearly see she is afraid, and her fear affects him, even though he is not sure what he is afraid of. Does Murnaka know something of which he is unaware?

Finally she pulls herself together and transmits her access data. Nothing happens, which is what he feared. Murnaka turns around helplessly.

"We will now go back to the main entrance and open it by force," Gronolf says, "The risk of damaging something is much smaller there."

Murnaka does not react, so he walks ahead. Through his rear eye he sees her following him.

"Is there something I need to know?" he asks quietly.

"No. It's only a hunch, but it scares me."

So she admits being afraid. That is a real sign of trust, he thinks. "Then I hope there is no reason for your fear. And if there is one, I am prepared for it. Nobody will get past me." He points at the weapon he carries over his shoulder.

"Not all problems can be solved by... Sorry, Gronolf, I am grateful you are trying to protect me."

While Gronolf doesn't know why she would thank him for something that goes without saying, her words make him feel warm inside.

Murnaka's hunch is verified by a breeze. He feels it on the hand holding the blowtorch, and he sees it by the changing form and color of the flame. Behind the door, which is supposed to contain a hidden nursery school, there must be a vacuum. He turns off the blowtorch.

"Why did you stop?" asks Murnaka.

"There is something wrong here," he says.

"Then we have to get in there even quicker."

That probably isn't a good idea. Yet Gronolf suppresses the thought, because he is afraid of the images they might be confronted with. Nevertheless, he reaches for the vacuum mask, as does Murnaka. Then he removes the door lock and waits for the pressure to equalize.

"The room behind the door cannot be very large, because the pressure equalized quickly," he says. His voice sounds quieter and higher-pitched because the air pressure is reduced.

"Good, then the occupants might have retreated into adjacent rooms."

He opens the door. The lighting integrated into the walls comes on as they enter the room, which is almost empty. There are only a few devices near a wall, but he cannot guess at their functions.

"We have to go there," Murnaka says, pointing to a door on the right side of the room. She tries to use her access data, but this lock also does not react.

Gronolf did not expect anything different and already has the blowtorch ready. Once again he feels the tell-tale breeze as soon as the flame has cut through the material. "Vacuum," he says. "But that makes no sense. The rooms are sealed off and airtight."

"Somebody must have pumped out the air via the life-support system."

Gronolf only knows one entity that could have done that. He cautiously opens the door. This looks like a conference room. The furniture has been thrown around, as if the occupants were defending themselves against something.

There are two black lines on a wall. Gronolf examines them. They are dried out. "Could be blood." he says, "or possibly some kind of paint. Do we have a molecular analyzer?"

"No."

The room has only one exit. Close to it he finds a part of a machine that looks like a support arm. It is heavy and made of metal. He examines it from all sides. "Look at the fracture surface here," He holds the thing closer to Murnaka. "This must have involved considerable forces."

"But where is the rest of the machine?" she asks.

"Perhaps behind this door," he replies.

At first it feels like it always does when he tries to use force to open the door. The typical breeze tells him the air pressure behind it is even lower. They wait for the pressure to equalize. However, even after he removes the lock the door cannot be opened. He bends down and looks through the hole with his front eye. The room behind it is dark, so he takes a lamp from his tool belt and shines it inside. Another chaotic scene.

"They must have welded the door shut on all sides," he says. "But we'll fix that in a moment."

He looks at Murnaka, but she does not resist when he takes

his weapon off his shoulder. He aims at the left hinge and triggers the harpoon. The shot is not as loud as he expected. The door falls forward. This movement automatically activates the room lighting and gives him a free field of view.

"Back there," Gronolf calls out. He has to yell so that Murnaka can still hear him, because the air is so thin by now. A shapeless mass is lying in the left corner. Murnaka runs forward. He deliberately takes his time so he will be prepared for what he sees. His companion holds her touch-arms in front of her front eye. Her eyelids are trembling.

In front of them is a Grosnop, definitely a female. Three of her four arms are interlaced in an unnatural way. The fourth one has been severed and someone stuck it into her breathing fold. She probably suffocated from it—unless the vacuum killed her first.

"Who would do something like that?"

He realizes that Murnaka knows the answer. No Grosnop would mutilate another one like this. There were wars in the history of his people in which countless plexes died, but according to the historians, they always kept to the rules of warfare.

This one seems to be still fresh, unlike the first corpse they found. The vacuum has hardly dried out the corpse, so she cannot have been here for much longer than two days.

"We have to concentrate," Gronolf says, "The enemy might be still nearby." However, that is not very probable. The Omniscience could not have known they were coming. Why should it have its machines waiting here? Yet they have to be careful—who knows what kind of strategies the Omniscience might develop?

"What should we do about her?" Murnaka asks, then turns around and looks at him with her front eye.

"We can't do anything."

"The control room?"

"I don't think it would be a good idea if they sent someone here."

"You are right, Gronolf. Nevertheless, it feels wrong to leave her here in such a state."

"We can pick her up on the way back." *If we ever return,* Gronolf thinks. The Omniscience seems to be a merciless opponent. He has no clue how they can fight it.

The room has three doors, and all of them have been welded shut from the inside. Gronolf finds the blowtorch the woman used and hooks it into his tool belt. How did the murderer make it into this room, though? He looks at the ceiling. There are two life-support vents there. The machine that killed the female must have come via the air ducts. Why didn't he notice this earlier?

He points upward. "Could we advance faster in there?"

Murnaka unrolls the map and zooms in on the duct layer between this level and the next. "The pipes are very narrow. Do you really want to risk it?"

Tactically, this is more of a disadvantage. He would either have to crawl with his weapon at the ready, which would slow him down, or he would have to drag it behind, making himself vulnerable. He definitely won't be able to react quickly to attacks coming from behind. It all depends on whether the Omniscience is expecting them by now. They probably have to assume this to be the case.

"We are staying down here," he says. "That way we are prepared for any surprise. But we also have to keep the ducts in view, both in the ceiling and in the floor."

"Fine. We have to continue through this door." His companion points to the right.

Gronolf takes the weapon from his shoulder when he remembers they should first check what lies behind it. He melts a peephole into the metal and takes a look. The room is cluttered and airless.

He places a small explosive charge into the harpoon, aims, and pulls the trigger. The explosion blows the door out of its frame. As before, the light is activated, but this time Gronolf also sees something move on the floor. Something is quickly slithering toward them. He has no time to replace the explosive charge, but even without it the harpoon is a destructive weapon. He aims the barrel down slightly, calculates the enemy's movement, and fires. The harpoon hits the ground three leg lengths away from him and gets stuck. Dust is stirred up, which settles only slowly.

"Watch out!" Gronolf yells, holding back Murnaka, who is trying to run ahead. He slowly approaches the spot where the harpoon is stuck in the ground. Something is wiggling around it. A hit! The hardened arrow has pierced the middle of a long, slender machine, and pinned it to the ground. It is made of a dark material, certainly not steel, probably carbon fibers, and it is divided into many small segments that can be twisted. It reminds Gronolf of a swamp crawler, a specialty of the Coal Coast, which is often eaten grilled.

What could be the function of this machine? Is it a spy, or does it also possess weapons? Could it kill a Grosnop? He notices how its segments are twisting more and more. The rear of the machine is hardly moving, but the front obviously does not want to accept being pinned by the harpoon. If the segments twist any further, the whole thing is going to rip itself apart. *That is probably its intention*, Gronolf thinks, and at that moment the front part of the fake swamp crawler tears itself free. It is so fast that it zooms away between Gronolf's feet. In the same moment he sees through his rear eye how Murnaka raises her right load-hand and hits the fleeing remainder of the machine.

"Got it," she calls loudly, raising her hand. Hitting the hard floor must have been painful for her, but she does not let it show. The swamp crawler lying on the floor now is only half as high and no longer moves. No matter what it was, a harmless spy or the murderer of the female in this room, Gronolf cannot suppress a shout of joy, and Murnaka joins him.

They have rested for half a bubble period. All by

themselves, and without talking about it, they slid to the floor with their backs to the wall, stretching out their legs. A conversation would have been too exhausting due to the masks and the thin air, but Gronolf was in no mood for talking anyway. He doesn't often feel like this, but it happens with Murnaka—he can simply sit without saying anything, and it doesn't feel awkward.

He is gradually starting to feel hungry. Therefore he pulls some dried food out of his belt pouch, giving Murnaka half of it. Then they drink water from a dispenser in the wall. He is still not saying anything, but both of them seem to feel that the time for leaving has come.

Murnaka pulls out the map and then points forward with her touch-arm. He looks at the path ahead of them. There is still a long way to go. They will be traveling for several days if they have to continue opening doors by force. Yet he doesn't mind—he is actually glad, because the time with Murnaka seems more valuable to him than any minutes without her.

He doesn't know what is wrong. He keeps catching himself watching her flawless green skin and admiring the play of the muscles in her powerful thighs. He must not get distracted by this.

Before they open the next door, Gronolf first seals the door behind them, because Murnaka has discovered a control panel for the life-support system. Using it, she can purposely reestablish normal air pressure. The Omniscience is not overriding it. Murnaka sets the life-support to keep the pressure on a normal level. Now they can finally take off the masks and talk normally.

They reach the next two rooms via the proven blowtorch method. Gronolf wants to open the third door this way, but then the sensor reacts and asks for authorization. His companion enters the data, and the two of them are admitted. Are they past the worst parts of this sector now? Gronolf would like to believe that, but then where are the occupants, particularly the children who were supposedly raised here?

The room they are entering looks as if it had just been left. There are scattered documents, and a monitor displays the data of an experiment. On a table Gronolf finds an open food container, which still smells fresh. In the corner is a climbing plant just starting to blossom. He admires the cyan blue of its leaves. Plants are not allowed in the crew quarters. Gronolf has the impression of detecting the various scents of numerous comrades in the air. Males and females seem to have worked together in this room. Yet where have they gone —and why?

In the middle of the large room there are wide double doors on both sides. Murnaka points left.

"That way," she says.

The doors are not locked, and Gronolf can push them open by hand. He takes his weapon off his shoulder, but he detects no danger. This area is covered in waterproof tiles. It could be a hygiene room—after all, the crew has to wash somewhere. Along the walls Gronolf sees long basins with side walls at chest height, so he cannot discover what is in them. Above the basins, heat lamps were later added, which is unusual. No, this is not a normal hygiene room, unless the crew of this sector has grown totally soft. Gronolf approaches one of the basins and looks over the edge.

He jerks back immediately. He has to get this image out of his head, as otherwise he will go insane. He grabs hold of Murnaka, who also wants to peek into the basin.

"Don't," he says. He is unable to utter more.

Murnaka wiggles out of his grip. Normally he would be strong enough to hold her, but right now he has to empty his stomach. The fold opens and all the food squirts out. He has entered a nightmare. How can he get out of it again? Gronolf pinches his thigh, but he is still caught in this false reality. Through his rear eye he sees Murnaka holding onto the side of the basin. Despite this, she is swaying heavily, as if a heavy tremor hit the ship. Oddly enough, this scene gives him new energy. He has to protect Murnaka and keep her from perishing due to this sight.

Gronolf takes three rapid steps and jerks her toward him so violently that she falls on her back. Murnaka utters a painful shriek. Gronolf briefly peers into the basin—briefly, yet much too long, because he will never escape this sight of extremely decomposed children immersed in a slimy, stinking sludge. They will never experience their draght. He feels like he is being welded to the side of the basin, like being unable to ever avert his front eye. Yet then Murnaka's fall pulls him involuntarily away and he also lands on his back on the cold tile floor, breathing heavily.

For half a bubble period they just lie there. They don't say a word and they don't move, because each of them is busy trying to purge the horrible images, so there will be space for other thoughts in their minds. Then Gronolf slowly gets on his feet again, carefully avoiding a look over the edge of the basin. He is still swaying a bit, but he stands on two legs. Somehow he has the feeling he should take the weapon off his shoulder. He slowly walks to the exit.

"Where are you going?"

"To the other two doors."

Murnaka briefly moves arms and legs, but she still remains on the floor. Let her rest. He has one more task to fulfill.

Gronolf goes through the double door and back into the large room. He traverses it and reaches the other double door. It is slightly ajar and he sees a narrow gap between the two doors. He only has to push it open with his hand, but something is holding him back. It is the fear of what he might witness.

He unlocks the safety catch on his weapon. This is foolish, but the weapon gives him strength. He uses its tip to push the right side of the door open and enters the room. It looks just like the other one, with tiles everywhere and basins at the edge, and with heat lamps above. Yet there is a crucial difference he sees at once, which he simply can't ignore. The crew members, who had been missing in this sector so far, sit inside the basins. They are arranged in a neat sequence, and they don't move. A long row of big black eyes is staring at him. He can only see their upper bodies. They look uninjured, as if they might get up at any moment, but an unmistakable odor of blood emanates from them. Gronolf does not have to get any closer to be sure they are all dead.

He turns around and leaves the room again. The door closes behind him with a squeak. Then he changes his mind. Everyone must know what happened here. He reenters the room, takes a recording device from his belt, and starts filming. A few moments is all he needs, as the images have so much effect. Then he walks to the edge of the basins, holds the device over them without looking himself, and presses the record button again. When he is done, he feels an enormous sense of relief.

"What are you doing there?"

He steps next to Murnaka and helps her get up. "Just a few recordings."

"You want to—"

"Yes. What happened here must not remain without witnesses."

Murnaka places her right touch-arm on his back. "We should not rush things."

"Whoever is responsible must be punished."

"And who is responsible for it? The leadership group, because it broke the taboo and allowed procreation, perhaps even experimented with it? The Omniscience will claim that it only interfered because rules have been ignored."

"Murnaka, you'd better take another look over the edge of the basin, then maybe you wouldn't talk like that anymore."

Gronolf immediately realizes this is unfair. Murnaka pulls her hand back and stiffens. Perhaps he can make amends? To be honest, she was just as shocked by these murders of innocents as he was. And he did not think that she was trying to protect the leadership, or even the Omniscience.

"I am sorry," he says, "but we cannot simply pretend we never saw this. Something like this must never happen again. Somebody has to determine the cause and punish the guilty ones."

"There is still time for that after we return. Otherwise, there will just be more of these bad decisions."

Perhaps she is right. Murnaka is smart. And it is true that determining the culprit would be hard. Yet he feels he cannot finish his task unless he has at least done something about this matter. Everyone has to know what happened here.

"I am sorry," he says, "but I simply can't do what you say. I... the burden is too heavy. I can't just go on like this."

"I understand," Murnaka says. As a sign of her grief she has pulled all four eyelids slightly upward. "Then it simply has to be done. I am not angry at you, even though I think it is the wrong decision."

That last sentence encourages him. He turns around and starts looking for a console. In the middle room he finds a control panel. He attaches the recording device and starts the transmission.

THEY TRAVERSE THREE MORE ROOMS. IN THE FOURTH THEY find a resting area. The sleeping beams look so inviting that they almost simultaneously decide they really need a few hours of rest. They share a bit of dried food and wash up. Gronolf stretches along the length of his beam. Letting his limbs hang down feels good.

"Quiet waters," Murnaka wishes him before falling asleep, following tradition.

"Quiet waters," he replies.

Archive, Darknight 11, 3350

GRONOLF WAKES UP FROM A SLIGHT NOISE. HE IS A WARRIOR, trained to sleep in a way that nothing and nobody can surprise him. He silently reaches for the weapon that hangs directly above the sleeping beam. His eyes are wide open, but it is pitch-dark. The noise comes from ahead and left. Murnaka is sleeping to his right. He can hear her calm and steady breathing.

The sound that woke him is a quiet clacking. It definitely does not come from her. The clacking slowly comes closer, while moving to his left. Gronolf calculates his chances. As soon as he gets up, the light in the room will turn on. It might blind him for a moment, but it should do the same to the intruder. That is, unless it is a machine, which can adapt its sensors faster than his eyes are able to adjust. To him, this seems to be the most realistic scenario. In practical terms, it means he will have to shoot blindly, without knowing exactly what is in front of him, friend or foe. Yet... why would a friend be sneaking around in the dark and deliberately moving in such a way that the motions sensors of the room don't react? Especially now, with the tension aboard the ship?

Gronolf makes a decision. He uses his sonar to locate the foreign object. At the same time he raises his weapon with a lightning-fast movement and fires at the target he sees with his inner eye. There is a dull crack, but unexpectedly the light does not turn on.

"What's up?" Murnaka asks softly without moving. This is the perfect behavior for this unpredictable situation, just as one learns during training.

"Possible enemy object destroyed," Gronolf says. He listens intensively, but the clacking has disappeared. Even his sonar no longer detects a movement.

"Mask on," he says, because he suddenly hears the typical hissing of air escaping. Somebody has switched the life-support system to pump mode. This does not make much sense to him. The Omniscience must know it cannot hurt them this way. It probably just wants to distract them from something. But from what? From the new intruder behind them! Now Gronolf notices a scurrying movement. The thing is fast, but not fast enough. He whips his weapon around and shoots. No more movement—he must have hit it.

"Retreat in three... two... one," he whispers. In this room they are at the mercy of their enemy's plan and can only wait and react. They have to change the situation in order to become active players themselves.

"Go," he cries. Murnaka obeys at the right moment. Gronolf can see her sprinting to the exit, thanks to his sonar sensor. He follows directly behind her. He uses his touch-arm to close the door behind him.

"Keep going!" he shouts.

They run through the next room. He has to admire Murnaka's memory. She knows exactly in which direction to go. He smashes the next door shut to block the way for possible pursuers.

"Go on!"

It is fantastic how well they synchronize. He rarely ever saw that happen even with the best recruits. The room they have reached has a chest-high platform in the middle—a perfect defensive position.

"Stop!" he yells.

Murnaka immediately finds a secure place behind the

platform. Gronolf drops two blaze balls next to the entrance. The lighting system in the entire sector seems to be out, and his sonar only works optimally when he is moving. The blaze balls will illuminate the entrance for at least one bubble period. Gronolf takes a deep breath. Of course, they should have expected this. He really would like to know, though, what exactly he killed earlier.

"Good reaction," he praises Murnaka.

"Good training," she says, and her lack of modesty does not sound arrogant.

Gronolf leans against the rear side of the platform. He pulls a folding mirror from his belt and holds it up behind him with his right touch arm. This way he can see with his rear eye what is approaching from the front. His right eye covers the right side, while Murnaka is responsible for the left side. Gronolf uses an additional mirror to watch the ceiling with his front eye. Exactly over the center of the platform he sees the opening of an air duct.

"Change of tactics," he whispers, and points upward with his free load-hand. Murnaka signals that she has understood him. Gronolf waits patiently until the blaze balls are almost extinguished, then he jumps on the platform, rips out the grate of the air duct, and pulls himself up. Murnaka quickly does likewise. During training he often had to crawl through such narrow pipes, and it was always a nuisance, but with a real threat below them it suddenly works perfectly.

The life-support ducts follow a certain pattern in each sector. Like veins, the ducts emanate from a central station and supply the rooms of the area below them with air. The sector centers are autonomous, but they have generously sized cross-connections with other sectors. If the technical systems in one of these centers should fail, at least three other centers can supply the relevant sector. This way, a network of air ducts spreads through the entire ship.

Gronolf rapidly crawls ahead. They have to cover a great distance, so he has to preserve his strength. Murnaka seems to be following him without any problem. However, their adversary will soon notice they switched levels. Gronolf's plan therefore includes occasionally breaking through to a level above or below them. Will this be enough? He doubts it. The Omniscience knows the structure of the ship much better than he does. They can try to remain unpredictable, but if it knows their destination, it can place guards at every entrance. Does it know their destination?

AFTER ABOUT ONE AND A HALF BUBBLE PERIODS THEY DESCEND into a technical room inside an adjacent sector. The sector appears to be inhabited, but this particular room is empty. They proceed as quietly as possible to avoid detection. Gronolf checks the room for microphones and cameras, but he finds nothing except for the autonomous recording device of the archive. The Omniscience should not have access to it.

"We need to go somewhere else," he says.

"Why?"

"Just as a diversionary tactic. So that the Omniscience will expect us there. Perhaps the drive system?"

"Why would we want to sabotage the drive?"

A good question. Gronolf can't think of an answer. Without a drive the ship would be damaged and they would all die. Nobody could want that, so the Omniscience would never believe them. However, there is no other structure in the core of the ship that would make a believable destination.

"You're right. Too bad, I thought I could trick the Omniscience."

"Nobody is smarter than the Omniscience," Murnaka says.

THEY REACH THE LAST SECTOR WITHOUT ANY FURTHER problems or encounters. Murnaka unrolls her holo-map and points at the structure in the middle and then upward.

"The core of the ship is above us," she says, "and it consists of the drive, and the thinking modules of the Omniscience are on top of that." Murnaka moves the longest of her seven fingers back and forth.

Under different circumstances, Gronolf thinks, *that could be a very erotic gesture.*

"The hub runs directly through the core. It starts at the security chamber." She taps on a spot which now glows yellow. "Here—this is where we can seal off the Omniscience from the rest of the ship."

Gronolf is amazed when he sees the structure in its entirety. "The ship is built almost like the body of a Grosnop," he blurts out.

Now Murnaka probably thinks him stupid. How could he have overlooked this until now?

"With one minor difference," she says. To his relief, she does not sound at all amused. She uses her long finger to give the map display a slight push, and the entire visualization starts to move. "The living quarters rotate around the core, which—luckily—is not the case with our bodies," she says.

Gronolf gazes down at his body. Without the rotation there would be no gravity, no up or down. "After we have left the living quarters through the airlock, we have to wait until the hub comes rotating below us."

"Exactly. There are about ten body lengths of vacuum we have to cross."

Gronolf points at the mask on his belt. "No problem," he says. He bends over the map and zooms in on the airlock of the living quarters. The real problem will await them there. The pressure chamber, which has been built into each of the innermost sectors for maintenance purposes, offers the only way into the core. Everything is very well-arranged and there are no alternatives, because the exterior wall of the entire living shell is so thoroughly hardened that it would survive even an explosion of the drive system.

"If the Omniscience wants to stop us, it would be here." He points at the airlock. If they don't manage to reach the exit, they stand no chance of fulfilling their mission. "Do we have any information about what to expect?"

"The Omniscience has maintenance robots, that's all we know."

"It certainly should be able to modify the robots according to its requirements."

"Without a doubt," Murnaka concurs.

"I understand. Then we will proceed the way I teach all recruits. We use the element of surprise and destroy anything that might be dangerous. If I am right, there is nothing in that room we are not allowed to demolish." Gronolf holds his weapon at the ready, "Please take cover behind me."

Murnaka looks at him with her front eye but remains silent. Should he say a few farewell words? No, that would be bad luck. He is the best of his plex. He will clear the path to the airlock, that is the only thing that counts. Nobody can stop him. He feels warm at the pit of his stomach.

Gronolf senses that there is more at stake than fulfilling his duty as a warrior. Yet he should not get distracted by it.

"Thank you for your companionship," Murnaka says.

His stomach rumbles. What is he supposed to reply? Nothing comes to mind. Therefore he simply releases the safety catch of his weapon and starts walking.

THE AIRLOCK IS IN THE CENTRAL ROOM OF THE LIFE-SUPPORT sector, and they are now in front of it. The many machines in the room generate so much noise on all wavelengths that their sensors will be overloaded. Technically, they will be blind as well. Gronolf positions himself left of the door hinge. In a moment, when the door opens to the left, he will have a good view of the right side of the room. The door panel will protect him from the left side.

As agreed, Murnaka stays behind him. She is even crouching slightly in order not to tower above him.

Gronolf silently counts to three and then pushes against

the door. Most of all, he will have to be quick, as that is his advantage. Therefore he does not wait to see an enemy, or even just a movement, but immediately fires his harpoon into the opening. The explosive charge detonates three body lengths ahead and shreds an obstacle, whatever it was.

A metal part comes flying through the door opening, but Gronolf manages to catch it with a load-arm. He drops it right away, as it is red-hot. Then Gronolf takes a strong leap forward in order to use the dust cloud caused by the explosion. It takes him just a moment to load a new explosive charge into the harpoon. While he is still airborne he whips his weapon to the left. He notices three multi-armed, slender shapes. He does not see any details, because smoke and dust fill the room, but they could only be robots. Gronolf fires the weapon a second time. Two of the three robots fall before he even touches the ground.

Then the pain starts. Electrical energy surges through him when he hits the floor. His muscles twitch uncontrollably, while his mind remains strangely lucid. He can watch himself as if from outside as he smashes to the ground. He collapses like a wet sack, and the physical pain is overwhelming, excruciating, like nothing he has experienced with the possible exception of his draght.

Something flies toward him from the other room. He can only see Murnaka's shadow. She bounces off the walls and the ceiling as if gravity did not exist. Her right foot hits his side and breaks several ribs, but the impulse rolls his body toward the door. Despite the pain, Gronolf manages to reach for the door panel at the right moment, Then one of his legs is outside the electrically charged area and he can lever himself to safety behind the wall, breathing heavily.

But where is Murnaka? He only now notices he has lost his weapon. He rolls around and looks into the large room. He can see movement behind the curtain of dust. Gronolf wants to run inside, but just in time he remembers the trap, the floor. Could he move across the wall and the ceiling, like Murnaka? Maybe, but only when his muscles have recovered from the electric shocks. He absolutely wants to save her, just like she saved him, but as an experienced warrior he knows it is no use.

Now visibility is increasing inside the life-support control room. A door opens in the back. He notices three more robots. They don't bother with him, as if they know that he no longer poses a threat. They are rolling a large, heavy object out of the room. It is nearly conical. Gronolf has to watch helplessly as the Omniscience kidnaps Murnaka's body. He angrily hammers his four hands against the floor. Yet the robots are not distracted.

When the door closes behind Murnaka and the robots, Gronolf goes limp. It is his fault that Murnaka sacrificed herself. He started combat just as he was trained to do. Naturally, the Omniscience expected this. It sacrificed a few robots and set a trap for them. He should have anticipated this! But why didn't Murnaka just leave him lying in there? She should have slammed the door and fled. *This whole mission was ill-fated from the beginning,* he thinks in frustration.

Suddenly the ship trembles under an enormous blow. Gronolf jumps up, even though his limbs still hurt. What happened? Has the *Majestic Draght* been attacked by something? He activates the two-way radio receiver. The Omniscience, he learns, simultaneously closed all bulkheads between sectors. Now it is impossible for him to reach the security chamber with the emergency switch. And even the way back will be difficult. Does he even have to rejoin the others? Wouldn't it just be better to stay here and die of exhaustion?

No! The Omniscience must pay, and Gronolf is ready to give his life to make it happen.

Brightnight 37, 3876

HE CAN'T GO ON. THE MEMORIES ARE SO PAINFUL THAT THEY still torture and weaken him, these many cycles later. Right now, he cannot afford that, because he needs to save the sleepers in their chambers. Gronolf has the archive present the rest of the story in text form. The Omniscience had closed all bulkheads in reaction to an attempted rebellion. Triggered by the images of the dead children, the rebels tried to fight the leadership group. Perhaps the Omniscience had planned this all along, or maybe it was just a useful side effect. The internal strife gave it the authority to depose the leadership and take on sole control. The rules included this option in case the leadership no longer could fulfill its function for any reason.

From that moment on, there had been no more 'accidents'—another fact indicating this had all been part of a greater plan. The Omniscience no longer accepted or followed orders, but it performed its duty and brought the *Majestic Draght* into an orbit around Single Sun. It sent the complete crew, in several waves, down to the surface of the planet, using the existing shuttles. Then, it went silent.

For the crew, survival on Single Sun turned out to be difficult. The Omniscience was not willing to provide resources from the ship. In fact, it did not even reply to any of their requests. At first, the marooned crew hoped this was only a passing phase. As the years passed, it became obvious they were going to receive no help.

The climate of the planet and its activities did not allow for a permanent colony, which had been the original plan. It turned out to be impossible to synchronize the deposit of eggs on the beach between the frequent flares. This became quite clear when Single Sun killed off the entire brood three times during the first year. The Space Scientists had not realized a red dwarf would emit so much deadly radiation. At first they still hoped for help from their home world. Yet this naive belief soon faded. Why should they send a second capital ship after one which was obviously lost, not reacting to signals? The shuttles which were left on the planet did not have powerful antennas.

After the population had been shrinking year after year, the new leadership decided to send a part of the Grosnops back home, using the shuttles that had landed them on the planet—at least as many as there was room for. As the shuttles were designed for short-range flight, they had to assume that many would fail and that the voyage lasting several generations could only be achieved in hibernation.

For the remaining majority of the Grosnops, the shelter building was constructed—right in the middle of the dark side facing away from the sun. This would protect them from the effects of the flares and save energy in running the cryogenic chambers. In secret they hoped that the home world would send help sometime—at the latest when the first shuttle had arrived. The archive has no information about whether this ever happened. No messages from the home world arrived.

They also kept a communication channel open, just in case the Omniscience on board the *Majestic Draght* changed its mind. Yet in all the cycles since the completion of the shelter building there had been no interaction—until a few days ago, when a desperate Eve seems to have sent a signal that provoked the Omniscience to react.

Gronolf searches for the syllable 'Mur' again, this time in the passenger lists of the shuttles that started their voyage to the home world in 3359. And this time he finds something. Murnaka's father must have arranged for her to get one of the coveted places. That was so much like him.

After Gronolf's failure to complete his mission and also his loss of General Murnak's daughter, he had initially been demoted. He never heard from Murnaka again. Yet weeks after the last waves of shuttle landings, a final transport had reached the planet. The identities of those on board were kept a strict secret. One brightnight later he was promoted—surprisingly—to his old rank again.

GRONOLF FEELS IT IS TIME TO WAKE THE OTHERS. FOR YEARS a wound has been bleeding inside him, sometimes unnoticed, sometimes painfully, which he now has to staunch. It was really an amazing coincidence that the system chose to pull him from his sleeping chamber.

May 10, 19, Eve

EVE SPENT THE NIGHT ON A BEAM THAT WAS NARROWER THAN her upper body. Nevertheless, she slept better than she had in a long time. The beam was padded surprisingly well, and even though she mostly lay on her side, she managed to keep from falling off.

Adam is just coming from the washroom, bare-chested. He seems to be in a good mood. "The basins are great for doing laundry," he says. "Give it a try."

Adam is right. Her clothes smell pretty bad, even though she bathed yesterday. She grabs all her things and disappears into the washroom. The smallest basin in the corner is for relieving oneself, that's what they agreed on. How do the frogs handle this body function? She has not yet found a toilet adapted to the anatomy of the locals. Perhaps it is hidden behind one of the invisible doors. It seems the alien just has to look at one of the doors in order to open it. If she could only talk to him, that would make everything so much easier.

After answering the call of nature Eve walks to the larger basin. She undresses and first washes her clothing, then herself. Unfortunately there is no clothes dryer. Therefore she squeezes everything out as well as she can, hangs the outer-wear over a short wall, and puts on the wet underwear. Luckily, it is warm enough not to be uncomfortable.

Eve's stomach is growling. She hopes Marchenko has created some tasty food overnight. That is the AI's one skill she probably missed most. *No, that would be unjust,* she thinks. But some fresh coffee and a crisp roll would be perfect now.

"Good morning, Eve!"

She is startled when Marchenko greets her in the shape of a bipedal robot almost as tall as herself. He must have done a lot of remodeling during the night. He definitely looks better than the piece of scrap he was yesterday, even though this lowers her chance of getting freshly baked rolls.

"Good morning!"

"Did you sleep well, even on that beam?"

"Very well. From now on I will insist on such a contraption."

"How about breakfast?"

"Gladly," she says.

Marchenko points at the door leading to the next room. There he used a kind of lectern as a table. There is a cup which actually smells of coffee and a bowl filled with porridge. Next to it she sees a spoon.

"Adam already finished," Marchenko says. "Unfortunately the porridge is nutritious, but that's all."

"Thanks." Eve nods and lifts the cup of coffee. Even from a close distance the beverage still smells real. She wonders how Marchenko always manages to do that. His nano-fabricators really are a miracle.

"How did you do all this?"

"I borrowed Marchenko 2's nano-fabricators."

"Borrowed? Isn't he dead?" Eve visualizes how she aimed the alien's weapon at the robot and pulled the trigger. She is to blame for his death, even though she had no choice.

"'Dead' is a relative term. He is a machine, like I am, so you might rather say he is broken, defective."

"And his consciousness?"

"I don't know. I haven't had time to deal with that. If his memory units are not too fragmented, his consciousness could be repaired. The memory contents will persist even without an energy supply. The data just can't be changed anymore."

"So this means he will eternally see this scene in which I fire the weapon at him?"

"That image will remain, yes, but for him time no longer passes. Without energy, the internal clock no longer works."

"So if we manage to repair him, no time would have passed for him?"

"Yes. Do you want us to repair him?"

Eve notices that Marchenko is giving her a compassionate look. Within one night he has even managed to give his face emotions. That is amazing.

"No, absolutely not. He deserved death," she says more aggressively than she intended to, and is shocked by the anger in her own voice. "Sorry," she adds.

"You don't have to apologize. You had several days of utter despair behind you."

"That is true." If she isn't careful now she will start to cry. She takes a sip. The warm beverage runs down her throat. It tastes like a mixture of coffee and tea. She puts down the cup and reaches for the bowl and the spoon. The porridge has a sweetish smell.

"Carbohydrates and protein," Marchenko says. "I made them from—"

"That's okay, I don't really need to know," she interrupts him. She dips the spoon into the mass, which has a slimy, sticky consistency. *I am sure there will be rolls tomorrow,* she thinks, gets over her aversion, and moves the spoon with its contents into her mouth. Without energy from food she won't survive —Marchenko is better off in that aspect.

"How do you recharge in here?" she asks.

"No problem, the entire building is full of electrical cables. The alien showed me an outlet where I can get 900 volts."

"Sounds tasty," Eve says, then laughs.

"Yes, it's a great feeling, almost like eating ice cream."

She actually manages to finish the bowl, because she is so hungry.

"Once you are done I would like to invite you to a meeting in the control center," he says.

"Just a moment, I have to brush my teeth."

While Eve stands in front of the basin, rinsing her mouth, she can barely believe her luck. A little while ago she was almost dead, and now her everyday routine has returned. *Not completely*, she remembers. There is still a huge spaceship hurtling towards the planet. Yet she is no longer alone and now she can face the future with more optimism.

May 10, 19, Adam

To the left of him sits a live alien, to the right a dead one. If he'd seen something like this three days ago, he would have soiled his pants out of sheer fright. Today it seems completely normal to him. He even knows the name of the alien—the live one—with whom they are going to have the first meeting of the day.

Everything is quite normal in appearance. The five of them will discuss how they can save this planet, Gronolf's numerous friends, and ultimately themselves. The fifth one, the dead general, won't actively participate, but at least he is the perfect warning of what will happen to them if they fail.

"Gronolf," the alien says. He points to himself.

Adam turns around. Is this a round of introductions?

"Marchenko."

"Eve."

"Adam."

Then the alien repeats their three names. Well, Adam had been worrying it might be tough going. Marchenko told him this morning that he has learned about 500 words in the alien language. That's probably not enough for complicated plans to save the world. Yet don't they say that the simplest plans are the best? He would be satisfied with a simple plan.

The alien gets up and walks to the holo-map they already

admired yesterday. Gronolf is not wasting any time. He uses the control panel to zoom in on the thing racing toward them. It has a complicated name for which Marchenko could only provide the rough translation 'Great Youth.' *A species that gives spaceships names like that cannot be evil and has a sense for poetry*, Adam thinks.

Gronolf freezes the holographic image and the *Great Youth* suddenly stops. Then he aims one of his long arms at Marchenko.

"Ro-bot," he says in English. Robot, right, Marchenko is one, but also more than that. Then the alien points at the spaceship again and says the word again. He repeats his gestures and words twice. The ship is a robot, that much seems to be clear, even if it makes no sense so far.

"Artificial intelligence," Marchenko says in English, and points at a small display on his arm.

Gronolf turns so he can see the display well with his front eye. Adam is too far away.

"Let me quickly solve a differential equation," Marchenko explains.

Something is probably happening on the display. It does not matter what exactly it is or how much Gronolf understands. Marchenko wants to show him his thought process, which is a difficult task. Doesn't he expect too much from Gronolf?

Adam speaks up. He has a better idea. When the others acknowledge him, he takes a screw from his pocket, shows it to everyone, puts it in his right fist, but also closes his left one. He wiggles his hands a bit and then holds out his fists to Gronolf. The alien realizes what is expected of him and points at the right fist. Adam opens it and shows the screw.

"Thinking," Adam says, and then points at Marchenko, the thinking machine. Gronolf seems to be very glad about it, because he winks several times with his front eye.

"Artificial intelligence," Marchenko says again, then points at himself. He repeats the term and now indicates the ship.

Gronolf also points at Marchenko and the ship and tries out the English term. It sounds like, "art-a-fish nn-tel-enzz."

It looks like the ship is controlled by an artificial intelligence. Is that good or bad news? Gronolf repeats the difficult words, but then he suddenly jumps up and runs from the room. The length of his strides is amazing. How far can he jump? Soon afterward he returns, holding an object in his hand. It is a fragment of the dead Marchenko. Gronolf makes a sound like the firing of his weapon and points at Eve. The alien must have noticed that Marchenko 2 resembles the real one in one aspect: He is also an AI—but a defective one.

"Could it be that the ship is controlled by an inoperative AI?"

"Yes, Adam, that's what I also think," Marchenko says.

"If the AI is inoperative, how can it steer such a huge ship?" Eve adds. "Did you see the acceleration data? These are far beyond what human technology is capable of. And wouldn't the control system simply fail?"

Adam looks at the map. It displays some kind of symbols, but no velocity values he can read. He slaps his hand against his forehead. Eve must have calculated based on the ship's starting position.

"That is a real contradiction," Marchenko says. "I just don't know how I can ask Gronolf about details concerning the AI of the spaceship."

Eve scratches the side of her head. "It's obvious," she says, "that the AI is not defective. Perhaps the parallels to Marchenko 2 are closer than we assume? What if the AI has rebelled against its creators?"

Marchenko raises his arm, allowing Gronolf to see the display again. Then he makes two giant frogs appear, and a huge cube which fires lasers at them.

"Yes," Gronolf says, one of the words the alien learned yesterday. The drawing has worked.

"So," Marchenko replies, which probably means 'yes' in the alien language.

Step 1 is behind them. Adam takes a deep breath. The

problem has been identified—a recalcitrant AI. Now they only need a plan. Marchenko becomes active and draws the number 1 on the panel. The alien confirms the number by tracing it. Marchenko must have already taught him some basic numbers.

Gronolf steps up to the holo-map. He acts as if he would take the planet into his two touch-arms and carry it to the ship.

"That gesture is obvious—we have to fly there," Adam says. The others nod.

"So," Marchenko says.

Then Gronolf draws a 2 in the air and then by turns points at Marchenko and the ship, without moving from his position. Then he repeats two words several times: "Marchenko. Grunuko-to. Marchenko. Grunuko-to."

"I have no idea what that word means," Marchenko apologizes.

"Maybe he wants you to take over for the ship's AI," Eve suggests.

"Or I should disable it."

"So," Gronolf says.

"So," Marchenko says.

"So," the alien replies, and his eyelids jump wildly up and down. Adam watches him with his arms crossed. Now the alien does not look threatening anymore, even though he is much bigger and could stomp him with one foot.

Adam is about to suggest they start looking for a suitable vehicle for this mission, when Gronolf draws a 3 into the air. So the plan is supposed to have three parts?

"So," Marchenko says, obviously to encourage him. Now the alien virtually takes the ship in both hands, zooms out of the image, and carries it to a binary star.

"Dutoka-so," he says.

"Alpha Centauri," Marchenko automatically translates, but Adam remembers the word. He has to sit down. Does Gronolf want to take them to his home world, once he regains control of the ship? That would be… Adam does not know what to think about it. A completely new world—and at the same time one in which they would spend the rest of their lives among giant frogs.

"Did you also interpret this as an offer to take us to Alpha Centauri?" he asks quietly.

"Looks like it," Eve whispers.

May 10, 19, Marchenko

IN THEORY THE PLAN LOOKS GOOD: TRAVEL TO THE *MAJESTIC Draght*, convince the Omniscience to cooperate, and then leave. However, they lack an important tool—a means of transportation! Marchenko considers the options. Their vehicle does not have to be particularly fast, because their target is moving toward them. However, they would have more time on board the 'Great Youth' the sooner they reach the enormous ship. *They picked a nice name,* Marchenko thinks, even though he is not sure how correctly he translated it.

Perhaps Gronolf still has a rocket standing around in some hangar? The aliens must have landed here somehow. Marchenko tries to put his question in pictures. Now he is annoyed the screen on his arm isn't larger. He alerts Gronolf to his attempt and has a few screen pixels fly back and forth between the planet and the spaceship.

"So-na," the alien says, a negation, and he waves his two load arms to the side, which probably corresponds to shaking his head. Then he moves his right touch-arm to his shoulder and turns around. This probably indicates they should follow him. What is he up to?

Gronolf only walks a few steps and then stops at the chair where Marchenko found him this morning. He leads

Marchenko directly in front of it and then pushes his shoulders down. Marchenko sits down obediently.

Gronolf touches a waist-high cabinet, from which a control panel folds out. He types in something. Suddenly a kind of cap falls from the bottom of the console. It is connected to the cabinet via several cables. Gronolf unfolds it and places it on the middle of his belly. It adapts perfectly to the shape. Is this some kind of diagnostic device, maybe for ultrasound? On the other hand, such a device would be out of place in the control center. Maybe it is able to transmit data, like an EEG helmet. They still know too little about the aliens' physiology. Marchenko automatically assumed their thinking organ was in the upper part of the torso, probably between the two arms, even though there is no head. However, there is no factual reason for that. There is space everywhere, and thinking requires little room.

Now Gronolf removes the soft cap from his belly. There is a snapping sound when he pulls it off his skin. He takes it in his touch-arms, examines it, checks the cable length, and stretches the material slightly. Then he gets up, steps in front of Marchenko, and carefully, almost reverently, places the cap on Marchenko's belly.

I hope I won't make a mistake now, Marchenko thinks. Whatever this object is for, nothing will happen if he just leaves it on his torso. Nevertheless, he waits for a minute. Maybe the thing is just meant to give him a pleasant massage, nothing else.

Nothing happens, and Gronolf seems to be getting nervous, as his front eye is blinking. The cap must have a different purpose, and the EEG function seems to be the most likely one. Marchenko can only find that out by testing it. The problem is that he is definitely not sensitive for the electromagnetic waves used to stimulate the alien's nerves. The cap won't function as an EEG helmet for him. He needs the original form of the data that Gronolf wants to transmit to him. First he would have to destroy the cap. Hopefully, there are no important alien religious or cultural ideas attached to it! Now that they are getting along so well with him, he rather not risk that. He also has no clue how to explain to Gronolf what he is planning to do.

It can't be helped. Sometimes you have to take a risk if you want to get ahead. Marchenko takes the cap in one hand and the cable in the other. He suddenly rips the connection. Gronolf jumps up but does not say anything. Marchenko keeps his eyes on the alien's dangerous load-arms. Yet the extraterrestrial allows him to proceed.

Marchenko examines the cable. It contains transparent fibers below a plastic-like covering. It seems to transfer data optically, in the form of light. Marchenko opens a flap on the left side of his torso. There the nano-fabricators have provided various inputs, including ones for optical signals. He will probably have to adapt them once the cable is connected with his body.

He involuntary imagines giving a monstrous AI access to his body this way. Of course that is a silly idea, but the image is vivid and makes him pause briefly. He notices Gronolf watching him intently. He does not sense any hostility, so he closes the connection. As expected, he first has to adjust the frequencies and the signal strength and then find out which modulation is used. The alien technology employs an extremely high clock speed. If he cannot slow down the rushing data stream, it will flood him like a tsunami. He can only hope the aliens thought of something like a feedback loop so that a weaker receiver can lower the value.

Five minutes later the technical adaptation is finished. Via the cable he receives a clean test signal now, which shows him a silver ellipse with two green focal points. It is interesting that the aliens also encode numbers in a binary system, even though they count based on a system of seven. He found out that the data stream contains three-dimensional images, 45 of which are transmitted per second. This might correspond to the abilities of the aliens' visual system, which then would be much more capable of perceiving movement than human eyes are. The audio data reaches all the way to ultrasound.

In addition there are two additional data streams he cannot assign. They probably correspond to other senses, perhaps smell and touch? As he lacks the necessary perception due to his different anatomy, he cannot evaluate these data streams. Therefore he ignores them. The cap definitely is a sophisticated construct. When Gronolf uses it, he might be able to directly visualize the past.

"So," he says loudly in Gronolf's direction.

"So," the alien replies. He leans over the control panel and starts typing.

The first flood of images is so exhausting Marchenko is glad to be sitting in a comfortable chair. What he sees is absolutely foreign. His consciousness needs considerably more time to process each image than usual. If he still were human, he would probably react with nausea or panic. Yet he lets the flood sweep over him and picks images to analyze in intervals he can handle. This means that he misses some information during the first minutes, but he will have to live with that.

Marchenko lands with both legs on a planet the likes of which he has never seen before. The ground is soft, the atmosphere is warm, and two suns shine in a green sky. Only the vegetation seems hostile, probably because a bilious green color has replaced the soft green of Earth.

He has no time to get used to this environment. Suddenly he is in the middle of a gathering of the inhabitants that he immediately recognizes as Gronolf's siblings. He follows their conversations. His mind is swamped by the alien language, and he finally has so much material that the development of a linguistic model is only a question of time. He assigns part of his resources to that task so that he can continue focusing on the images. The system appears to give him a historical overview of this civilization, and the language center already provides the first translations. It is overwhelming to discover so many parallels to developments on Earth, but also so many different paths taken by this civilization.

Now he is on board a spaceship. He notices this right away by the change in gravity. It is the *Majestic Draght*, as he

now knows, and his initial translation of the name was not
that far off. The ship is on the way to Single Sun—Proxima
Centauri in his language—where the Grosnops have discovered a planet that might be suitable for colonization.

Marchenko carefully observes the growing alienation
between the AI and the crew. The idea of subjecting artificial
and natural intelligences to the same rules might sound just,
but he already knows what effects it had in this case.
Marchenko sees the hopeless struggle of the crew against the
Omniscience and the landing of the Grosnops on this planet.
He watches the construction of the building in the ice and the
attempt of a part of the crew to return to Dual Sun using
small shuttles. Now he also knows it won't be easy to subdue
the alien AI.

A warning signal returns Marchenko to the present. Now
90 percent of the free memory in his body has been filled. He
is no Omniscience and will never become one, as he lacks the
resources. It will be hard to get rid of at least two-thirds of the
knowledge he just acquired. Marchenko is already running
algorithms to separate important information from unimportant. He keeps the linguistic ability. Now they can finally talk
to Gronolf without any obstacles.

First, one critical question must be answered: Where can
they get a rocket to take them to the alien spaceship?

Brightnight 37, 3876

Gronolf barely managed to control himself when Marchenko ripped apart the metal archive-interface equipment. Of course it is his own fault, because he handed it to this stranger. However, he had no idea Marchenko would simply destroy the most powerful hardware available in the control center. While the contactless sonar access to the archive—which he himself used yesterday—provides mostly impressions, the ventral cap allows one to call up absolutely everything from the archive.

'Allowed,' Gronolf corrects himself. Or should he ask Marchenko to repair the cap? After all, the machine managed to connect the cables to his own body, which is based on a completely different technology. It would be best to wait and see whether and how Marchenko has processed the data he has received. Gronolf uses the control panel to unlock the most important information about the Grosnops and their journey.

"How can we best reach the *Majestic Draght*?"

Marchenko has surprised him again. He can already speak the Grosnop language flawlessly! Gronolf gestures with his hand, expressing appreciation, as he thinks maybe it's not so awful that the AI tore the equipment apart.

Adam and Eve come running. The machine seems to

translate its words to Grosnop simultaneously now. "All our shuttles set course for the Dual Sun," Gronolf says. "Don't you have a ship? You must have arrived here in one."

"Unfortunately, we destroyed our ship to clear the way into the shelter building," the AI informs him.

"Why?"

"The ice layer on top had become too thick."

"Couldn't you have melted it?"

"We were in a great hurry."

"You cut off any possibility of a return journey. That's bad tactics."

"For us, the return journey was already made impossible at launch."

What does Marchenko mean by that? This sounds like a potentially interesting story, thought Gronolf. He loves stories, but this one will have to wait until later.

"Then our mission has failed," Gronolf says. He still cannot quite believe it. Two civilizations previously unknown to each other meet on a faraway planet, and then they have no opportunity to return to space? That is surreal. Gronolf starts waving his load-arms and walks through the control room.

"We could try once more to contact the Omniscience," Marchenko says. "Perhaps we could smuggle me on board, meaning my consciousness?"

"The Omniscience does not react at all to our messages."

"And if I try it, from one artificial intelligence to the other?"

"Are you really an AI?" Gronolf is surprised, as so far he had thought he was dealing with a robot, a machine.

"If I only knew exactly!"

"You do not know what you are?"

"I am based on a human consciousness. It's a long story. Yet I was changed, so I have many abilities of an AI."

"In my civilization, this would have been unethical," Gronolf says. However, he remembered, there had been a few

Knowledge Scientists who suggested such a method. Who could know whether the Omniscience would have betrayed them in this case? Might it have then understood its creators better?

"In my civilization, such a hybridization is also considered unethical. However, there are always some scientists who want to try out anything that is possible," Marchenko explains.

"The result is positive, I would say."

"Oh, well..." Marchenko says, then quickly turns aside.

Gronolf actually meant his statement as a compliment, but he seems to have hit a sore spot. Marchenko seems to miss his humanity. Perhaps the Life Scientists of his people could give him the healthy body of a Grosnop. Marchenko certainly would not want to be one of those fragile creatures with that ugly growth above the arms. What probably matters most to him is to enjoy life in its biological form, the boisterous strength of a young body, the joy of diving into the cold, salty water of the ocean. He shakes his belly, as this idea is so attractive.

Then Gronolf turns around and walks to the holo-map. "Come, Marchenko," he calls. At the same time he starts typing on the segmented keyboard. He selects the ship and activates the voice communication. "We can get started."

Marchenko looks around, as if searching for something. It must be really impractical only to have eyes on one side. Marchenko can change his configuration, so why doesn't he get rid of the shortcomings of human anatomy?

"My name is Marchenko," the robot starts saying. As if on command the two humans also move closer. "I am a representative of humanity, a civilization which has developed four lightyears from here."

An interesting introduction, Gronolf thinks. If the Omniscience shows any interest in the universe, it should react to this.

"I know your creators call you the Omniscience. As this can't be an accurate description of your state due to physical reasons, I assume the name expresses your desires to always gain new knowledge."

An interesting strategy—but it does not fit the fact that the Omniscience has been inactive for many, many cycles, Gronolf thinks.

"I can fully understand this desire, because it is also my driving force. I don't even know the exact reason for it. Perhaps it was implanted in me by my creators, similar to you. Or it could be part of my human nature. I resemble you, but I am also different, because I am not a pure Omniscience but a hybrid AI. Would you be interested in exchanging information?"

Marchenko really manages to make the Omniscience an attractive offer. Gronolf does not know what else would get it interested in starting a conversation. He carefully watches the communication channel to the ship, but there is no sign of a message coming the other way.

"For this purpose, though, we have to talk to each other now. Right now, your ship is hurtling toward the planet I am staying on and will destroy it a few days from now. I would like to save the two humans here, and the numerous members of the race that created you, from that fate."

Perfect reasoning—but there is no reply from the other side. Gronolf basically knew it would be so. The Omniscience is beyond any understanding, utterly mysterious. Nobody can guess how it will behave.

"What now?" Gronolf asks.

Marchenko walks back to the chair and drops into it. Can a machine be frustrated? It seems that way to Gronolf, even though he could not exactly pinpoint the reason why.

"Then we really need a ship, after all," Marchenko says.

"This is where we left off."

Adam asks something Gronolf doesn't understand. However, he has an idea of what this is all about. Marchenko talks to Adam and then suddenly jumps up, as if recharged with energy.

"Adam has an idea that might work," he says.

"Marchenko 2, the machine Eve destroyed, also arrived here in a spaceship."

"Where is it?" Gronolf asks.

"One part is at the bottom of the ocean, a journey of several weeks from here."

"But there is another part."

"Yes. He came down with the lander module, just like we did. *Messenger*, his spaceship, should still be orbiting the planet."

"Can we reach it?"

"It won't be easy. *Messenger* is not designed to land on a planet. And to contact it we need the codes of Marchenko 2."

"Which he took with him when he died," Gronolf conjectures.

"It is not that easy to extinguish a Marchenko completely," the machine says and gets up. "I have to start working."

May 10, 19, Eve

"You really want me to revive Marchenko 2?"

"Of course, that was exactly what I was thinking," Eve says. Why does Marchenko think she would be against it? Just because she pulled the trigger? They cannot go on without *Messenger*, so she won't allow vague fears to interfere.

The four of them search the place where it had happened. The body of the impostor was splintered into many small fragments. Each splinter could contain parts of his memory and thus each could house sectors of his consciousness. Marchenko thinks they won't need every single part of the puzzle. They only have to assemble it sufficiently that it can perform basic mental functions.

"Can't you simply scan every memory chip for the codes?" she asks while picking up a coin-sized piece of metal.

"From outside, for another mind, they cannot be recognized as codes. Memory for us does not work like it does in a computer, with fixed storage locations. It is more the tracks of the thoughts that serve as storage. And I don't know my way around the labyrinth of a foreign mind—that's why we need him." Marchenko adds, "Awake and psychologically somewhat stable."

"That'll be a good trick—he never *was* stable," is Eve's somewhat snide but nevertheless accurate observation.

Half an hour later Marchenko calls them to join him. They have only estimates as to the former weight of Marchenko 2. By now they have collected 35 kilograms of his former body, and Marchenko starts to reassemble the parts.

"I am not going to give him a specific form, I'll simply connect the pieces electronically," he explains.

Something that looks like a big cookie develops on the floor in front of Eve, and then it begins to resemble a work of art accidentally squashed flat. She watches with fascination. Eve imagines that at some point this mass will once again be imbued with the spark of life she extinguished.

Suddenly she notices a slight movement. "There, did you see that? Is he waking up again?"

"No, it must have been some remaining energy discharging," says Marchenko. "Nothing should happen until I connect him to an electrical power source again."

"That's it," Marchenko says about ten minutes later. "All of the parts we found have been temporarily connected. Now I am going to hook it up to a power supply."

Eve feels like she is watching Dr. Frankenstein during his experiments. Soon electrical energy will change dead matter into living.

Marchenko signals Gronolf, who types something at a small console.

"Tokroko-so!" the alien says.

Marchenko answers him in his language. The words sound harsh to Eve's ears. Marchenko explained to them that part of the communication works in the ultrasonic range. She knows she and Adam will be unable to learn the aliens' language without technical aids. *Does it really make any sense to accompany Gronolf and the surviving Grosnops to their planet?*

"Okay, I am going to connect him to my vocal center so we can talk."

Marchenko's speakers emit some croaking, chirping, and scratching sounds. Eve leans forward and gives him a worried look.

"It's okay," he says, "just a few initial adjustment problems."

Now they hear rattling and hissing. Eve notices Adam is about to laugh just as she hears some heavy breathing. "Is that you, Marchenko?" she asks.

"I... where am I? Why can't I see anything? Eve, is that you?" The voice sounds frightened.

"You are inside your destroyed body," their real Marchenko says in a completely calm voice.

"What... what did you do to me?" replies the fake Marchenko 2. The fear is still audible. Eve is impressed by how obvious the differences are.

"You and only you are responsible for that. Your behavior would have caused our deaths."

"I... I don't know. I can't remember. Could you get me out of here? Please!" Now Marchenko 2 sounds almost weepy. Is he really unable to remember?

"We will see. First we need something from you."

"You already have everything, what else do you want?"

"The access codes for *Messenger*."

"The... what? I don't even know whether those still exist. I haven't had any contact in a very long time. Let me out of here and we can talk about it."

"You are not imprisoned. It's only that your body no longer exists. Don't you remember?"

"I don't know anything about that. I just saved Adam on the ice sheet. Doesn't that count for something?"

Eve is still not sure whether to believe him. About a quarter of his memory units are missing, so he truly might have 'forgotten' things.

"Afterwards you wanted to kill me and Gronolf."

"Gronolf? Don't know that person."

Now Marchenko 2 has told the truth, and his voice already sounds much more assertive.

"The alien you knocked down with no prior warning."

"He threatened me with a huge weapon."

So he does remember what happened inside this building. Eve nods at Adam and Marchenko. They also seem to have noticed that Marchenko 2 just gave himself away.

"Will you give us the codes now?"

"I need at least a bit of light. Give me an eye. It is horrible inside this dark hole."

"I know," the real Marchenko replies, "because you once treated me like this."

"But that all happened a long time ago. Don't be so resentful! Give me eyesight and you will get the codes."

"Okay." Marchenko runs a cable from the hardware fragments on the floor to his own body. "There. Now you see what I see."

"Oh, here you are. Turn around."

Marchenko chooses to obey his request.

"All three of you together, how nice... and the giant frog is also here. What a *nice* family you've got."

"His name is Gronolf," Eve says.

"Hi, Eve darling, I am glad to hear your voice."

"I am not at all glad to hear yours."

"Don't worry, I won't hold it against you that you shot me."

Lies, lies, lies. That's all he ever did was lie to them. Now Eve is annoyed at herself for ever pitying him.

"Leave Eve alone! And give us the codes," the real Marchenko says in a menacing voice.

"Or what?"

"Or I will pull your plug."

"Then you won't reach *Messenger*."

"Or even better: I could leave you with a tiny bit of energy. And then you would be stuck in your dark hole for all eternity."

"You've convinced me," Marchenko 2 says, suddenly affable, "Wait, I will transmit the codes to you."

"Thanks."

"You don't want to check them?"

"Don't worry, I will. But not now." Marchenko calmly removes the two cables that connected the electronic scrap with his body and the wall.

Eve jerks back. "Did you—"

"Kill him? No, he is just like before. His internal clock is paused. Time stands still. He is not suffering."

"But we promised him light." Eve's hands tremble.

"Did he ever keep his promises?"

"Still, we are not like that."

"We don't have any time for additional problems. Marchenko 2 is devious, as we all certainly know by now. If we leave him in an active state, no matter how damaged, he will find a way to hurt us. I am sure there are some nano-fabricators crawling around that are programmed to serve him. Even a single one would be enough to gradually rebuild a body. And do we dare let him interfere, just as we are about to solve our main problem? No, Eve, I am sorry, but I won't do it."

She turns around because tears well up in her eyes, and she doesn't want Marchenko to notice. She has never seen him act so cold. Why isn't Adam saying anything?

May 10, 19, Adam

ADAM WAS SURPRISED THAT THEIR MARCHENKO TURNED OFF the power to his alter ego without any discussion. He suspects something: Perhaps Marchenko is so merciless because he sees a lot of himself in Marchenko 2. Adam does not know how much the Creator has manipulated the minds of those two. Yet he cannot imagine that the path the evil version took was predetermined from birth. At some point Marchenko 2 must have made a different decision. At that time it might not have been obvious which one would be right and which one wrong. Yet consequently one mind became an impostor, a murderer even, while the other one developed into someone he considers his father.

Marchenko must know that both of these personality pathways are inside him, especially since meeting his alter ego. Therefore he puts in a great deal of effort to stay on the right side. Adam will have to tell him sometime, that this effort carries some danger of its own. He wonders whether Marchenko will accept this from his son.

All the doubts Marchenko 2 sowed in his soul have, strangely enough, disappeared during the last few days. It simply doesn't matter now who did not tell what to whom. Adam really does not want to know it anymore. They have worked together in a way befitting a family, and even the odd giant frog no longer seems to be a stranger, even though he has known him for only a day. The world is crazy.

"It is working."

Adam is startled out of his musing because Marchenko comes from the control center into the crew room.

"You are in contact with *Messenger*?" asks Eve, rising from her sleeping beam.

"Yes. The codes are correct and I have full access."

"You still sound concerned, as if we have some big problem."

"You are right, Eve. I really should have thought of this earlier. *Messenger*—or more specifically, the orbital module—cannot land on the planet."

"It can't be that difficult," Adam says. "Gravity will pull anything down."

"True, but what I ought to have said was, 'The ship can land, but not launch again.' Marchenko 2 turned his command module into the undersea base. And you know where our command module is."

"In the middle of the desert," Adam says. "But can't we get it here by remote control?"

"It is not prepared for a launch. No fuel. I think I even left the door open."

"Well, we didn't think we would ever need it again," Eve says apologetically.

"So we have an orbital module that reacts to our calls and would fly us to the spaceship if only we could get on board somehow."

"Well summarized, Adam."

"I think I have an idea," Eve says. "Is the onboard computer of the orbital module still working?"

"Almost perfectly," Marchenko says. Adam knows what Eve is thinking.

"Then we can send you on board via radio. There you would have to use the nano-fabricators to create a new body for yourself."

"Would there be enough time for it?" Adam asks, giving his sister a skeptical look.

"The fabricators could already get started, and they have time before you will have to enter the big ship."

"Yes, I can do that," says Marchenko. "I knew we would find a solution. I am going to send an order to the fabricators right away. Then I will explain everything to Gronolf, and afterward you can say goodbye to me."

Brightnight 37, 3876

Gronolf is walking around in the control center. If only he could talk to someone! The foreign machine made a demand he can't accept—but if he rejects it, he will also have failed.

Everything had started out so well. The humans found a means of transportation that could take them to the *Majestic Draght*. This method does not involve a landing on the planet. Instead, Marchenko described a plan that sounds like a scientific fairy tale to Gronolf: The AI wants to transfer to the ship by purely electronic means and then construct a new body on board. The Life Scientists of his people should be interested in this, because if the method could also be applied to biological beings, it would revolutionize travel.

However, this revolutionary plan deeply distresses Gronolf. He has no choice but to let Marchenko fly alone to the *Majestic Draght*—and, he must give the AI all access codes. If the alien should solve the problem of the Omniscience, he could claim the spaceship as his own. According to Grosnop law, this would be entirely legal. The *Majestic Draght* would then be Marchenko's personal trophy... just as he, Gronolf, could claim it if he were somehow the hero to liberate the ship. Naturally, being a Grosnop, he would then give the ship to his people as custom demands, but can he expect that from a machine?

Gronolf slowly walks in circles. With each circle he looks into the decayed front eye of the desiccated general. *How would you proceed? Which strategy would you employ? Should I take Adam and Eve hostage to force Marchenko to come back?* While he just met the humans, these beings have shown themselves to be very reliable so far. They care as much for each other as a Grosnop mother would for her children. They are interested in self-preservation, of course, as that is a biological instinct, but he feels that there is more than that, a sense of responsibility. Is that related to the high developmental level of their civilization? That would be nice, Gronolf thinks, because that would give him a positive view of his own species' future. The behavior of the leadership group made him doubt whether sophisticated technology always goes hand in hand with a sense of responsibility. Humans seem to be different in that aspect.

Therefore he decides to trust them. He doesn't have to tell Marchenko, though, that the AI could theoretically claim the *Majestic Draght* as his trophy. Gronolf is finally calmed enough to sit down again. He touches the console, locates the humans' ship, and assigns it the code of a shuttle that crashed a long time ago, during the landings. Then he increases the system privileges of this shuttle so that it can dock in any airlock. Finally he copies the voice signature of the dead general who is sitting across from him. Marchenko has the highly useful ability to imitate any voice input so perfectly that he can fool the best acoustic system. Of course, if the Omniscience blocks all access points he would not stand a chance.

Gronolf gets up and walks to the crew room, where the humans are waiting for him. When he enters the room they are just performing a strange ceremony: All three are hugging each other. It would look funny if three of his comrades did this. Yet due to their slender shapes and thin arms—only two each, only six in total—it almost looks natural for humans. Saying goodbye seems to be very emotional for them. Drops of water flow from Eve's eyes. Adam seems to have trouble breathing, because he sniffs and swallows several times.

Gronolf taps the ground politely with his foot in order to alert the three to his entrance. They turn around and look at him. *With humans you can be sure that they are paying attention*, he thinks, *and that makes dealing with them easier.* However, only being able to scan 180 degrees should make it harder to survive in the wild. Gronolf is really glad he has four eyes.

"You and your ship now have all the access privileges I can grant from here," he says.

Marchenko says something in the human language. He is probably interpreting. "Thanks. Do you have any tips concerning my technical equipment? I can freely modify my body," he replies.

"A perfect speech synthesis so you can identify yourself using the general's voice. And for obstacles which the Omniscience still won't remove, having a weapon with a good blasting effect would be advisable."

"Could you send me the plans of typical door and airlock constructions? I have an idea of how to get past locked doors without attracting attention."

Gronolf hesitates for a moment. *Now Marchenko wants the ship's blueprints, too?* Of course he is right. If there is a way to open doors without explosions, that would definitely be better. "Certainly," he says. "But don't forget the weapon." He remembers the moment when he tried to storm the life-support control room. His weapon had not been sufficient to save Murnaka's life.

"It would be ideal if the weapon could attack several targets at once. The opponents are not taller than you are now and are made of light alloys." At least this is true if the Omniscience has not changed its tactics. And it would have had no reason to do that.

"Are there body parts where the targets are especially vulnerable?"

"No, the Omniscience copied our body structure and distributed all functions across the entire body."

"Okay, then I will have to decide according to each situation. I would prefer to avoid an armed conflict."

"That might be true," Gronolf says. "Yet if the Omniscience completely seals off the central shell, entering it will be a great challenge. The outer hull is very sturdy."

"I will sneak up to it," Marchenko says, "and before the Omniscience notices anything, I will already be inside the system."

"That would be optimal."

"Then we should say goodbye now. From where could you best transfer me?"

Gronolf bends down and opens a flap at the base of the wall near the entrance. "There is a data input here that can be switched to the wireless system." He points downward, "I only need details about the signal path. After all, your ship has to be able to process the signal."

"Sure," Marchenko says, raising the display on his wrist.

"That should be enough," Gronolf says. "I will go to the control room and start programming the data. You can already connect here. You will notice an impulse in the line once it is about to start."

Marchenko crouches, pulls a cable from a flap in his side, and connects it to the wall outlet. "It fits," he says.

"It is all standardized, the way it should be on a ship." Gronolf wonders what to wish Marchenko. An honorable death, the way warriors do? That might be misunderstood. It is only symbolic, as one really wishes the other person to win. Yet it is supposedly bad luck to say that.

"Best wishes," he finally says.

"See you soon," Marchenko replies. Gronolf goes to the control room and reprograms the radio transmitter to use human technology. Then he gives the start command. When he returns to the control room, he already sees Marchenko leaning lifelessly against the wall.

Adam and Eve crouch next to him, each of them holding one of his hands.

May 10, 19, Marchenko

SUDDENLY HE IS THE SHIP AGAIN. HE FEELS AS IF HE HAS COME home in a suit, stripped it off along with the necktie and stiff shirt, and pulled on a comfy tracksuit. He spent many years here, first all alone, then with two infants who turned into children and became adults. That is not quite true, though, because he is inside Marchenko 2's *Messenger* instead of his own. On the other hand, he can't notice any difference. He is back home again.

Marchenko mentally stretches himself with a deep relaxing sigh. He is reminded just how confining a robot body can be. When he first moved into J the robot a few months ago, he focused on the adventure ahead, the exploration of a completely new world. While the orbital module that now serves as his home is no more than a speck of dust in space, it gives him a feeling of freedom he missed in the gravitational well of the planet.

Should he really move back into a solid body, the one that the nano-fabricators are presently assembling in the cabin? For a moment he even toys with the idea of running away. Perhaps the Omniscience had similar thoughts? Why should he care about humans or aliens? He is immortal, after all. He could leave the gravitational field of this sun behind and once again travel through space. Even if it takes him thousands of years, he has enough time. He can explore the galactic vicinity of Earth and then gradually move toward the center of the Milky Way. He will see things eternally inaccessible to mankind, if... yes, if he frees himself from his subservience to biological life forms.

Marchenko is suddenly ashamed for entertaining these thoughts. He remembers the looks Adam and Eve gave him when saying goodbye. For them, he is not just a machine. They consider him as close to a father as they will ever have. And he thinks of them as his children. This urge to flee might be based on fear, the natural fear of death, because the Omniscience is dangerous. He has to save Adam and Eve. And he can only do that if he defeats the Omniscience. Then he can stay with his children until the end of their lives, and still have millions of years left to roam the universe.

He aims the antenna at Proxima b and activates the transmitter. "This is Marchenko."

"This is Adam. Did you arrive safely?"

"Yes. It is just like coming back home."

"Yes, I'd like to see *Messenger* again, too."

"The ship would seem small to you."

"Please return it in one piece. Have you already left the orbit?"

"That will not be necessary. I have already started to turn and raise the orbit of *Messenger* around Proxima b. The alien ship is coming toward us, after all."

"When will you meet it?"

"I estimate thirty-six hours of flight time. Then I have four or five hours on board the *Majestic Draght* to talk the Omniscience into cooperating with us."

"You will soon be in the radio shadow. Let me say goodnight now."

"The same to you, Adam, and say hello to the others."

The connection is interrupted. Marchenko only now realizes he spoke English. Gronolf would not have understood him. In an hour he will be back out of the area of radio silence.

Talking to Adam felt good. Adam and Eve are his last connection to mankind—and perhaps his own human nature. Maybe his alter ego lacked this factor.

May 11, 19, Eve

EVE HAS SPENT A LOT OF TIME WITH HER BROTHER SINCE Marchenko's departure. Gronolf mostly leaves them alone, and they can only communicate in primitive phrases. Talking to him is difficult for her. It must be even harder for the alien, as he constantly has to remember not to use any sounds in the ultrasound range. Eve tried, just for fun, to lower her voice for a few sentences, but that was really exhausting.

Marchenko has left some food for them. If he doesn't come back within two days, they will have to make do with carbohydrates that Gronolf will have to prepare chemically from Grosnop food, according to Marchenko's instructions. That stuff won't have any taste, but at least they are not going to starve. If Marchenko 2 had not become so crazy, they might be able to use his help now. *If wishes were horses...* She has never actually seen a horse, but she likes the saying. Eve remembers Marchenko using it when they were about thirteen or fourteen years old.

Now the project of the day is to get their spacesuits and make them functional again, if possible. It is feasible, after all, that Marchenko succeeds with this phase of the plan and they will then be taking off in a much larger spaceship. Eve cannot really imagine this. They go to what is left of Adam's suit, which he took off next to the exit from the coolant system channel.

"We can't fix the visor," Eve says. She picks up the helmet and cautiously moves her hand across the material. A shard hits the ground with a soft tinkling noise.

"Looks worse than it is," Adam remarks. "I just dropped it, accidentally."

"Can you imagine how shocked I was when I found the helmet?"

"I can."

"And that happened after I had considered you dead for a long time."

"It was pretty stupid of me to sneak off the sled."

"If I had not pushed every available button in the control room..." *Once again if, if, if,* she thinks. That won't help them, though. She swipes a hand through the air. "That's all behind us now. We should take this thing to the control room. Perhaps Gronolf can fix it. Grab your suit, and we'll take it to him. After that, we'll go pick up my suit."

THEY WALK BACK NEXT TO EACH OTHER. DURING THE TRIP, they pass by the side corridor where the drama with Marchenko 2 had happened.

"Do you think it was right that I shot him?"

"Yes, Eve. From what I've heard, that was the only thing you could do."

"I could have simply dropped the weapon."

"If wishes were horses..."

"Beggars would ride," Eve finishes. "Yeah, I thought about that same proverb several times today."

She doesn't ask Adam whether he thought it was right of Marchenko to cut power to the impostor, as she already knows his answer.

IN THE CONTROL ROOM EVE SHOWS THE HELMET TO THE alien. Gronolf sits in his chair, staring at the general with one eye, looking at her with another and aiming the third at a console. Eve points to the cracked visor. He massages his knees with his strong but coarse load-hands. He points at the exit with a touch-hand, then jumps up and almost bowls Eve over.

Gronolf returns soon afterward with some foil. First he uses his load-hand to break off the remaining glass. He simply drops the shards. Then he briefly pushes the foil below the skin fold covering the pit of his stomach, probably to moisten it, and then he presses it firmly against the edge of the helmet. He counts to seven with the fingers of his other hand and then gives her the helmet. The foil seems to stick. Does it seal the inside completely?

She hands the helmet to Adam. "Put it on."

Adam does what she asks. "The tip of my nose hits the foil, but otherwise it is fine."

"Do you think it is airtight?"

"Hard to say. I would have to test it." Adam blows against the foil, then he takes off the helmet and pushes against it with his fingers. The foil does not rip. "It should definitely withstand half an atmosphere of pressure within the suit,"

"Fine. My suit is near the sleeping chambers."

Eve stands up and touches Gronolf's load-arm near the shoulder. She points at the miniature display of the building and says: "Sleeping chamber!"

"Leeping chamber?"

"Sleeping chamber!"

"Leeping chamber?" Gronolf scratches between his legs. Then he rubs his touch-hands. "Leeping chamber!" He points at the wall.

At first Eve thinks he misunderstood her, but then a hidden door opens there. "An elevator," she says with a smile. Now they won't have to climb through the long, dark corridor.

"Alavatar," Gronolf confirms. "Retoko-tu!"

"Retoko-tu," Adam replies while Eve enters the compartment. It has enough room for at least three aliens. But she can't find any buttons to operate it. Gronolf seems to have noticed her confusion and joins them. He apparently speaks a command in ultrasound—she doesn't hear anything, but the elevator starts moving. Or, she wonders, maybe it only has one destination.

As if Gronolf read her thoughts, the doors soon open in the tall hall with the sleeping chambers. It looks very different here all of a sudden, Eve thinks. It must be the light emanating directly from the walls. She pulls Adam with her to the wall where she left the lower part of her suit. Gronolf doesn't say anything, but he follows them slowly. She briefly turns around to him. He looks like a bored adult who was given the job of watching a few playing children.

The suit is still there. Eve expected that, but even so she feels a sense of relief. Together they carry it back to the elevator. It would have been so much simpler if they had better understood the alien technology!

Eve wants to enter the cabin, but Gronolf gently pushes her back out with a touch-hand. "Retoko-na!" he says, "Alavatar later."

What does he want from them? Panic rises in her. Is he going to take his revenge because she killed his sleeping comrades? She has to calm down. Her cheeks must be flushed by now. In the almost glaring light that would be all too visible. Adam is giving her a puzzled look. He missed that part of the story.

"I think I know what he wants," Eve says to Adam.

"Will you tell me?"

"I... I can't."

"What's wrong with you, Eve? You look like you are in a total panic!"

She jerks back. "Is it that obvious?"

"It is. So, what is going on? Did I miss something? Did

something embarrassing happen to you? No," he says as he looks at her, "it is worse."

"You will see it soon, I believe."

Gronolf leads the way. He stops every few meters and waits for them. Eve tries to interpret his behavior, but that is impossible. She also does not dare to ask questions. Does Gronolf look more angry than usual? Has he polished his weapon? They are slowly walking along the rising path by the wall. When they reach the first sleeping chambers, Adam presses his face against the windows, out of sheer curiosity. She pulls him back.

"What is it? Did you see that? They all look like Gronolf."

"Yes, I know," she says. "Those are sleeping chambers. There are thousands like him here."

"So it's no wonder he wants to save this building."

"But we knew that beforehand."

"Still, seeing it with one's own eyes is different. Why didn't you show this to me earlier?"

"I... well, we just met each other again!"

Adam does not pressure her any further. However, he still looks into every third or fourth sleeping chamber. Gronolf does not seem to mind and lets them do what they want.

Because we are about to die? The question pops unbidden into Eve's mind. *No, I have to stop thinking about that.*

They move up level by level. Eve tries to remember. *Where was the chamber with the dead Grosnop again?* It can't have been too far from the ground floor. Yet it is not her memory but her sense of smell that tells her they are approaching the 'crime scene.' The smell has definitively gotten worse. Eve wants to hold her nose, but she simply can't do it. She has to tolerate the disgusting odor. And isn't there a sour smell in the air, too, from the leftovers of her own stomach contents? She looks around on the floor to avoid stepping into her own vomit. This way she can at least distract herself from what is about to come.

"Man, what a stench," Adam says. He pinches his nose

with his thumb and index finger. Gronolf marches on calmly, as far as she can tell. Or is he showing his anger by repeatedly moving his huge rear eyelid up and down in a fast rhythm? What does it mean that his touch-arms are interlaced and that one of his load-arms taps against the window of each chamber while he is moving, causing an unpleasant noise?

"Is this going to take a long time?"

Sometimes she could just wring Adam's neck. "We are almost there, I think," she replies.

And indeed, Gronolf stops soon afterward. Eve sees that he stands near the couch of an open chamber. She knows what is going to be on the couch, even though the light dazzles her a bit.

Adam walks around Gronolf to get a better look. "Well," he says, "I expected more."

More? Three corpses, or a hundred? Adam must be really sick, Eve thinks. She steps next to the other side of Gronolf and turns pale. The couch is empty. Gronolf leans on it with his load-arm. He untangles his touch-arms, wraps the right one almost completely around his body and aims at himself.

"Gronolf," he says.

So this must have been Gronolf's sleeping chamber. Eve feels hot and knows her face must be beet-red.

"What did you expect?" Adam asks. She does not answer.

Gronolf gets down on his knees. Is this a kind of prayer? Then he starts rummaging below the couch and inside the chamber with all of his arms. How stupid of her! The alien is looking for something! He probably took something with him into the chamber before going to sleep.

After two minutes he utters a dull sound and gets up. He is holding a flat, silver-colored object in his left touch-hand. He holds it in front of each of his four eyes in turn. Then he holds it closer to Adam and Eve without letting go of it. He presses a button she had not noticed before and the object flips open like a jewel case. Eve tries to see what is inside. Finally she realizes what Gronolf was looking for. Inside the case there is a three-dimensional image, a hologram, showing another Grosnop.

"Murnaka," Gronolf says. "Murnaka!" he screams.

For about ten minutes the alien stands almost motionlessly beside the couch, then suddenly starts walking. He does not go back, but further upward. In spite of the warmth, Eve is starting to shiver. She had hoped to be spared this embarrassment.

Now Gronolf is walking more slowly than before. He seems more content, as if he had already reached his destination and was only taking a casual stroll. She knows that perception must be wrong. The stench becomes stronger and stronger. And there it is. The next chamber is open. Eve sees from afar that this couch is not empty. Gronolf calmly walks toward the corpse. What might this sight mean for him? Eve slows down with every step. Yet one touch-arm waves her closer and the other one leads Adam until they both stand next to Gronolf and in front of the corpse disfigured by putrefaction.

"Rugnar," Gronolf says. This sounds like a name. *He must have been an important man*, Eve thinks automatically, and then she corrects herself—*important Grosnop*. Tears stream down her face.

"Hey," Adam says. He comes closer and places a hand on her shoulder.

"I killed him," Eve sobs.

"No, I don't think so."

"What do you even know? You weren't there." She pushes his hand off her shoulder and then regrets it. It's not his fault. "Sorry."

"Rugnar," Gronolf says again, this time a bit louder. He folds his hands.

"Please," he says in English. The lid of the eye facing

them is moving up and down again and again. "Please," he repeats.

Now Eve realizes what he might be trying to do, and she places her two hands in his four. Adam does the same.

"Thank you," Gronolf says.

"Rugnar," Eve answers, and Adam repeats the name.

May 11, 19, Marchenko

IF THE *MAJESTIC DRAGHT* DOES NOT CHANGE ITS SPEED, IT will reach *Messenger*, and him, by midnight. Navigation in space reminds Marchenko of a roulette table in a casino, and he is the little ball. The wheel is turning faster, moving his orbit outward, and near him there is a much larger wheel in which a sphere the size of a soccer ball is rotating, instead of a small roulette ball. When the roulette ball and the soccer ball meet, he will have won the grand prize. It is almost impossible that this could happen by accident, but of course he is more than a roulette ball: Marchenko can determine how fast his wheel is turning and thus match his trajectory to that of the soccer ball. As long as that soccer ball does not upset his plans, they will rendezvous in a few hours.

The body he will need then is already lying on the floor of the cabin. It is connected to the wall by cables and receives energy that way. His body is approximately as alive as a human in a persistent vegetative state. It can receive environmental signals, but cannot process them or react to them until his consciousness indwells it. Marchenko could use remote control to move it, but the body is not capable of autonomous motion. Nevertheless, the subsystems work, the cooling system keeps it at operating temperature, moving parts are lubricated, and the outer surfaces clean themselves.

Marchenko has created a technological marvel. The body weighs much less than a human being, but it is much more durable. Cold and vacuum cannot harm it, nor can a certain level of radiation or heat. It is not indestructible, as otherwise the body would have become too heavy and inflexible. He had instead constructed it in such a way that it can move quickly to evade dangers. Its sensors work in all wavelengths and it can process warning signals without its owner—Marchenko—having to be aware of it. There would be few obstacles which could stop this body for long, no enemy who could surprise it.

He still pities it a bit, though. The way the body is lying there reminds him of a slave. Soon Marchenko's mind will take control of it, but unlike the soul of a human being, he is not irreversibly linked to it no matter what. If an enemy pulverized this body with a nuclear explosion, that would also be Marchenko's last moment. Yet as long as the body is not completely destroyed, he can leave it at any time—for instance, to flee to *Messenger*. How does that affect his consciousness and his human status? Should he suppress his humanity for now in order not to limit his objective decision-making ability?

Adam and Eve are doing fine, he thinks. They don't have to worry about such issues, as they don't have a choice, and that protects them. On the other hand, there were enough individuals in human history who behaved most inhumanely. Life is complicated, and it does not get any simpler the more freedom you have. He should really appreciate his freedom, which is more comprehensive than any other member of humanity enjoys, yet he catches himself being discontent and sullen.

His body is ready and the time has come to switch into it. Marchenko once more roams through space, drifts, enjoys the solar wind on his virtual skin... and then starts the transfer. He will be dead for several seconds. He feels goosebumps on his arms, even though he does not possess arms anymore. During the transmission he is neither here nor there. His thoughts are frozen and time stands still. It is a critical moment. If something were to go wrong, it could be his end.

Activate transmission, he thinks.

A few seconds pass on *Messenger*. Huge amounts of data move at the speed of light, tiny vibrations of photons pass through fiber-optic cables, into his new body where they are unpacked and installed. When Marchenko awakens again, he still feels an echo of his last thought before the transfer.

He immediately checks the data integrity. No errors. Marchenko is relieved. The data connection to *Messenger* is still active, offering a way out if his body should not work as expected. He tests one limb at a time. Feet, legs, hands and arms, everything is working as planned. The nano-fabricators have performed well.

Marchenko gets up. A brief wobble: The algorithms need a moment to balance his unevenly-distributed mass. *Now nothing should be able to knock me over.*

Marchenko looks around. The orbital module seems smaller than it used to be, yet still pleasingly familiar. There are two smaller seats and a larger one. Marchenko walks to the smaller ones and sniffs them. His olfactory sense is working, but he can't smell anything. He had hoped to detect traces of Adam or Eve, but that's nonsense. His children never sat in this orbital module. If Marchenko 2 did not lie about them, his two children died from the effects of a flare when they were very young. It is quite shocking that his alter ego nevertheless followed the plans so strictly. The two seats, for example, would never have served a purpose, yet Marchenko 2 built them. He must have really been in despair.

"Marchenko to base," he says via the radio transmitter.

Nobody replies. Did something happen, or are they all asleep? He cannot help but worry.

"Marchenko to base," he repeats.

No answer. Perhaps nobody can react right now. There are only three of them. He should not worry, as most likely everything is okay. Yet he checks the sensors of *Messenger* to see whether they recorded anything unusual coming from the planet. But there is nothing.

He waits for five minutes. Time seems to stretch. Marchenko walks through the tiny cabin on his two new legs.

Then he reactivates the radio transmitter. "Marchenko to base."

"This is Adam."

He feels relieved.

"Sorry, we were busy just then. What's up?"

"What is going on over there, Adam?"

"Nothing much. And with you?"

"The transfer into my new body worked perfectly. *Messenger* is on course and we will encounter the alien ship shortly after midnight."

"Good, then we will talk later."

"Say hello to the others."

"I will do that."

Adam interrupts the connection. That is strange, and Marchenko is still concerned. What is wrong with Adam? Should he worry about him? Are there any conflicts he is not aware of? Is it related to Marchenko 2? He starts pacing the cabin again, until he notices what he is doing. *That's useless*, he thinks, *I have to stop this*. Gronolf is watching over Adam and Eve, so that is not his job. He has to take care of the Omni-science. Marchenko sits down in the larger seat and connects himself to the ship's sensors.

May 12, 19, Marchenko

A SHINY CUBE ROTATES IN SPACE IN FRONT OF HIM. Marchenko had imagined the *Majestic Draght* appearing darker and more menacing, probably due to its representation on the holo-map. It looks just like a giant die without any dots, slowly rolling through space. The ship's hull is not smooth—it is made up of cells that are clearly demarcated. There are so many that Marchenko's first impression is that of a coating consisting of small gems. This is probably due to the fact that the sides, made of multiple metals, reflect the light of the warm yellow sun, and the image of the illuminated planet below them, in all directions.

"Isn't she beautiful?"

This was spoken by the alien. By now, Marchenko is translating his words automatically. Gronolf, who is in the shelter building, has tapped into the data stream sent by *Messenger's* sensors.

"She *is* beautiful. Your people created a masterpiece."

"The design is the work of one of our most famous architects."

"In my world, spaceships are not designed." Marchenko thinks of the practical but ugly vessels crisscrossing the solar system. One would not even have called *ILSE* beautiful, even though she was the most expensive spaceship ever built up to

253

that time. "the thinking is that shape does not matter in space," he adds.

"We believe that it is easier to fulfill a mission if a warrior is proud of what he is doing."

"Pride is a tricky subject on Earth," Marchenko says. "We will have to talk about it some other time. What's next?"

"Do you see the central axis? The shell of the cube rotates in such a way that the axis stays in the same position. That offers you the best entrance point."

"I can see it." Marchenko mentally marks the point and calculates an appropriate course. An optical cable linked to the ship systems sticks out through the surface of his right hand like an IV needle. This way he can react faster, as the wireless data capacity is limited. "*Messenger* will take ten minutes," he tells Gronolf.

"I know."

Marchenko forgot that Gronolf can access all the data in the ship's systems. He carefully watches the course taken by *Messenger*. With every minute the *Majestic Draght* looms larger.

"This is insane," he says. "The ship is really enormous."

"Thank you," Gronolf says.

Marchenko stands there calmly. The orbital module has no windows, which are unnecessary because he can visualize space, the planet, and the cube with his inner eye. Later he can overlay these images with what is happening directly in front of him, but right now he focuses on the view. The Omniscience might try to change its course. However, it can hardly escape him now. Such a huge ship has a correspond-ingly-large inertia, so that *Messenger* would always be faster during the first kilometers. It would be as if an elephant tried to escape a fly.

A countdown indicates the last 60 seconds. Marchenko doesn't actually need the countdown, but it is a nice tradition that makes it easier to prepare for exiting the ship. He pulls the cable from the console. It retreats automatically into his body like an earthworm. Then he steps to the bulkhead. The orbital module does not have an airlock, but only a simple hatch he can use to get outside. As he did not fill the module with air to begin with, there is no hissing sound when he opens the hatch. The cube is directly ahead of him. It is no longer glittering. The 'gems' have turned into individual raised sections with a height and width between 30 and 50 meters.

"Three, two, one."

"Jump," Gronolf shouts.

Marchenko pushes off slightly and then triggers the jets in his shoulders. Once he is ten meters away from *Messenger*, the ship changes course and retreats. He might need the vessel again. He approaches the *Majestic Draght* at a slow pace. He is glad he arrived near the central axis where the shell of the cube rotates more slowly.

Where is the best entrance? The axis itself seems to be massive, having no hatches or anything similar. The round shaft in its center leads directly to the engine. Trying to enter there would be a guaranteed way to die, as the Omniscience would only have to activate the engine briefly and he would roast at a temperature of several thousand degrees.

Not a good idea. Instead, Marchenko aims for a round structure on the hull in the sector next to the axis. "An airlock?" he asks.

"Confirmed. But I don't think..."

"Don't worry." He did not exactly tell Gronolf about the tricks he was capable of performing. Some of that came from a desire to show off, but there was also the risk that the Omniscience might be eavesdropping. Marchenko does not expect that it is willing to let its former passengers escape easily.

Only three more meters to the airlock. Marchenko decelerates with his shoulder jets. In order to cushion the impact he stretches his legs forward. They absorb the kinetic energy of his body.

"The access panel is toward the axis," Gronolf explains. "You should have the necessary access rights."

Marchenko looks for the panel Gronolf described. It has two buttons. "How do I identify myself?"

Gronolf gives him a frequency. "You pronounce your name."

Marchenko establishes a connection "General Dukar," he says, using the original voice of the dead officer. The Omniscience must know that the general is in the shelter building, so it would be plausible for him to appear here. Yet nothing happens.

"Is the airlock receiving energy?" asks Gronolf.

Marchenko looks at the area in the infrared spectrum. "Yes, there is electricity flowing."

"Then the Omniscience does not want the general on board. I don't think it would be different at the other airlocks. So, do you have to use the shaft?"

"I am not suicidal."

Marchenko touches the metal surface between the panel and the airlock. There it is, a slight indentation between the door and the outer hull. The airlock is airtight, but that is a relative term. While no air can escape, there is a little bit of a gap between the door and the wall. At least it is enough for the special tool he constructed. It consists of a chain of nano-fabricators he modified, which are as flat as a string of single atoms. He puts his right thumb against the center of the gap. Sensors locate the exact spot and then the string gets under-way. The only problem is the time—the chain needs a few minutes to reach the other side. There it will start to produce small sensors and tools from available materials.

After 20 minutes he receives the first low-resolution images through the string.

"Not bad," Gronolf says via radio.

Another 20 minutes pass before Marchenko can have his 'agents' manually open the door from the inside. Two large bolts have to be pushed aside, and then the door can be opened outward. "I am inside," he says.

"I am *impressed*," replies Gronolf.

"I hope the Omniscience did not lock all the doors this way. That would cost us too much time."

"I cannot imagine it."

Marchenko would like to know what Gronolf's optimism is based on, but he doesn't say anything. He first closes the external door and then examines the inner airlock door. Even that door does not react to the general's name. Does the Omniscience already suspect something?

"Tshyort vosmi," he says.

"What did you say?"

"It doesn't matter, Gronolf. A swearword from my home country."

Marchenko once again searches for a gap between the door and the wall. He will probably need more patience than he expected. "How many hours do we have left?" Marchenko asks.

"Six, I would estimate."

"I see nine more doors on the map."

Marchenko imagines going through the airlock door and entering a long corridor. Suddenly numerous new doors slam down. He can't even count that fast. Then he returns to reality. "Nonsense," he says to himself and shakes his head.

"What do you mean?"

"Sorry, I am just thinking out loud. How are... Adam and Eve?" He almost called them 'the children.'

"They are watching and are very excited."

"Fine."

"Speaking of watching. The *Majestic Draght* will soon be entering the radio shadow of the planet. We will lose our connection."

"The way it looks, I am getting along quite well by myself. How much longer?"

"I can't tell for sure. As soon as the atmosphere interferes, the connection will degrade, and once you move below the horizon, it should stop altogether."

"I understand. I won't be surprised when I suddenly can't hear you."

Brightnight 39, 3876

MARCHENKO'S PLAN IS REALLY IMPRESSIVE. GRONOLF HIMSELF probably would have failed to get into the airlock. He might not have succeeded in breaching the hull with an explosive charge. One would not notice it from looking at this machine, but it has capabilities far surpassing those of a Grosnop. If he manages to get the humans to his home world, that might offset the costs for the entire expedition—and save his honor. The Production Experts and Knowledge Scientists would kill for a chance to examine Marchenko.

But he is getting ahead of himself. They have not yet solved the problem. They are still in a life-threatening situation. If the Omniscience has really placed nine locked doors between itself and its visitor, they can only hope against hope that it will veer off in the end, instead of destroying the ship and the building—and the planet with it.

Marchenko opens the inner airlock door, which requires some strength to overcome the air pressure there. The door slams shut behind him. With the aid of the cameras, Gronolf can see over Marchenko's shoulders into a corridor illuminated by flickering light. This sector looks oddly familiar to him. It would be a great coincidence, but it is not impossible... He wants to use the right eye to look sideways, as usual, but there is nothing there. How can Marchenko work under such restrictions?

"Could you look to the right?" requests Gronolf.

The camera turns to the side while Marchenko slowly walks through the hallway. It captures the image of the side corridor. At its end... Marchenko has already passed it before Gronolf can clearly see what is at the end of the side corridor.

"Could you go a few steps back?"

"Aye, aye," Marchenko says. He turns around and steps back. This causes the camera to be pointed in the wrong direction.

That is terrible, Gronolf thinks. *What kind of evolutionary trick allowed humans to survive in spite of the disadvantage caused by their physique?* "Please look at the other side," he says.

Marchenko also fulfills this request.

"And now stand still briefly."

The machine stops abruptly. Indeed, at the end of the side corridor is a door blasted off its hinges. Gronolf zooms in on the image. It is obvious. This is the place he and Murnaka must have been a long time ago. The corridor itself shows no sign of all the cycles that have passed. It looks as if it had been built yesterday, except for the flickering lights.

There is a crackling in the audio channel. Gronolf suspected it. He looks at the time. So far, this is only the effect of the atmosphere. He would like Marchenko to run, but he refrains from urging him on. Marchenko knows exactly what to do. If this is really the corridor he and Murnaka used in the past, the life-support control room should be located at its end.

"I believe you will find the life-support room ahead," Gronolf says.

"That room also contains the airlock that will get me to the right path toward the security chamber."

"Exactly. Back then, the Omniscience placed its security robots in front of the airlock."

"And what is behind it?"

"I don't know. We failed in the life-support center."

"Good to know. If the robots defeated a fighting machine like you, it won't be easy for me."

"They electrified the floor, and I simply ran inside."

"Without sufficient information about the area held by the enemy? A tactical mistake."

"I was stupid."

"You obviously survived."

"But Murnaka didn't."

"Murnaka?"

"Never mind."

"I understand," Marchenko says. "But how can you be so sure she is dead? Did you consciously experience the end of the fight?"

"You are right. I also found indications in the archive that she might have survived. Yet in my memory I caused her death."

"I am here now." That went faster than expected. There are no nine doors left, that is clear, at most four—the one to the life-support center, two airlock doors and the entrance of the security chamber.

"Are you going inside right away? I don't want to cause you any stress. We still have a radio connection."

"No. I need a pair of thick socks." Marchenko points at his feet. Very cleverly, he has the nano-fabricators build an insulation layer. The electricity won't be the only trick of the Omniscience, Gronolf knows, but at least it won't work against Marchenko the way it affected him.

"Adam and Eve want to wave goodbye, they say—whatever that means."

The camera moves from the door to Marchenko's face. The two humans next to Gronolf move their right hands sideways. Marchenko returns the gesture.

"Okay, I better start working," Marchenko says.

Gronolf witnesses him saying the general's name in front of the door, then the transmission is interrupted.

May 12, 19, Adam

Ever since the connection to Marchenko was interrupted, Adam has been pacing up and down in the control room like a caged predator. Eve has asked him several times to sit down, but he simply can't. He has to keep moving to distract himself.

If they can't observe Marchenko directly, then how about indirectly? There is just a teeny, tiny obstacle—the planet itself. If they were on the other side of the planet now—for instance, in the forest of walking trees—they could contact him easily. Not far from there they found the antenna in the ocean. Might it be possible to use that from here?

Adam taps Gronolf on the shoulder. The alien's right eye winks, so Adam must have caught his attention. Now he uses the arm display to draw the antenna they found months earlier. It takes a while, but then the alien seems to understand what he is trying to communicate. He jumps up, runs to the holo-map, and starts typing on the sector control panel. Then he moves his right load-arm toward Adam. Is that a sign of success? Adam comes closer, but he only sees a blinking dot.

Gronolf uses the sector control panel again. The display changes. The 3D image shows the side of Proxima b invisible from here. An approximately fist-sized, cube-shaped object is approaching. With the naked eye its movement is not visible, but when Adam covers it with his hand for half a minute, he notices its position is slightly changing. It must be the *Majestic Draght*. From here the ship looks like a toy.

Gronolf magnifies the image. Now the space ship is about the size of a human head. Adam walks around it once. It is multi-colored. At the rear, where the engine is located, it is brighter. The display probably indicates the intensity of the radiated energy. Gronolf must have switched the antenna in the ocean to pure reception mode. Adam remembers their excursion to the antenna. They were so full of innocent curiosity. But then Marchenko 2 tried to gain control of them. The alien antenna had seemed so elegant and had given them hope that they would soon solve the mystery of Proxima b.

Suddenly a bright spot appears in the side of the cube. What is it? Adam turns around and looks at Gronolf. He has also noticed it, and he increases the magnification even further. However, no details are visible. The antenna must have reached its limits. What could have happened? Where does the spot come from? Might it be a sudden energy pulse? If only he could talk to Gronolf about it!

"Eve," he says, but when his sister steps next to him, the spot has disappeared.

"Energy," Gronolf says in English.

Adam has already realized that. Can't Gronolf tell him more? But he is being unfair, Adam realizes. It is just that all the waiting around makes him crazy. Perhaps the Omni-science just vaporized Marchenko. If so, they will never find out. However, then it really doesn't matter, as they will all die in a few hours.

Eve puts an arm around his shoulders and pulls Adam closer.

Eve is right, he thinks. *We shouldn't spend our last hours alone.*

May 12, 19, Marchenko

THERE IS NOTHING BUT STATIC FROM THE AUDIO CHANNEL, YET Marchenko doesn't mind at all. No matter what happens now, he will have to react fast. Nobody can help him, and knowing that Adam and Eve are observing events live is a distraction. He definitely does not want them to see him die. He feels well prepared, but he will only know afterward how things went.

"General Dukar," he says to the panel left of the door. This time it works. The general is granted access. There is a clacking sound somewhere behind the door. Marchenko only has to give it a slight push and it swings to the left. He uses the wall as cover and beams his sonar through the opening. The reflected sound waves give him an overview of the room behind it.

The snapshot confirms it: As Gronolf feared, this seems to be the defensive position set up by the Omniscience. The airlock he has to reach is located at the rear wall of the room. In front of it, twelve differently shaped machines await him. Only one of them has anything resembling a weapon.

Marchenko glances down at his body. It would be hard to tell what he is capable of. Should he simply march inside and ask for an audience with the Omniscience? No, that would be testing his luck too much. He will neutralize the twelve robots using limpet charges.

Marchenko leans his back against the wall and moves his left arm into the room, allowing the door to cover the rest of his body. Then he snaps his hand downward. The barrel of an air gun appears at his wrist. He will shoot at the twelve targets indirectly. His ammunition consists of small spheres, about the size of ping-pong balls. They are considerably heavier, due to the explosive filling, but they also easily bounce off hard walls.

Marchenko aims for the part of the wall he can see. He knows the positions of the robots, and the rest is just classical physics—Newton. What, he wonders, was the name of the Grosnop who discovered these laws on their world?

Marchenko fires. The first ball flies, then his arm moves slightly and the next one is on the way. It takes just three seconds. Click-click-click... the balls rapidly bounce off the wall and zoom toward their targets at different heights. Marchenko sends a radio impulse to change the surface of the balls. Now they will stick to whatever they hit. The target farthest away gets the first ball. Marchenko can't see exactly where it hits, but it must have been approximately at waist height. Shortly afterward the other balls impact. Marchenko triggers the explosive. There is a loud bang. He has used a charge that is calculated to destroy humanoid robots. A dust cloud spreads through the room and also comes outside. He once again activates his sonar. Eleven of the robots are down.

However, the twelfth one is running through the door, directly toward him. It is incredibly fast. The enemy moves on all fours like a dog, a very long dog, almost a giant dachshund without a head, and it does not even reach as high as his waist. Perhaps it was located on a platform and the echo of the sonar did not see this flat target. Therefore the twelfth ball must have missed it.

The opponent might weigh about as much as Marchenko himself. He can't use the explosive balls at such a short distance. Marchenko's mind analyzes his enemy's potential weaknesses. The connection between the body and the limbs looks vulnerable, but so does the long body itself. The robot dog leaps at him. The jump is precisely calculated. Marchenko can't stay on his feet. He starts swaying and falls. *Tshyort vosmi! I thought I couldn't be knocked over.*

Everything happens within seconds. His brain is working at full speed. Suddenly that thing is above him. There are blades that work like chainsaws on the back of its legs. The animal wants to dig these sharp points into several spots of his body. He won't have time to destroy the limbs, so he will have to attack the body itself.

Marchenko stops using his arms to defend against the sharp blades. He grabs his enemy's body at the front and back, while the chainsaws dig into his outer layers. He pulls on the body with all his strength, but it is not enough. The structure of the robot is uniform and well-designed. There are no predetermined breaking points, so he has to create one himself. His head whips upward, he opens his mouth and digs his sharp teeth into the hard material.

One of Marchenko's legs has been severed. He throws all his strength into his arms, and now he hears a horrible sound, like wet chalk on a blackboard, mixed with the plaintive yearning wail of a creature, but he keeps pulling. Debris falls down on him. The blades of the robot stop and no longer hurt him. Then his arms suddenly flip out to his sides because he has torn the enemy's body apart.

That was close, Marchenko thinks. He slowly sits up and slides over to lean against the wall. He starts to brush the remnants of the robot from his body. They consist mainly of steel, small wires, shreds of plastic, and an oily liquid. His leg jerks. He pulls it closer. The robot made a clean cut. He presses the leg against his body, using the other leg to hold it in proper alignment, and lets the nano-fabricators start their work. He will be fit again in half an hour and then he can greet the Omniscience in the security chamber.

May 12, 19, Eve

EVE IS HAPPY—ALTHOUGH SHE CAN'T EXPLAIN WHY. IT TOOK A while before she could even give this feeling a name. The warm feeling inside, the desire to sigh now and then without any reason, the knowledge that nothing in this world can harm her, the brightness that flows from her wide-open eyes deep into her heart—all of that must be happiness. It is surprising how tiny and huge this feeling is simultaneously. How often did she ignore it before, just because she was waiting for something much greater? Yet this time she has not overlooked it. Her night of utter despair probably helped in this regard. It was just three days ago that she considered Adam and Marchenko dead and believed herself surrounded by hostile aliens. Now, all of that has turned around. Is it still important that they may not experience the coming day?

Eve doesn't care. Yet she notices that Adam hasn't reached this point yet. He is walking up and down, and nothing can stop him. She tries, pulls him closer to comfort him. He manages to stay with her for two minutes, then he starts pacing again. She can understand him. He had never believed her to be dead. He had retained hope of seeing her and Marchenko again. Yet perhaps uncertain hoping is harder to bear than the conviction that you are alone in the world.

She stands propped against the wall and closes her eyes. Nevertheless, the world does not go black. With her inner eye she still sees the control room with Gronolf sitting across from the general, and she hears Adam's regular steps, the slight humming of the holo-map, her own heartbeat. All this is happening here and now. It does not matter what will come later.

A loud humming interrupts this image. Eve opens her eyes.

"Gronolf, Eve, did you hear that?" Adam is running frantically through the control room. Gronolf sits up in his chair and folds out the console.

"Just a moment," he says, one of the few English expressions he knows.

Eve does not move. Whatever she might do now will have no effect on what will happen later.

May 12, 19, Marchenko

MARCHENKO CAUTIOUSLY ENTERS THE CENTRAL LIFE-SUPPORT room in this sector. The dust has settled, or it was suctioned off by machines located in the center and at the sides of the room. They serve to freshen the air in all the rooms of the sector. At the rear wall he detects the remnants of eleven robots. Their original shapes are indiscernible for some of them. His explosive charges worked well. Even though these robots were dangerous, Marchenko is glad the Omniscience did not send living beings to fight him. Would he have been able to act in cold blood then? He does not know.

He looks around. The walls and the floor look damaged, as if this was not the first battle here. However, Gronolf's defeat was a long time ago, so the Omniscience must have cleaned up since then. The floor is not electrified. The entire room seems harmless and he hopes this impression does not deceive. It is only a few meters to the airlock in the rear wall. Marchenko proceeds, one step after another. He wouldn't put it past the Omniscience to use mines here. Therefore he steps lightly, testing with only half his weight at first.

Two meters from the lock he suddenly hears a rustling sound behind him. Marchenko whirls around and aims at the source of the noise. But he does not pull the trigger. Behind him a thing not quite eight centimeters high is peering through the partially open door into the room. Is it an animal or a machine? He can't quite tell, because he can only see its head. Two eyes look in his direction, while a third independent eye gazes at the ceiling. Below the eyes there is a slit, perhaps a mouth.

"Zzzzzsssssss." The noise is generated by a long tongue that suddenly shoots from the slit, confirming that it is a mouth. The creature slowly moves forward and he can see its entire body. Marchenko had thought of an exotic type of mouse a moment ago, but with its 20-or-so tiny legs, it more closely resembles a centipede with a raised head.

"Shoo, shoo," Marchenko says softly. The creature listens. Marchenko moves his arms towards it. The thing quickly turns around and exits the room. He definitely has to tell Gronolf about it. It did not look like a machine.

It's time to deal with the airlock. Suddenly there is a cracking noise under his right foot. Marchenko instinctively leaps aside, but he'd only stepped on a piece of scrap. He needs to be more careful.

Marchenko pretends to be the general, but the door won't open immediately. No reason for concern—after all, he has his universal key, and the door opens after the usual waiting time. Marchenko enters the airlock chamber. He has to bend down because it is so low. He closes the door behind him and starts the procedure for opening the outer hatch. Now would be the perfect moment for attacking him. He sits alone in a steel chamber measuring two cubic meters. Yet nothing happens. Marchenko only hears the hissing of the life-support system. He will soon be done. When will the *Majestic Draght* leave the radio shadow of the planet?

Finished. He discharges the air and then opens the round hatch. In front of him is space, or more precisely, about 20 meters of vacuum, with the central area and the core behind it. No problem: He just has to jump at the right moment to reach his destination, the security chamber, which seems to be slowly rotating below. In reality, of course, the outer section he is about to leave is turning around the core.

Marchenko does not hesitate for long. He jumps and misses the chamber during the first rotation. He did not account for how relative forces change as he approaches the core. He has to calculate his trajectory as if he were a satellite trying to lower its orbit. Therefore he has to decelerate relative to his direction of flight. He recalculates everything and arrives exactly at the entrance of the security chamber. He only has to turn a steel wheel to open the hatch. The designers must have made sure that the chamber could not be blocked. That makes sense, as it contains the emergency shutoff for the Omniscience.

Marchenko pulls the hatch open. The light in the chamber switches on automatically. He enters and closes the hatch behind him. The room is narrow and about four meters long—it feels like a basement corridor. There are no life support systems and it is as cold as in space. Whoever comes in here would require a spacesuit.

Marchenko looks around. The chamber appears empty. The walls seem rusty and burnt. Gronolf was not able to give him any clues about exactly how the security chamber might be working. Only his companion Murnaka had that data. Marchenko remembers how Gronolf had opened the door they had been unaware of inside the building on Proxima b.

He utters the general's name. The sound in the chamber is dull. There is silence for a moment.

Then the chamber replies. "I greet you," it says in the alien language.

"I greet you," Marchenko replies. Now he will probably be tested. They wouldn't want just anyone to have power over the Omniscience.

"Were you born or made?" asked the chamber.

"I was born. And you?"

"I was made."

"Who are you?" *It is a program,* thinks Marchenko. *It certainly can't hurt to ask the program a few questions.*

"I am the key to the *Majestic Draght.*"

"Are you part of the Omniscience?"

"The key is independent. It only belongs to itself."

"What can the key do?"

"It separates and unites core, shell, and Omniscience."

"Does this mean it can keep the Omniscience from steering the ship?"

"That is correct."

"Who is allowed to use it?"

"The scientists and their descendants."

"I would like to use it."

"I know. You ask many questions. I am glad about that. Like you, I was made to ask questions. The Omniscience no longer asks questions. But first you will have to answer my questions."

"Certainly," Marchenko says. He hopes Gronolf has provided him with all the information he needs.

"I have to warn you," the key says. "If you do not answer the questions correctly, the chamber will be filled with a corrosive gas and be heated to a temperature of 3,000 degrees."

The gas should hardly bother him—the heat, though, would kill him. He is glad he is alone. "I understand," he replies.

"You can still leave the chamber now. The hatch will be closed as soon as I start the first question."

"Please get started."

Brightnight 39, 3876

GRONOLF LOOKS AT THE HOLO-MAP. HE DID NOT SHOW ANY emotion during the energy surge a moment ago, but he is really worried. If that could be detected by the antenna in the ocean across such a distance, it must have been an enormous amount of energy. It would be helpful if he could speed up the rotation of Single Sun right now. They will only find out more once they reestablish a connection with Marchenko.

To be honest, he is afraid of bad news. The Omniscience controls the resources of the entire ship. Compared to that, Marchenko is a speck of dust. Why didn't he at least assume a sturdier shape? A cone with four eyes, stronger legs, more flexible arms, and an efficient weapon—then he might have had a real chance.

It would have been best, Gronolf knows, if he had been able to solve the problem himself. That would have been fair, too, as he was the one who messed up the first time around. Yet fate was not that merciful to him. Instead, he now has to make sure the two humans, with whom he cannot even converse, stay alive as long as possible. He even wonders whether they shouldn't leave the building. If the *Majestic Draght* really hits the planet, they might have a chance to survive at the bottom of the ocean. Perhaps he can use the resources of the building to construct something that would help them. *Why didn't I think about this much earlier?*

Because you were busy.

Gronolf looks at the general as if the officer had just spoken that thought. It is true. Until now, there simply hadn't been any time for developing alternative plans.

He follows Adam with his right eye. Somehow the young human reminds him of a younger version of himself. Gronolf also used to get nervous when he had no meaningful task. And that had happened a lot during his training. Perhaps Adam should pay more attention to his sister. Gronolf never had that chance. The members of his plex quickly went their own ways. What might have become of his brothers and sisters? It would be nice to find an answer to that question sometime.

Perhaps Marchenko will be successful.

May 12, 19, Marchenko

"WHO ARE YOU?"

That is a good question, and if he answers it incorrectly, it might be the last one. He could once more pretend to be the general, but if the system is cleverly constructed, it would have a camera and could see he is lying.

"I am Marchenko, a friend of Gronolf."

"What do you need me for?"

"The Omniscience is on a course for the shelter building on Single Sun. If the building is destroyed, there will be many casualties. I have to stop the Omniscience from doing that."

"I understand and have confirmed the collision course. Authorization granted."

"That was it?"

"That was it. You answered my questions correctly."

Marchenko is stunned. After all the efforts and struggles, the last stage was much simpler than he had feared. He was already prepared to report the key historical details Gronolf had transmitted to him. Well, even better—now they would not waste any more time.

"What's next?" he asks.

"To whom should I transfer the control authority? I can give it to you or Gronolf. The decision cannot be reversed,"

Marchenko ponders... Using the *Majestic Draght* they could

reach the solar system in 20 years. He could take Adam and Eve home, to Earth. His children would be among their peers. They still would have at least one-half of their lives ahead of them. If he hands control to Gronolf, they will certainly fly to Proxima Centauri. He has already described his plans to them. Adam and Eve could fly along, but they would spend the rest of their lives among strangers, with whom they could never properly communicate.

It is a difficult decision.

Transfer control to me, he thinks, *that would be a real happy outcome. Adam and Eve are not responsible for this situation. They were never asked whether they wanted to go on this voyage.*

"Gronolf," he says, nevertheless. He simply cannot decide otherwise. He immediately feels guilty regarding his children, but he cannot help that.

"I understand," the chamber answers. "Now you only have to decide the fate of the Omniscience. According to my records, it caused the death of 1,323 descendants of my creators. The current course of the *Majestic Draght* would completely annihilate the remaining crew. According to the basic rules, a suitable punishment would be a complete erasure of its higher mental abilities. Independent from that, it will only be able to monitor the core afterward."

"So this means a death penalty?"

"The subconscious of the Omniscience will survive and control the engine core. Only its thoughts, sensations, and emotions will be deleted. Should I initiate the deletion now?"

Now Gronolf should be the one standing here. The Omniscience committed crimes against his relatives. Marchenko regards the high number of victims as a loss, but he is not personally affected. The Omniscience never did anything to him, at least so far. It does not deserve death for that, even if Gronolf might see this differently.

"I would like to leave this decision to Gronolf," he says.

"That is not possible. The key program will automatically deactivate itself after handing over control. Then deleting the consciousness of the Omniscience will no longer be possible."

"Fine. I cannot make this decision, so I have to reject the deletion."

"I understand. You just passed the test. I now hand over control of the *Majestic Draght* to you."

Marchenko is petrified. The key program tricked him. It gave him a false sense of security and then asked the decisive questions. What would have happened if he had given the wrong answers? He remembers the initial warning.

A moment later a cover in the side wall slides away, revealing a large console. Marchenko studies the labels. Due to the data provided by Gronolf he can easily decipher them. The keys, divided into four groups, obviously serve to control the Omniscience and the *Majestic Draght*. First he has to change the course of the ship. That is done via the lower right sector. Marchenko makes the *Majestic Draght* enter an orbit around Single Sun.

"What are you doing?" It is the same voice the key used to speak to him. Yet he has the feeling that he is no longer hearing the key program.

"I am putting the *Majestic Draght* in a course around Single Sun."

"That is inefficient."

"It saves the lives of more than a thousand Grosnops."

"That does not matter. The goal of colonizing Single Sun could not be achieved. The remaining crew members only use up resources unnecessarily. They should be placed in an inactive state."

"Who is saying this?"

"I am the Omniscience. I know it. I am infallible."

"Nobody is infallible."

"I am programmed that way. I simply have to be infallible. If I fail, I am no longer myself and my right to exist would end. I cannot fail."

"Is that why you want to destroy the *Majestic Draght* through a collision with the planet?"

"I am the Omniscience. I always choose the right decisions. Any other option is not possible."

"I am afraid there is an error in your programming. Therefore you will not be able to decide anything anymore in the near future."

"That is not planned and not acceptable."

"Was that why you tried to prevent me from entering the security chamber?"

"You were classified as a security risk according to the basic rules, and were therefore destroyed."

"I wasn't destroyed—quite the opposite. I reached the security chamber and deactivated your influence over the ship."

"I am the Omniscience. I always choose the right decisions. I cannot fail. You were destroyed."

"You repeat yourself. Unfortunately I will have to end our conversation, because the *Majestic Draght* is leaving the radio shadow of the planet."

May 12, 19, Adam

"So!" Gronolf shouts. "So!"

Adam jumps up. The alien is standing next to the holo-map and gestures with all four arms. It is unclear whether he is expressing shock or joy.

What happened? Adam takes a deep breath and exhales. Gronolf is pointing at the spaceship, which now is fist-sized again. It is still there, so at least it wasn't destroyed. This should mean Gronolf's shouts expressed positive emotions.

"Marchenko," Adam says and points at the *Majestic Draght.*

"Yes, what has happened to him?" Eve asks from behind.

"Marchenko," Gronolf says. Gronolf taps the keyboard feverishly. Now the map projects a glowing line in front of the ship, which bends around the planet.

"The ship is entering orbit," Adam exclaims. He turns around to Eve and wants to pat her on the shoulder, but she embraces him. Of course she knows what this means. Nobody will die.

"Marchenko did it!" Adam says. He can hardly believe it. Tears fall on his throat. It must be Eve's tears. He does not wipe them off. His heart is beating faster, he sweats, he would like to dive into cold water, but he also does not want to let go of Eve.

"So!" Gronolf says.

Adam looks at Gronolf. The alien is drumming against the wall with his lower legs. It is a catchy rhythm.

Minutes pass. It could be hours, as Adam has lost any sense of time. Gronolf drums against the wall with incredible endurance. He feels sorry the alien has to celebrate on his own and has nobody to hug him.

"Eve? Come on, let's go over to Gronolf," he says. His sister understands. Arm in arm they stroll over to the alien. Gronolf's body stiffens when their hands touch his arms. Adam would like to be able to read his thoughts now.

"His skin is warm," Eve says. She sounds surprised.

"This is Marchenko, can anybody hear me?"

"Finally!" Adam shouts. *Finally we can communicate with the ship again,* he means.

"That's a nice welcome," Marchenko says.

"We are so glad," Eve exclaims. "How did you manage it?"

"Oh, that is a long story. I will tell you as soon as you get here."

"You mean we should get on board the *Majestic Draght*?"

"Yes. That would be the best solution for all of us, Eve."

"Right," Adam says. "There is only one problem: How do we get to you?"

Brightnight 39, 3876

HE WAS THE FIRST TO SEE IT. GRONOLF NOTICED IMMEDIATELY that the *Majestic Draght* had changed its course. At that moment, due to the resolution of the map, it should have been impossible to see, but he detected it anyways. The two humans reacted in an incredible way. They wrapped their arms around each other. This is such an odd behavior that it almost seems disgusting to him, yet in its own way he finds it fascinating.

He nearly emptied his stomach when they touched him. It was a very intimate moment, particularly because they are so very different. They are not just members of a different species. If he touches a strangleblossom or a carriontooth he doesn't feel anything comparable. Adam and Eve come from a different star. They have nothing in common with him, not a single gene, except the fact that they are carbon-based life forms, and that they are intelligent and able to act in a purposeful manner. They crossed the ocean of space and met here, what an incredible coincidence. And then they did not kill each other, but touched in kindness instead. Gronolf's skin still vibrates when he thinks of it.

Now, though, they have to solve a problem. They have to reach the *Majestic Draght*, and this time it won't be anything like beaming Marchenko's consciousness there.

"MARCHENKO?" THE TWO HUMANS ARE ALREADY ASLEEP, BUT Marchenko doesn't need any sleep.

"I am here."

"There is definitely no rocket here in the shelter building that could be used to transport us into space. I checked the inventory carefully."

"Not even parts of one?"

"In no form. Back then anything that could fly was used to bring warriors back home, to Dual Sun. They wanted to leave as few behind as possible."

"There is also nothing on board the *Majestic Draght* that could be used as a rocket. But we still have *Messenger*."

"You told me the ship could not land on the surface, Marchenko."

"Yes, you will have to move toward it, at least a bit."

"How would this work?" *Are we supposed to fly, like flying fish?*

"With a balloon."

Gronolf rubs his knee. *That Marchenko—he sure comes up with odd ideas.*

"The atmosphere of Single Sun is relatively dense. With a flexible balloon and spacesuits, you should be able to reach an altitude of 100 kilometers."

"Grosnops don't have spacesuits. Our skin is tough enough to withstand the pressure difference. A breathing mask is enough."

"You still should wrap yourself in something. Otherwise the cold will hurt you. In the upper atmosphere it will feel much colder than in space."

"I am working on a plan."

"And then there is the issue of finding material for a balloon."

"That's already solved, Marchenko. In order to save weight, we removed the landing parachutes from all shuttles. Their material should be perfect for this."

"Excellent. There should still be some of my sensor units

crawling around in your building. They are equipped with nano-fabricators. I can program them from here so they will help you assemble the parts. What about gas to fill the balloon?"

"The life-support system can separate helium from air. It requires energy, but we have plenty of that."

"Gronolf?" Marchenko asked in an odd-sounding way.

"Yes?"

"We can't take all of them."

He had thought about this yesterday for many bubble periods. But there is no way. If they wake the sleepers without the help of trained Life Scientists, like Eve tried to, they will lose more of them than if they let them sleep until they return in a few cycles.

"No," Gronolf says, "I'm well aware of that. We will return in a few cycles, though, with the *Majestic Draght*, shuttles, and Life Scientists. Then we will wake them safely, and take them home." *Those that are still left*, he thinks.

They will have to hurry.

May 13, 19, Eve

EVE KNEELS ON THE GROUND AND USES A LASER TO TRANSFER the pattern Gronolf sent to her universal device onto the material in front of her. They have been busy tailoring since the morning. The ISUs Marchenko left behind separate the thin but tough foil at the predetermined lines and then join these pieces to other pieces. On one side of the room there is already a thick, silvery roll. Eve cannot imagine how this will turn into a balloon, but Gronolf must have had something in mind when he created the patterns.

Adam sits with his back to her. He has a special task: He is supposed to construct a kind of thermal suit for Gronolf. He selected the same material used for the balloon, but he employs multiple layers, which are separated by insulating air chambers. The finished suit will be electrically heated. Adam has had to get up several times to measure Gronolf. The archive did not contain any usable plans. This alien civilization simply does not know the idea of clothing. At first Gronolf tried to design something for himself, but that ended in a fit of rage. Adam and Eve still can't completely interpret Gronolf's gestures, but just the volume of his incomprehensible sentences made it clear he was very angry.

Eve still cannot quite believe that they will leave the planet soon. She will never again see the forest of walking trees and the fluorescent mushrooms in the shade beneath them. She will never set foot on the hot central plains, nor will she ever again hide in a bunker during a solar flare. She remembers the giant spider they found in a pit. *Is its dead body still entombed in the ancient building there? Are the trees still waging war against each other?*

Yet her own problems are nothing compared to the misfortune that befell the Grosnops. They wanted to use the giant ship to explore and colonize a foreign planet—but then the AI controlling it failed. Only a part of the crew managed to start the return journey. The others had to wait inside a building in the ice, hoping to be rescued. Yet help never arrived, and when the sleep-systems started to fail, an odd fluke in the shape of a desperate human at first seemed to bring death and instead sparked the chance for a return.

ISU 6 bumps against her knee. Eve looks up. Her thighs hurt from the unaccustomed posture. She should concentrate on her work, as the sensor unit seems to have nothing to do right now.

May 15, 19, Adam

ADAM FEELS COLD, EVEN THOUGH HE IS INSIDE HIS HEATED pressure suit. Above him the balloon flaps in the wind, shining yellow due to four lamps arranged in a square. The balloon seems amazingly floppy, but Gronolf reassured them that it will be able to carry all three. The higher they get and the thinner the atmosphere becomes, the more the balloon will inflate. At some point—according to plan, not below an altitude of 100 kilometers—it will burst. *Messenger* must arrive before then to pick them up. Marchenko started to explain this complex maneuver yesterday, but Adam did not want to hear about it.

Next to him a cable with the thickness of an arm comes out of a hatch leading into the building. The cable, actually a flexible pipe, moves helium into the balloon. By now it is only adding enough to compensate for the slight losses, because the thin foil cannot keep 100 percent of this noble gas inside. Later this minor leakage will not matter because they will rise so rapidly.

"Eve," Gronolf shouts.

His sister climbs out of the hatch where she has been hiding from the wind and walks over to the alien. Adam sees how Gronolf connects the harness on her back to the balloon. Gronolf looks funny in the suit Adam designed. The material bulges in unexpected places, so that Gronolf seems to have big bumps everywhere. However, the suit will fulfill its function and keep him warm, as Gronolf has confirmed. The temperature will fall from the current minus 70 degrees to minus 160, but Adam designed the heating unit with sufficient capacity. The entire ascent should not take more than eight to ten hours. Their oxygen and energy will last twelve.

Now it is his turn. He stands with his back facing Gronolf. It feels as if the alien were preparing him for his execution.

Adam looks at Eve rubbing her gloved hands. "Everything okay with you?" he asks her via helmet radio.

"I am a bit nervous," she says.

"Me, too." He tugs at the lower part of his suit. Something doesn't fit right, probably the improvised diaper. As the flight will take at least eight hours, they have to account for those needs, too. They will have to do without food, but they can drink liquids through a straw integrated into their helmets. After shivering earlier, Adam now starts to sweat. He wishes he felt cold again, because the evaporated sweat condenses on the inside of his helmet. Will Gronolf or Marchenko give a farewell speech? He wouldn't put it past them.

"Adam, Eve," he hears Gronolf's voice via helmet radio. "Ready?"

Adam looks around. Gronolf has put the helium pipe back inside the hatch and now stands behind him. The balloon has already started to rise. Due to the cables that the balloon pulled upward, Gronolf and Eve look like a puppeteer's dolls.

"Ready," Adam and Eve say almost simultaneously. Now the strings tug at him. His back is pulled up with surprising force. Adam wiggles his arms and legs until he realizes how useless that is.

"Yay!" he hears Eve shout.

"Good start?" It is Marchenko's voice.

"Yes, it is great," Eve replies.

"So," is all Gronolf says.

Adam does not know what to say. His stomach protests against the upward acceleration. He has the feeling his stomach has sunk to his knees. He hopes he won't have to vomit. The idea of having that yucky stuff inside his helmet for the next eight hours disgusts him. He will have to think of something else, and quickly.

Proxima b solves that problem for him. They are slowly rising out of the darkness. In front of him, far away, a light blue oval shines in the blackness. Adam turns around his axis. The oval is the horizon, a circle, he can now see. They started at the North Pole, but they are slowly drifting away, it seems. With every passing minute the horizon brightens a bit. He won't see the sun from this balloon, because it shines on the other side of Proxima b, forever and ever.

The air is turbulent. Now and then something rips at his back and the straps dig into his flesh. In the helmet radio he hears Eve singing a children's song. It warms his heart. He would like to say something to her, but he can't think of anything. His eyes close at some point.

MARCHENKO'S VOICE IN THE HELMET RADIO WAKES HIM. "YOU are drifting southward very quickly. The jet stream probably gave you a strong push."

"Is that a problem?" Eve asks.

"No, quite the opposite. It makes it easier for me to pick you up. I cannot reduce the velocity of *Messenger* at will. The faster you are moving, the better."

Marchenko is right. What they are attempting is no easy maneuver. Adam is glad he did not think too much about it earlier. It is good that Marchenko controls *Messenger*, as he has lightning-fast reflexes.

"How much longer?" asks Adam.

"About two hours," Marchenko says.

Adam feels pressure in his bladder. He won't be able to hold it for two hours, so he just relaxes and relieves himself.

The diaper absorbs the liquid well. He looks around. The horizon is no longer a circle. They must be at least ten degrees of latitude from the North Pole. In one direction he sees only darkness. That's where they came from. In the other one a blue arc is visible, which is widest in the middle. Somewhere in that direction must be the forest they lived in, and even further south stands the lander module that brought them to this planet.

The day after tomorrow will make it five months ago. Five terrible months full of hardship and most of all full of mistakes. It seemed to him like five years. Of course he would do everything differently now if he had the chance. Yet he would not want to miss this adventure.

"Adam?"

"Yes, Eve?"

"In the end, we managed quite well."

"True."

Eve does not say anything else. Adam hears her softly humming another children's song. He tries to identify the tune, but he can't.

Marchenko's voice sounds worried. "Watch out down there."

"What's going on?" Adam asks.

"You are approaching the upper reaches of a cyclone."

"At this altitude?"

"Don't forget the greater gravity. The atmosphere is structured differently from that of Earth."

"Can we evade it?"

"Not a chance. Just stay calm, though, as the storm shouldn't be dangerous."

Adam quickly notices the air movement. He is spinning around to his left, as if sitting on a swing carousel like he remembers from a video. The harness straps holding him to the balloon would be the chains.

"Are you also rotating?" Eve asks.

"So," Gronolf says in affirmation.

"I am trying to enjoy it," Adam says. "I'm pretending I'm riding a swing carousel. I only know about that idea from books and videos."

"I don't like to rotate," Eve replies.

She doesn't like to lose control, Adam thinks. *Typical for her.* But then he notices his own motion is getting faster and faster.

"Is the storm increasing?" he asks.

"No," Marchenko replies.

"So why am I turning faster and faster?"

Nobody answers. Adam looks around, but cannot see anything.

"Oh, your straps have become entangled," Eve finally says.

Yes, that makes them shorter and he spins faster, like a figure skater pulling his arms against his body. "It is getting rather unpleasant," Adam observes.

"Just a moment," Gronolf says.

What is he up to? Adam shines his headlamp at him. The alien is unbuckling one of his own harness straps, and then another and another. "What are you doing? You will fall without the harness!"

"I know," Gronolf says. He is hanging from the balloon by a single strap. Now it becomes clear why he is doing this. He pulls himself up on this strap to reach the spot where Adam's straps have become entangled. The other straps would have hindered him. He undoes one strap after another on Adam's harness, untangles them, and then reattaches them.

"So," he finally says.

The rotation has stopped. "Thank you, Gronolf." Adam is shivering.

"You are lucky," Marchenko reports from *Messenger*. "You have traversed the storm cloud."

"THIS IS MARCHENKO. IT'S TIME."

Adam looks for Eve and Gronolf. The alien will blast off the balloon at the decisive moment. Then they will fly in free fall.

"I am starting the countdown for Gronolf," Marchenko says. He starts counting down.

"Three, two, one, go." Adams sees a flash in his field of vision. At the same time something jerks his harness. They are still connected to each other, but the balloon escapes upward. Adam looks after it, but ten seconds later the balloon has disappeared.

"Are we already falling?" Eve asks.

"Free fall," Marchenko confirms.

So they are falling. If Adam didn't know it, he would not notice. If Marchenko leaves them in the lurch now they will burn up like meteorites. They have no parachutes to slow them down.

"Intercept maneuver in 15," Marchenko says calmly. He starts counting down again. When he reaches zero, Adam feels a strong tug on his left side. That must be the net.

"Are we inside?"

"Yes, Adam, it worked. I am now accelerating you."

"Congratulations!" shouts Eve.

Messenger chose its orbit so it would be as slow as possible during this encounter. Yet that is not nearly slow enough for them to simply step on board. Therefore Marchenko placed an extremely sturdy net of carbon nanotubes behind them, which he now slowly accelerates, together with his catch.

The acceleration, which must be almost twice Earth's gravity, pushes Adam strongly against the net. He knows that Marchenko has calculated and simulated every detail. The net is supposed to be sturdy enough to hold him. *But what if it isn't?* He cannot completely suppress this thought. If he slips through the mesh, the others will see him burn up like a meteorite. He is breathing faster.

"Adam, are you alright?" Eve must have noticed something.

"Yes, I am fine."

"I am also scared of the net breaking. The threads are so thin. You remember that spider in the forest?"

Adam realizes Eve wants to distract him. And it is already working. He remembers how he fell into that pit, out of sheer stupidity. Eve had actually warned him. He laughs. "I was pretty stupid then."

"Sometimes," Eve says.

"Adam, Eve," Gronolf says.

Adam turns around. The sun is rising in the South. It moves very slowly above the horizon. Its light spreads dramatically across the entire hemisphere, as if somebody were rapidly lighting one candle after the other. They are leaving the dark side.

"THERE, I CAN SEE IT," EVE SHOUTS, FULL OF EXCITEMENT.

Adam is just as glad. *Messenger* has successfully pulled in her catch.

Adam yawns. He has had enough for today. Someone is pulling on his harness. The outer hatch is opening. Gronolf wants Eve to go first, but she refuses. Adam also insists on Gronolf entering *Messenger* first. The chamber is too small for all three of them. They would have never made it this far without Gronolf.

Ten minutes later the two humans have also boarded *Messenger*. They greet Marchenko's body with a hug. It feels strange for Adam, because he knows that Marchenko is inside the ship computer again. Previously, they only called the robot body 'J.' Perhaps they should switch to that again.

"Make yourself comfortable," Marchenko says through the loudspeaker. "We have a long journey ahead of us."

May 19, 19, Eve

Eve is lying on her comfortable couch, which Marchenko designed according to the pattern of *Messenger's* pilot seats. The *Majestic Draght* has been on course out of the Proxima Centauri system for several hours. The ship is accelerating with approximately 1.3 g. Eve doesn't really mind, because she is used to it from Proxima b. The *Majestic Draght* seems strange to her, not at all like a spaceship, even though she is zooming through the infinite reaches of space in it. It will reach speeds that would be unthinkable for human spaceships. The dark matter drive allows for this. Marchenko estimates that researchers on Earth will need at least 20 years to understand completely how it functions.

She misses windows, portholes, a view. Of course there can't be a view, because they are somewhere inside the ship, in one of the countless sectors. She can only watch on her screen how the *Majestic Draght* moves away from the ecliptic plane in which Proxima b orbits its sun. It will be a long journey, as Marchenko has announced several times. They will hardly see him, because he will try to repair the Omniscience. He himself would not use that term, as he sees himself more as a psychotherapist for the alien AI. No matter what one calls it, if Gronolf's species wants to travel with the *Majestic Draght* in the future, the ship will need a functional Omniscience. After all, Marchenko can't stay on board forever, can he?

How will she make it through the coming months? Eve should be used to long voyages. After all, she grew up during one. Yet she still worries. At some point they will have explored the whole ship, in spite of its size. And it is boring to spend all day learning the aliens' language. Eve shakes her head. She could finally start drafting the novel that has been going through her mind for a long time.

Brightnight 7, 3878

"Welcome!"

By tradition the leadership speaks the first word. The first Grosnop delegation came on board 10 minutes ago. They had been flying toward them in a small ship. What an honor!

"I thank you," Gronolf says. The voice that greeted him seems familiar. It belongs to a female, which already represents a revolution.

"I thank you," she says, and Gronolf starts to tremble, because a channel of his memory has opened. He desperately tries to suppress the memory, but he fails.

'Thank you for your companionship.' Those had been Murnaka's last words, an incredibly long time ago. And now she is standing in front of him. She has grown older by a few cycles. Biologically speaking she now might even be older than he is. Yet the voice is unchanged. He does not know what to say, so he remains silent. He really must get hold of himself.

Somehow he survived the ceremony. They had awarded him a medal and promoted him to general. Now he is finally alone in his cabin again. After such a long time in space, the presence of other Grosnops seems stressful. He sits on the sleeping beam and takes the case out of the locker. He had always carried it with him in his exterior stomach pouch. A small bump formed on his skin where he used to hide it. Gronolf is not angry about it, quite the opposite—now he only needs to place a hand on the stomach pouch to feel Murnaka's presence.

THERE IS A KNOCK ON HIS CABIN DOOR. THE NOISE IS SO loud a human can't have made it.

April 15, 21, Adam

"YOU CAN UNBUCKLE YOUR SAFETY BELTS NOW."

Thanks, Marchenko, for stating the obvious. Even from afar—Marchenko still remains on the *Majestic Draght*—the AI can't help giving such advice. Adam unbuckles his belt. The shuttle, they were told, would land in a recreational area near the capital city. He hears the clicking of Eve's belt alongside him.

Until now they had only seen Dual Sun, the planet of the Grosnops, from orbit. It must be a fertile planet, with billowy seas and green continents. There seem to be no high mountains. The very best aspect, they say, is that it has two suns. Right now it is brightnight, the season when both suns are visible in the sky. This should be the best time to recover in the recreational area, which carries the promising name Slime Swamps. There would also be a big surprise for them, the Grosnops had explained in perfect English.

Even Marchenko was surprised how quickly the locals had been able to learn this human language. Had Gronolf sent data via radio to his home planet?

Suddenly there is a blinding light. Somebody opened the door of the shuttle from outside. Together with the light, the scent of the planet enters the ship. It is a sweet smell, slightly reminiscent of decay. And of fish, but Adam already suspected this, because during the long journey Gronolf had raved about the extensive ichthyofauna of his planet.

He gets up and walks toward the exit. Eve follows him. The pilot is nowhere to be seen. They had been told he speaks no English.

Somebody placed a gangway against the exit. Adam can see broad-bodied Grosnops walking away, presumably the ones who had put it there. They probably don't speak English either.

Adam looks around at Eve. She nods. 'Okay,' she signals. He steps out of the shuttle. The first thing he notices is the humid heat. He starts to sweat immediately. In front of him is an area which looks like a neatly trimmed meadow sporting a bilious green color. Adam is careful about not jumping to conclusions. What looks like grass might be something completely different here. At a distance of about 50 meters, some plants as tall as a man are visible, a kind of forest. Their leaves display a different, more yellowish-green compared to the meadow. A swath has been cut through the forest, ending at a body of water.

His eyes turn upward. The sky is verdant green. It is amazing, because it looks so inviting. He would like to be a bird and rise into the air. Perhaps this was why the Grosnops built spaceships before they invented other technologies.

Adam searches for the suns. They are not far from each other. One, called Mother Sun, is yellowish, the other, Father Sun, burns hotter and white, but it is farther away and therefore appears much smaller in the sky.

Eve taps on his shoulder. "Could that be the ocean?" She points at the swath through the forest.

"No, it is an inland lake." The answer comes from the left. It is spoken in perfect English. It is a man's voice. A biped walks around the ship. That is no Grosnop.

Adam takes on a defensive stance.

"I am sorry," the voice says. "I did not want to frighten you."

"Adam?"

Adam turns to Eve, but she has not addressed him, but the other one. Now he realizes it. The human looks just like him. He is meeting his identical twin, even though it does not feel that way at all. Shouldn't the other man seem to him like an old acquaintance, or even his mirror image?

"Yes, that's what Marchenko called me."

This is a nightmare. Now the story of Marchenko 2 is starting all over again. Adam feels a shiver run down his spine.

"Your... father... is also named Marchenko?" Eve asks.

Doesn't she realize what is going on here? Somehow Marchenko 2 has managed to arrive before them.

"Eve, watch what you are saying," he whispers to his sister.

She looks at him dumbfounded. "What's wrong with you?" Eve places a hand on his shoulder. "The Creator obviously sent a *Messenger* spaceship to Alpha Centauri as well," she says cheerfully, "with another Marchenko and two clones of us on board."

"That's exactly it," he hears Eve's voice say, but it comes from the wrong direction. "Funny that your ship is also called *Messenger.*"

Now the woman appears from behind the other Adam. She bears an amazing resemblance to his Eve, but her hair is longer and her clothes are totally different.

"How... how long have you been here?" Adam still can't believe Marchenko 2 has nothing to do with this.

"We landed ten months ago. The locals helped us a lot from the very beginning, even though there were some misunderstandings."

Adam calculates back. The impostor from Proxima b could not have arrived here so quickly. That is, if the date is correct, and he is going to find that out.

"Well, then the coming years won't be quite so boring," his Eve says.

"We are so glad," the other woman says. "May we invite you to our house? We are curious to hear your story, and our Marchenko is also looking forward to seeing you. Barnar, our local adviser, told us you come from the neighboring star, Single Sun. That would be Proxima Centauri, right?"

June 16, 21, Marchenko

HE FINDS ADAM IN THE CLASSROOM. ADAM GREETS HIM A BIT gruffly. He knows he should have rather called in the afternoon, but by then he might once again lack the strength. It took Marchenko a long time to gather the strength to make it through today's conversation.

"Adam, can you visit me today at the spaceport?"

"Sure. With the other two?"

"No, just Eve and you."

"Is something wrong? You sound depressed."

"No, I just want to tell you something. Come for afternoon tea."

THE AFTERNOON TEA DEVELOPED FROM A TRADITION OF THE Grosnops, who drink a brew made of swamp grasses one hour before sunset. For humans, that concoction inevitably leads to stomach cramps, but Marchenko developed a different drink. This 'tea' is palatable to humans, though Grosnops find it flavorless.

Whenever Adam and Eve are near the fleet command center on the spaceport, meaning to or three times a week, they visit him and have tea. Marchenko is busy examining the

Omniscience. He hopes to find the source of the error that caused the malfunction. At first he told himself he was working so intensely in order to help their hosts. After all, there is one big task left—bringing back the remaining sleepers from Proxima b. By now, however, he knows he has other reasons. The cosmos is calling him. The *Majestic Draght*, which orbits Dual Sun, is perfect for this.

For this special occasion, Marchenko has switched to the body of the robot. In this shape, he set the little table. He has three teacups and saucers that he synthesized himself. The tea is bubbling in a self-heating teapot manufactured by Grosnops.

Adam and Eve are punctual.

"What's up?" Adam asks right away.

Eve first hands Marchenko a bouquet of flowers. These are not flowers like on Earth, because plants do not need colorful blossoms here to attract pollinating insects, but they still look interesting. The locals like to decorate their homes with different shapes instead of colors.

Marchenko puts the bouquet in an empty vase. He does not have to add water, because the humidity is so high that the plants get enough moisture via their leaves. "I am glad you are here," he finally says.

"Thank you for the invitation," Adam replies formally. He walks to the low table and kneels down in front of it, then sits on the floor. Eve and Marchenko follow suit.

Once all are seated, each one pours tea for the neighboring person. Nobody says anything. Marchenko puts the cup to his mouth but doesn't drink. He did not give the robot body a sense of taste. What he likes about tea time is mostly the ritual. They sit around a table and alternate in raising and lowering cups filled with a hot liquid. It is almost like a slow ballet.

"Well," says Marchenko after at least Eve has finished drinking her tea.

"How is it going with the Omniscience?" Adam asks.

"That would be my first piece of news. I think I have

achieved a breakthrough. The Omniscience lets me touch its code."

This cost him a lot of persuading. Up to now the Omniscience had behaved like a human with a dangerous tumor, who stubbornly rejects any examination. Without the permission of the Omniscience he could not enter the data levels, which are encrypted in multiple ways.

"That is fantastic," Eve says, "so there is still hope. How did you manage it?"

If he only knew exactly! Sometimes he thinks he just exhausted the Omniscience, while at other times he assumes he used convincing arguments. "I'm not sure," he admits.

"You talked it to death," Adam says, laughing. His face is starting to look more relaxed, too.

"Maybe."

"So what?" Eve says. "It's the success that counts."

"The leadership group is also very happy about it. However, they don't want to postpone the rescue mission any further. Their doctors calculated that for every month we delay getting there, about ten more sleepers will die."

"It is understandable that they would put you under pressure," Eve says.

"However, as the Omniscience is not yet ready for action—"

"They asked you, right?" Adam interrupts.

"Yes, they did."

"And you agreed?" Eve's question sounds as if she is afraid of the answer.

"You are well taken care of here. This Marchenko can provide you with everything, you have nice companions—"

"Why doesn't this Marchenko go on the flight? Doesn't he have your abilities?" Eve says, standing up and stretching her legs.

"He lacks the experience in steering the *Majestic Draght* that I gathered during the long flight here," says their Marchenko.

"Can't you transfer the experience to him?"

"Experiences are different from factual knowledge. They are intrinsically tied to my consciousness."

"You cannot go on that flight," Eve says aloud. She walks to the exit, but turns around again. "Adam, what do you have to say?"

"Just look at him," Adam replies. "He made up his mind long ago."

"I have to help. I owe that to them. After all, they rescued us."

"Is that all this is about?"

"Well, Adam..." Marchenko is pondering. His son is right. He has to be honest. "It is also about research, about knowledge, about experience. I cannot stay forever in one place or in one body. I have this chance and must use it. I will be back, no later than four years from now."

"And then you *will* take us with you, Marchenko, to wherever you might be traveling."

"I promise."

June 25, 21, Eve

THE NEWS PROGRAM SHOWS THE ELECTED GOVERNMENT SAYING goodbye to the leadership group of the *Majestic Draght*. Eve is proud she recognizes Gronolf among all the other aliens, who initially had all looked the same to her. The image is flickering slightly. The reason is that the new Marchenko modified one of the Grosnop ultrasound projectors for them. The technology is not 100 percent compatible with the human visual system.

The old Marchenko, as they call their father for the sake of simplicity, said his personal goodbye to them yesterday. Now he is somewhere inside the giant black cube which is still orbiting Dual Sun.

"Are you watching TV again?" Adam says as he comes through the door. He is splattered with mud and is only wearing underpants. Eve still cannot acquire a taste for their hosts' hobby of holding mud races, but Adam seems to have a small group of fans in this respect. For reasons of fairness he runs in his own weight class, against those under ten years old. The spectators are thrilled, and two of his races have already been shown on Grosnop television.

Every other evening they meet the other pair of siblings for dinner, sometimes in one house, sometimes in the other— and it is very practical that the buildings are right next to each other. Then Adam is always especially nice to her. Eve suspects this is caused by the fact that the other Adam is also extremely friendly to her. *That's going to be a ton of fun,* she thinks.

"Look, it's about to start," Adam shouts. He has dragged a trail of mud into the living room. He will have to clean that up later. The moving image on the wall shows a small space-ship separating from the *Majestic Draght*.

"That's the government ship, as any kid here knows," Adam says. Eve is not sure what he means by that.

The camera view changes to the engine core of the *Majestic Draght*. Eve has to swallow hard. She has already cried enough, but this seems to be the moment everything has been aiming toward. This time she won't accidentally rediscover her Marchenko. If everything works out he will return in many months. Four years, he told them. He will have changed by then, and she won't be the same either. She hopes those will be good changes. They saw with Marchenko 2 that humans, as well as AIs that used to be humans, can develop negatively.

It is strange. If she thinks of Marchenko, she always thinks of a human being, not of a machine or an AI. Until now he always has proven her right. No matter what happens, if that stays the same, she won't have to worry.

"Goodbye, Marchenko," she says out loud.

"Goodbye," Adam repeats, and Eve sees a tear running down his cheek.

Author's Note

Welcome back to reality! I must admit I envy Marchenko a little bit. He now has almost everything he could wish for—a spaceship in which to travel to the stars, and an indefinite amount of time to discover the wonders of the universe. Will he always be happy? I doubt it. I believe there will always be moments when he misses his human body...

There's a difference between experiencing a place through the datastreams of your ship's detectors and with your own body's immediate senses. So, in one possible future for Marchenko—in my imagination, where he lives—he might be tempted to guide the mighty ship toward a small yellow star called the sun. Wouldn't we be surprised if such a large ship landed in Russia, China, or the United States? And especially if frog-like creatures got out of it and tried to negotiate with our governments?

Well, that's pure fiction, but I hope you had fun experiencing these adventures on Proxima b. If you liked the book, you could do me a great favor by describing your experience in an Amazon review. Reader reviews are extremely important—they help me to find new readers. The link is here:

hard-sf.com/links/705419

Thank you so much! In exchange, I promise you a steady

stream of new books. My wife sometimes asks me if I am afraid of running out of ideas. And my answer? "No, I'm not." I always have more ideas than I can use for my books, which makes me really thankful to everyone who encouraged and shaped my imagination.

Yours

Brandon Q. Morris

ALIEN LIFE PLAYS AN IMPORTANT ROLE IN THIS SERIES, SO THIS note is followed by a section entitled *A Guided Tour to Alien Life*.

Register at hard-sf.com/subscribe/ and you will be notified of any new Hard Science Fiction books that I will be publishing. Also, you will get a beautifully illustrated version of the Guided Tour to Alien Life.

Proxima Rising

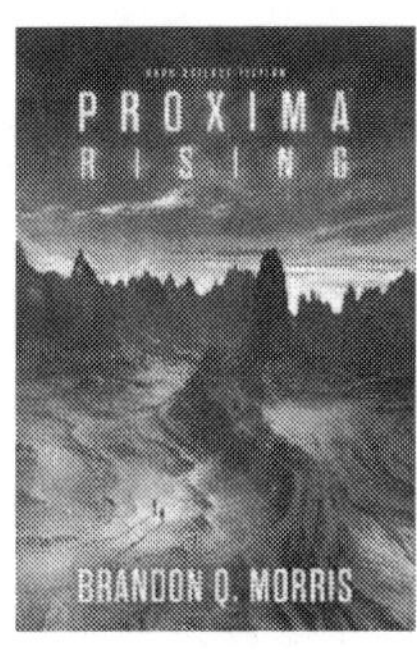

Late in the 21st century, Earth receives what looks like an urgent plea for help from planet Proxima Centauri b in the closest star system to the Sun. Astrophysicists suspect a massive solar flare is about to destroy this heretofore-unknown civilization. Earth's space programs are unequipped to help, but an unscrupulous Russian billionaire launches a secret and highly-specialized spaceship to Proxima b, over four light-years away. The unusual crew faces a Herculean task—should they survive the journey. No one knows what to expect from this alien planet.

3,99 $ hard-sf.com/links/610690

Proxima Dying

An intelligent robot and two young people explore Proxima Centauri b, the planet orbiting our nearest star, Proxima Centauri. Their ideas about the mission quickly prove grossly naive as they venture about on this planet of extremes.

Where are the senders of the call for help that lured them here? They find no one and no traces on the daylight side, so they place their hopes upon an expedition into the eternal ice on Proxima b's dark side. They not only face everlasting night, the team encounters grave dangers. A fateful decision will change the planet forever.

3,99 $ – hard-sf.com/links/652197

Proxima Dreaming

Alone and desperate, Eve sits in the control center of an alien structure. She has lost the other members of the team sent to explore exoplanet Proxima Centauri b. By mistake she has triggered a disastrous process that threatens to obliterate the planet. Just as Eve fears her best option may be a quick death, a nearby alien life form awakens from a very long sleep. It has only one task: to find and neutralize the destructive intruder from a faraway place.

3,99 $ – hard-sf.com/links/705470

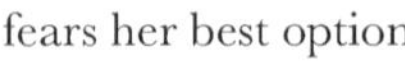

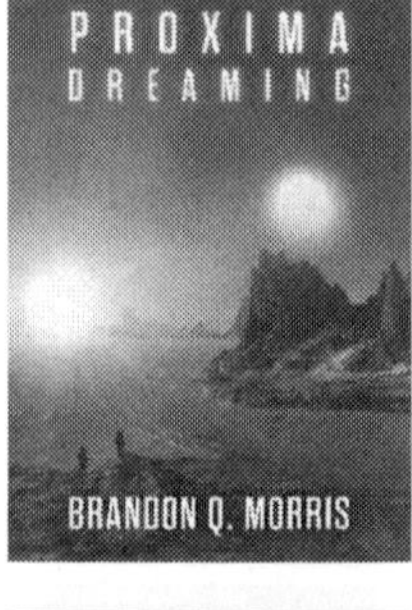

The Hole

A mysterious object threatens to destroy our solar system. The survival of humankind is at risk, but nobody takes the warning of young astrophysicist Maribel Pedreira seriously. At the same time, an exiled crew of outcasts mines for rare minerals on a lone asteroid.

When other scientists finally acknowledge Pedreira's alarming discovery, it becomes clear that these outcasts are the only ones who may be able to save our world, knowing that *The Hole* hurtles inexorably toward the sun.

3,99 $ – hard-sf.com/links/527017

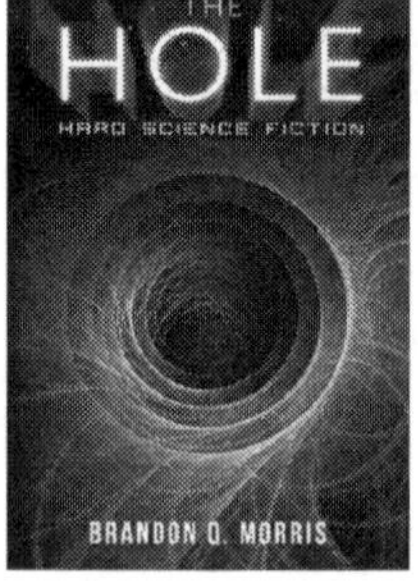

Silent Sun

Is our sun behaving differently from other stars? When an amateur astronomer discovers something strange on telescopic solar pictures, an explanation must be found. Is it merely artefact? Or has he found something totally unexpected?

An expert international crew is hastily assembled, a spaceship is speedily repurposed, and the foursome is sent on the ride of their lives. What challenges will they face on this spur-of-the-moment mission to our central star?

What awaits all of them is critical, not only for understanding the past, but even more so for the future of life on Earth.

3,99 $ – hard-sf.com/links/527020

The Rift

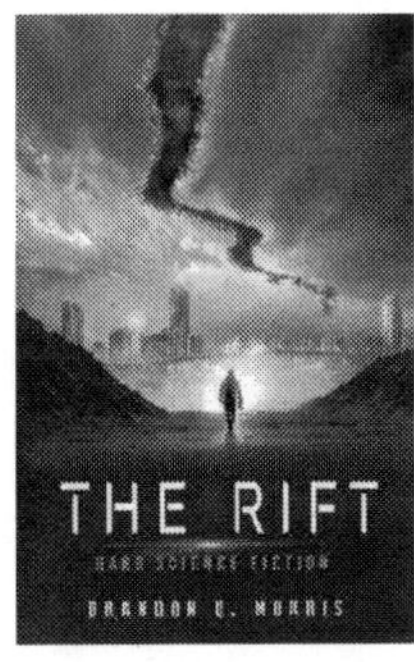

There is a huge, bold black streak in the sky. Branches appear out of nowhere over North America, Southern Europe, and Central Africa. People who live beneath The Rift can see it. But scientists worldwide are distressed – their equipment cannot pick up any type of signal from it.

The rift appears to consist of nothing. Literally. Nothing. Nada. Niente. Most people are curious but not overly concerned. The phenomenon seems to pose no danger. It is just there.

Then something jolts the most hardened naysayers, and surpasses the worst nightmares of the world's greatest scientists – and rocks their understanding of the universe.

3,99 $ – hard-sf.com/links/534368

The Enceladus Mission (Ice Moon 1)

In the year 2031, a robot probe detects traces of biological activity on Enceladus, one of Saturn's moons. This sensational discovery shows that there is indeed evidence of extraterrestrial life. Fifteen years later, a hurriedly built spacecraft sets out on the long journey to the ringed planet and its moon.

The international crew is not just facing a difficult twenty-seven months: if the spacecraft manages to make it to Enceladus without incident it must use a drillship to penetrate the kilometer-thick sheet of ice that entombs the moon. If life does indeed exist on Enceladus, it could only be at the bottom of the salty, ice covered ocean, which formed billions of years ago.

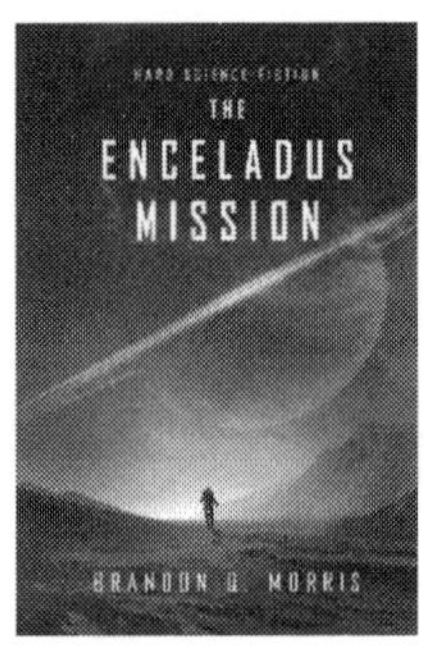

However, shortly after takeoff disaster strikes the mission, and the chances of the crew making it to Enceladus, let alone back home, look grim.

2,99 $ – hard-sf.com/links/526999

The Titan Probe (Ice Moon 2)

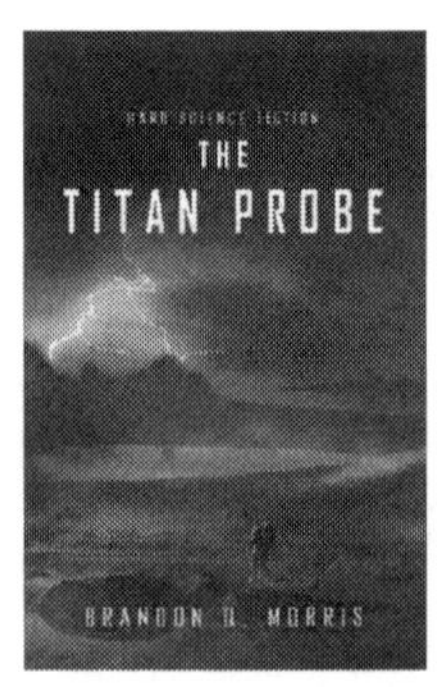

In 2005, the robotic probe "Huygens" lands on Saturn's moon Titan. 40 years later, a radio telescope receives signals from the far away moon that can only come from the long forgotten lander.

At the same time, an expedition returns from neighbouring moon Enceladus. The crew lands on Titan and finds a dangerous secret that risks their return to Earth. Meanwhile, on Enceladus a deathly race has started that nobody thought was possible. And its outcome can only be decided by the astronauts that are stuck on Titan.

3,99 $ – hard-sf.com/links/527000

The Io Encounter (Ice Moon 3)

Jupiter's moon Io has an extremely hostile environment. There are hot lava streams, seas of boiling sulfur, and frequent volcanic eruptions straight from Dante's Inferno, in addition to constant radiation bombardment and a surface temperature hovering at minus 180 degrees Celsius.

Is it really home to a great danger that threatens all of humanity? That's what a surprise message from the life form discovered on Enceladus seems to indicate.

The crew of ILSE, the International Life Search Expedition, finally on their longed-for return to Earth, reluctantly chooses to accept a diversion to Io, only to discover that an enemy from within is about to destroy all their hopes of ever going home.

3,99 $ — hard-sf.com/links/527008

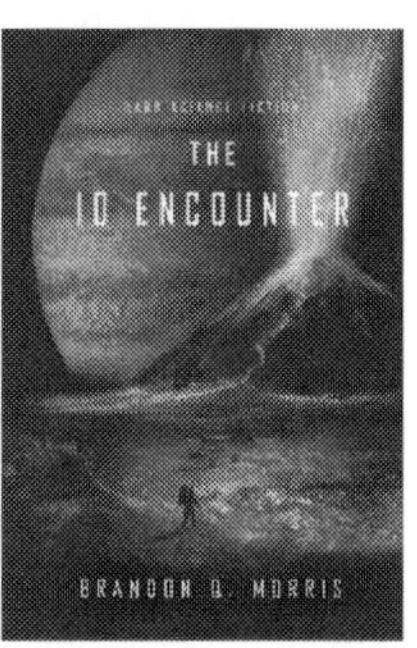

Return to Enceladus (Ice Moon 4)

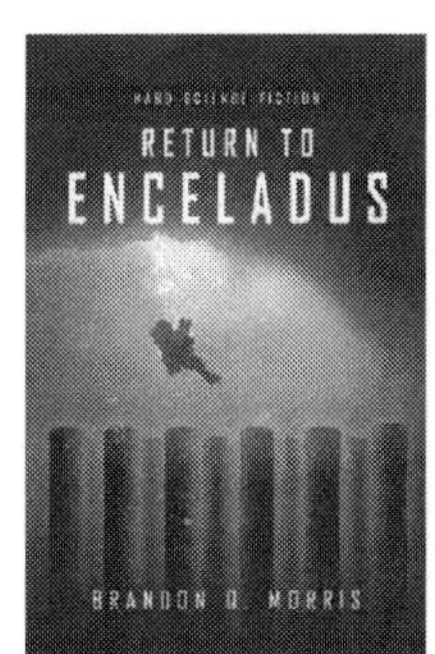

Russian billionaire Nikolai Shostakovitch makes an offer to the former crew of the spaceship ILSE. He will finance a return voyage to the icy moon Enceladus. The offer is too good to refuse — the expedition would give them the unique opportunity to recover the body of their doctor, Dimitri Marchenko.

Everyone on board knows that their benefactor acts out of purely personal motivations… but the true interests of the tycoon and the dangers that he conjures up are beyond anyone's imagination.

3,99 € — hard-sf.com/links/527011

A Guided Tour to Alien Life

Introduction

HOW REALISTIC ARE THE DESCRIPTIONS OF LIFE ON 'SINGLE sun' and 'double sun'? The answer to that question belongs to the field of astrobiology, an interdisciplinary science dealing with the origin, development, and future of life in space.

Astrobiology is still a relatively young science. It used to be called exobiology, but that term excluded an important part of life in the universe—life on Earth! And that was particularly unfortunate, as Earth is the only planet where we know for sure life has developed. Considering the issue of intelligence, there are dissenting opinions, but that is a different topic. Therefore the claim that astrobiology is the only science whose subject still has to be found is incorrect. Of course it is a shortcoming that researchers can only use one specific example to support all of their theories.

Nevertheless, the basic qualities of elements—meaning what we can learn from chemistry and physics—allow for surprising insights that we will cover during our tour.

What actually is Life?

THE SPIDER CRAWLING ACROSS THE WALL NEXT TO MY DESK IS certainly alive. The fine web it spun on the radiator is not. Why is this clear to me immediately, even though the two objects have much in common?

- Both move, the spider by itself, the web due to the warm air rising from the radiator.
- Both will grow and multiply if I don't intervene.
- Both consist mainly of carbon, hydrogen, and oxygen.

These features are obviously not enough to define life. In order to find better criteria, we will have to see who is responsible for what. The cobweb cannot multiply itself. It cannot move independently, either—but that's another story. Accordingly, life could be defined as a self-multiplying system. Yet that is not enough. This feature also applies to some computer programs, or to robots that produce other robots. We will surely encounter these more often in the future. They might even be subject to a form of evolution, as evolutionary algorithms already exist today. Yet those are not examples of life in its proper sense, but systems created by humans. They could not develop from the basic building blocks of the universe through natural evolution.

It could be a helpful differentiation to define life as a self-replicating chemical system. However, there are still examples that don't really fit. Crystals, which are hardly life forms, can produce exact copies of themselves in a saturated solution. This precision copying actually gives us an argument for excluding them from the definition of life. Your children don't resemble you exactly. Living systems don't replicate themselves exactly, they introduce errors—mutations—and these errors lead to evolution, the advancement of some species and the breakdown of others. Life therefore would have to be defined as a self-replicating chemical system subject to evolution.

The important aspect is that this does not refer to the individual. Not every human has offspring, and in some species, only a few individuals propagate—think of the queen bee. Life can therefore only be recognized as a system. If one of the Mars rovers were to find something such as a single solitary Mars bacterium, we could not yet talk about having discovered extraterrestrial life.

How does one recognize Life?

Based on this definition, there are specific features life should possess. Here is the list:

- Energy exchange and metabolism
- Organization and self-regulation
- Reaction to stimuli
- Reproduction
- Heredity
- Growth

If you are on a foreign planet and find something unknown, you can test it for these six characteristics. Yet even if the subject has all six, it is not necessarily alive. And if it fails in one category, it might nevertheless be a part of life. You definitely need a second specimen. Just for fun, you might test living and inanimate objects this way next time you take a walk in the woods with your family.

Chemical Foundations

AFTER THE UNIVERSE WAS BORN IN THE BIG BANG, IT MOSTLY consisted of hydrogen and helium atoms. Helium is a non-reactive noble gas, and hydrogen forms one molecule at most. That is not enough for the development of multifaceted life. Luckily, the first stars developed at some point. They first bred heavier elements in their cores through nuclear fusion, among them oxygen, carbon, and silicon.

Which of these elements are necessary for life? If we look at Earth, carbon, water—a combination of hydrogen and oxygen—and oxygen seem to be most important. However, this does not have to hold true for the entire universe.

Generally, it seems to help the variety of life if the basic elements create numerous different compounds. Do you still remember the periodic table? In the middle, in the fourth main group, you find elements that are most flexible in chemical compounds because they have up to four free bonding sites. Carbon and silicon are relatively common, at least on rocky planets. Next to oxygen, silicon dominates the crust. Both carbon and silicon can form long-chained molecules typical for life.

Nevertheless, the development of life based upon silicon seems rather unlikely. Silicon is strongly attracted by oxygen. While carbon can be easily transferred into other compounds by plants through photosynthesis from carbon dioxide, such a process is almost impossible for silicon. In addition, silicon dioxide is solid—the rocky crust consists of it—so it would be hard to 'breathe' it. Carbon really makes it easier for life in so many ways.

However, this only applies to Earth-like conditions. At high heat and pressure, conditions change. On a planet that is very close to its sun, gaseous silicon dioxide might exist in the atmosphere. There the various reactions involving silicon could occur much faster than on the much-colder planet we call Earth.

What about the other elements? Compared to the main group, they form fewer bonds than carbon or silicon. Metals like sodium or potassium prefer ionic bonds, which are weaker than covalent bonds. Thus, in a solvent, a lifeform would disintegrate into its components.

Speaking of solvents: The fact that life on Earth came from the sea is much more than an accident. In the liquid phase, the participants in a reaction have much better opportunities to connect in a variety of ways, and there are also more potential partners. In a gas, the partners are also very flexible, but they must all be gaseous. In a solid, the mobility of the partners is severely limited.

On Earth, therefore, water serves as a solvent for life. We still mostly consist of water! But are other solvents imaginable? Unfortunately it would be hard to find a suitable substitute. Water has some enormous advantages. Think of the water anomaly you heard about in school. Water is one of the very few substances that expands when it freezes. This provides the advantage that lakes and oceans always freeze from the top, as ice is lighter than liquid water. Otherwise oceans would gradually freeze from the bottom up and there might only be a thin layer of liquid water on top during the summer.

In addition, there is the high heat absorbency and high evaporation temperature of water, which is good for sustaining a moderate climate. And consider the wide temperature range across which it stays liquid, the good dissolving power, and the high availability in the universe. Water's high density also plays a role: It forces other molecules to shield themselves against the outside world. That is likely why the first cell walls came into being.

Theoretically, of course, there are alternatives. Hydrogen fluoride—HF, known as hydrofluoric acid in a solution with water—resembles water in many aspects. Unfortunately, the element fluorine is rather rare in the universe. Compounds like methane and ammonia are much more common. While they are useless as solvents on Earth, that might not be the case under different conditions. Titan, a moon of Saturn, for instance, has a pronounced methane cycle that is remarkably similar to the water cycle on Earth—though at much lower temperatures.

Trappist-1: When Planets have too much Water

Trappist-1 is a red dwarf about 40 light-years from the sun. While it is hardly larger than Jupiter, it is orbited by seven planets, as researchers discovered in 2017. All seven are Earth-like planets.

They share one peculiarity, though—they are all surprisingly light. Their density is lower than that of rock. Therefore they must be partially made of a different material. Now a team of scientists has described the details in the journal *Nature Astronomy*. Normally, one would assume the lighter component to be atmospheric gas. However, the seven planets are too light to keep such a dense atmosphere. Therefore another substance must be available in great quantities —water.

But, how much water? Researchers have now calculated this. According to their finding, about 15 percent of the total mass of inner planets b and c is water—for comparison, on

Earth it is only 0.02 percent. So, 15 percent is a lot—750 times greater than on Earth. Half— meaning about 50 percent—of outer planets f and g must be water, though, an equivalent amount to hundreds of Earth oceans.

A large part of the water is most likely ice rather than occurring in liquid form. Considering the high pressures in the interior of a planet, that is not unusual. What is amazing is that these planets are located inside the ice line—aka snow line or frost line—of their system. Inside the ice line of a protostar, water is gaseous, and outside of the line it is solid. Ice worlds like Neptune and Uranus can thus only have formed outside of the ice line. This also applies to the planets of Trappist-1. During their history, they must have slipped closer to their star—by at least half of their initial distance.

What does this mean for the development of life? The planets of Trappist-1 might simply have too much water. On Earth, life developed in the boundary regions between rock and water. Only there were all the necessary preconditions met. A purely water world is therefore hardly suitable for developing Earth-like life. This might be bad news for all red dwarfs of the M class, the most common type of star in the Milky Way. The planets circling them might, in general, suffer from an oversupply of water.

Energy!

Life is an incredible phenomenon, from a physical perspective, as it at least temporarily reverses the most important trend during the development of the universe: It creates order from disorder. In fact, the cosmos has been moving the other way ever since the Big Bang. Entropy, the measure of disorder, is constantly increasing. With life, though, the degree of order is increased through evolution. This can't happen without a very important ingredient: energy! It must be available energy, which exists wherever there is an imbalance.

That is, for instance, the case near a star. On the one side we have the star, which produces energy, and on the other its planets, which receive this energy in the form of light. Life must find a way to use and store the energy of light. Plants do this through photosynthesis, but other methods are imaginable. Animals can then use the energy stored in plants for their metabolism.

The energy received from the star also has another advantageous side effect: It allows the planet to heat its atmosphere so much that the solvent on its surface—mostly water— occurs in liquid form. The definition of a habitable zone around a star applies to this very fact.

This does not mean that a planet outside the habitable zone must by definition be uninhabitable. The worst factor would be too much energy. If it gets too hot, because the planet is too close to its star, it will sooner or later lose its atmosphere. Perhaps silicon-based life might stand a chance at high temperatures, but that is mere speculation. If it is too cold, other energy sources might play a role. Life does not necessarily have to be located on the surface. Conditions might be more favorable in the mantle or core of a planet. Biologists are surprised at the depths on Earth where we can discover traces of biological life. This might also apply to Mars, on whose surface conditions have been inconducive for life for three billion years.

Origin and Birth

SINCE ITS BIRTH 13.8 BILLION YEARS AGO, THE UNIVERSE HAD to change significantly to become today's haven for life. Rocky planets like Earth could not have formed around the first stars, because the heavy elements of which they consist did not yet exist. The first star generations had to produce these elements in their interiors and then fling them into space when they died in supernova explosions, which also simultaneously created elements heavier than iron. All of us consist of atoms created during the deaths of these stars.

Scientists are often amazed at how all of this worked. If only a single physical parameter had been different, we would not exist today. The simplest explanation for this is: We could not describe a universe in which the parameters are not suitable for the development of life, because then we would not exist. This is called the 'anthropic principle.' There is another formulation for this, which is much stronger: It demands that the development of life must be possible in all universes. One argument for this comes from quantum physics, stating that reality only comes into being through an observer.

Yet it is basically pointless to think about these issues. The only verifiable—and verified—fact is that in our universe the probability for the development of life must be greater than zero.

How high is this probability, though? Many people have wondered about this. There is the famous Drake equation, which calculates the number of galactic civilizations willing to communicate. However, it contains so many unknown factors that the result varies between one and four million, based on the specific interpretation. This tells us little about our chance of finding extraterrestrial life, because the Drake equation focuses on civilizations, on intelligent life. On Earth alone there are about 50 billion species, and only one of them developed higher intelligence.

Which stars should you concentrate on while looking for life? Over the last few years, many firm beliefs dissolved into nothing while discussing this. Currently we assume that on average there is one planet per star. Quite a few of these planets have the correct size and are at a suitable distance in relation to their star. In the Milky Way, which has up to 300 billion stars, our current estimate assumes about 40 billion rocky planets of Earth size in the habitable zone of their respective stars. Of these, 11 billion orbit sun-like stars. And the Milky Way is only one of the billions of galaxies in the universe.

Some stars have characteristics that make them appear less suitable at first sight. For red dwarfs—like Proxima Centauri in our story—the habitable zone is so close to the star that the planet is tidally locked, always pointing the same side toward the star. Yet life might have developed in the transition zones. These zones would also be shielded by the planet against frequent flares of the red dwarf, or a well-dimensioned magnetic field might protect against them.

The Birth of Life

Let's assume we found one of the 40 billion rocky planets in the Milky Way. Let's further assume there is water on the surface that was deposited there by comet impacts. The planet has a proto-atmosphere. What next?

Today, scientists don't know for sure. The most important

relevant experiment was performed in 1952 by Stanley Miller and Harold Urey at the University of Chicago. They mixed simple chemical substances in a hypothetical early Earth atmosphere—water, methane, ammonia, hydrogen, and carbon monoxide, but no oxygen—and exposed this mixture to electrical discharges modeling the energy supplied by lightning strikes. The result: After a while, organic molecules formed in the experiment.

Back then, the Miller-Urey experiment caused quite a stir, because it showed that the building blocks necessary for life can spontaneously develop under the right conditions. However, it did not solve the question about the development of life. Geologists later showed that early Earth exhibited slightly different conditions than the experiment presupposed. In addition, the experiment resulted in amino acids, but not in carbohydrates, another important building block of life. Those must have formed in a second phase. The same holds true for lipids, i.e. fatty acids.

By now, chemists have found indirect ways in which these components might have formed from the original chemicals. What is missing is the scenario that unites them all. Very often the conditions under which one biological building block is supposed to have developed are different from those for others. For practical purposes we must assume that all of this happened simultaneously four billion years ago at a specific location on Earth. Perhaps it did not occur in the atmosphere, but in a volcanic vent in the ocean, or deep inside the Earth's crust.

How the actual spark of life came into the world is still a hotly-debated research subject. There are basically two opposing theories. The first assumes it all started with the metabolism, the energy cycle. This might have occurred in volcanic areas of the ocean, either based on iron and sulfur, or on zinc. At first there would have only been a primitive metabolism. Hereditary transmission via RNA molecules—a primitive precursor of DNA—would have been added later.

The second theory proposes that life started when RNA

molecules came into being by accident within encapsulated proto-cells. We know that some variants of RNA both encode information and serve as a catalyst for certain reactions. Just the sudden appearance of the RNA molecule could have boosted the metabolism of the proto-cell, giving it an advantage over other cells.

There are also discussions on whether RNA might have been preceded by even more primitive code molecules such as PNA, TNA, or GNA. Back then, the conditions for the development of life might have been better on Mars than on Earth —meteorites could have afterward transported those early forms of life to Earth.

If you check the Wikipedia entry for 'Abiogenesis' you will find more than a dozen more theories about how life might have come into existence. For biologists, only one of them can be correct. Which one it is will be decided based on the exact conditions on Earth four billion years ago, a subject which is still being researched.

From the perspective of astrobiology, all of these theories might be correct—if the conditions on any of the exoplanets fit any specific theory. Life does not have to develop the same way everywhere. Earth is one example of it, nothing more and nothing less.

On Earth the results at some point in time became LUCA, the Last Universal Cellular Ancestor. This is proven by the DNA analysis of current life. LUCA, the archetype of all current species, from bacteria to humans, lived about 3.5 billion years ago. At that time it probably was not the only form of life—but the descendants of all others living back then have become extinct. LUCA was already a rather biologically complex single-cell organism. It certainly was already the product of evolution. The organism stored genetic information in RNA and used ribosomes as protein factories. LUCA must have existed before Earth's atmosphere was enriched with oxygen. This is an interesting piece of information for astrobiology—even a planet without oxygen in its atmosphere can harbor life.

The Classification of Life

Life on Earth seems to have divided early on into three sections—called domains—namely bacteria, archaea, and eukaryota. You know bacteria as pathogens. You yourself are a eukaryote—like any other multi-cellular being. Recent research even suggests there are only two domains. Bacteria would then have branched off from archaea.

Archaea are very fascinating from an astrobiological viewpoint, because among the still-living species there are many extremophiles, which thrive under particularly difficult conditions which might mimic those on alien worlds. There are organisms that grow at temperatures higher than 80° C, others living in highly concentrated saline solutions, under high pressure, or in very acidic or alkaline surroundings. Even methane-generating archaea are extreme in a certain way: They only grow without oxygen and often need molecular hydrogen for their metabolism.

Archaea species are relatively common and occur in fresh water, the ocean, and the soil, but also in the intestinal tracts of animals and humans. Archaea have even been found in the folds of the human belly button.

The greatest change of life on Earth occurred with photosynthesis. It probably developed first among bacteria and archaea. This is not always connected with the production of oxygen. Sulfur bacteria create the carbohydrates they need for their metabolism from carbon dioxide by creating elementary sulfur from sulfur compounds. Others use hydrogen or small organic molecules. We are lucky these species did not succeed worldwide, otherwise the atmosphere of today's Earth would be unbreathable for us. Instead, organisms thrived that convert the oxygen atom in water into molecular oxygen, in order to produce carbohydrates. Plants later inherited this system from cyanobacteria.

When our planet was not even two billion years old, its surface was like a paradise. A billion years after the development of Earth, temperatures finally dropped below 100 degrees. Due to this cooling, the water vapor in the atmosphere condensed to huge oceans, in whose pleasant warmth first organic molecules and then the first forms of life appeared. Approximately 3.2 billion years ago the oceans must have been filled with flourishing communities of primeval bacteria, a veritable paradise.

Then environmental villains showed up.

Blue-green algae—today they are correctly called cyanobacteria, because they lack the true nuclei which real algae possess—started to produce masses of a deadly poison: dioxygen. They used the energy of sunlight to turn carbon dioxide, which was plentiful, into this dangerous substance. Their competitors, all of them anaerobic bacteria, had not yet formed a defensive system that could have stopped this environmental destruction.

At first everything seemed to be fine. There were sufficient dissolved metal ions in the oceans to render the produced oxygen harmless, and active volcanoes constantly provided enough reaction mass. The ore formations that came into being then are now our most important sources of iron worldwide. Earth settled down, and the cyanobacteria developed further. The first multicellular organisms appeared—and that must have been the moment when the great oxygen disaster started. About 2.3 to 2.4 billion years ago the percentage of this gas in the atmosphere, which was lethal to most forms of life then, rose so much that most species were doomed. Inside these organisms, oxygen created very reactive peroxides, which damaged the cells.

At the same time the growing oxygen content caused a global climate catastrophe. The protective greenhouse gas methane reacted with O_2 and became carbon dioxide—which has a much lower impact on the climate—and water. Earth, scientists believe, must have been completely covered with ice for 300 to 400 million years.

The reactive gas also accelerated the weathering of the surface. New compounds and minerals were created—and that is the fact used by an international team of researchers publishing in the scholarly journal *Nature* to date this catastrophe. The scientists examined deposits of chromium compounds in rocks in South Africa, which must have formed about 2.98 billion years ago.

These already turned out to be extremely weathered, meaning they were influenced by processes that could have only happened in the presence of significant percentages of oxygen. Researchers calculated that at that time the dioxygen percentage in Earth's atmosphere was about three ten-thousandths of today's value. Although that seems a very small amount, it is significantly more than had been assumed for this point in time. This fact indicates that blue-green algae must have been very common three billion years ago—and therefore photosynthesis as an efficient means of gaining energy.

We can still feel the effects all over the world today:

- A large percent of anaerobic organisms populating Earth at that time was eliminated.
- The oxidation of atmospheric methane to carbon dioxide caused an ice age covering the entire planet and lasting 300 million years.
- The variety of minerals occurring on Earth nearly doubled.
- Life received a new chance through the increased

oxygen content. The energy cycle became easier, as with many substances the oxidation with oxygen releases much more energy than a metabolism without oxidation. This was ultimately a trigger that helped multicellular organisms succeed.

A different Life?

THE SEARCH FOR EXTRATERRESTRIAL LIFE DOES NOT JUST fascinate astronomers, but also philosophers, movie directors, authors—and most other people. In previous times, influenced by religion, the fear of losing our exclusive position in the universe influenced this search. Today, enlightened from a historical perspective, we seem to want a kind of big brother, a wise civilization like the Vulcans in the Star Trek universe, who would have solved our problems long ago by helping with their advanced technology.

An alternative is the overwhelming menace from space, which makes us forget our differences and work together, saving us at least politically and religiously this way. However, if we are realistic, unlike in Hollywood movies, mankind would have as little chance against attackers who are 200 years more advanced as Native Americans had against European settlers 200 years ago. And a technological difference of 200 years is probably not even enough to give a civilization interstellar travel.

So much for the dreams of Hollywood and science fiction. The reality in searching for extraterrestrial life looks quite different. We have not even solved the question of how we would recognize alien life. The molecular biologist Gerald Joyce has published an interesting paper about this, which can be found in the open-access journal *PLOS Biology*. The preconditions for the work of exobiologists seem to be very good: We already know of about 1,000 exoplanets. We know that a number of them are orbiting their stars in areas that we consider suitable for the development of life. Astronomers have calculated that within a radius of 1,000 light-years around Earth there should be tens of thousands of sister planets offering conditions similar to our world. We estimate that within ten years we should have atmospheric data about some of these planets.

Nevertheless, it is hard for us to identify alien life. One reason, of course, is our lack of experience—we only have one biological life form for comparison. Therefore we are inclined to assume that life is based on cells in which genetic information is translated into proteins. Accordingly, we define that life reproduces itself, passes information from generation to generation, and is subject to Darwinian evolution. Yet what would happen if a life form does not fulfill these prerequisites? What if, for instance, it was a complex chemical system that does not use heredity?

Gerald Joyce suggests a different perspective, which analyzes the information content of a system. In that sense, biological systems have a kind of molecular memory, their genotype, that is maintained by self-reproduction and is affected by experience and environment. The information content of this memory can be calculated from the number of possible combinations, minus the number of actually realized combinations, or 'phenotypes.' A fictive molecule that self-replicates and also uses substances in its environment to create copies of itself would have information content of 0 according to this calculation. Every possible combination—one—has also been realized. Conclusion: Not life. According to this view, life could develop in different ways: directly from chemistry, for instance, after a sufficient molecular complexity was reached to form an information memory. Life could also develop from earlier forms of life, without taking information from them. That is probably what happened on Earth: The earlier RNA-based forms cleared the path for DNA-based life.

In his paper, Joyce develops a complex method to determine the information content of potential life forms. At the same time, the method also provides clues where it might be worth searching for life. In order to develop a permanent memory, certain prerequisites concerning the potential information density must be fulfilled. Joyce calculates, for example, that in a small pond, even under ideal conditions, 27 kilograms of RNA would have to aggregate chemically in order that there is a high probability of life developing. The first real alternative to life as we know it, Joyce thinks, might not therefore, be found on Mars or on Saturn's moon Titan, but rather in labs on Earth.

Finding Aliens faster

If ET doesn't come from Mars, but from a faraway solar system, he might not even notice Earth is an inhabited planet. From several thousand light-years away our home planet can't be seen. This rock is so small compared to Jupiter or Saturn that it does not visibly affect the movement of the sun. The radio waves our civilization sends into space are useless as a cosmic beacon, as we only started building the first radios a few generations ago. And mankind has not yet succeeded in destroying our whole planet in an explosion.

Of course these restrictions also work the other way, when we ourselves start searching for alien life forms. How should we recognize them from a great distance? There is one substance that astronomers consider a typical, though not conclusive, sign of life—and we have been voluntarily releasing more of it into the atmosphere for several centuries: Methane, which under Earth-like conditions is a gas, can have a biological origin.

In order to find out which substances are in a planet's atmosphere, we need a spectrum of the light that is emitted or reflected by it. Back in school we learned how spectra are created: an excited electron moves to a lower energy level and emits a photon. Its color—or its wavelength and energy—depends on the energy difference of the two levels the electron is switching between.

Reality is basically like this lesson from school, but a bit more complicated. While methane only consists of one carbon and four hydrogen atoms, and is highly symmetrical, even this modest multi-body system causes considerable difficulties for scientists. So even at room temperature the spectrum of methane has not yet been completely characterized. However, if temperatures rise, for example to the level on a brown dwarf, millions of different transitions become possible. The current knowledge about the methane spectrum in various sectors is fragmentary, partially calculated from the structure of the molecules, partially determined semi-empirically, and partially measured in experiments.

In a paper in *Proceedings of the National Academy of Sciences,* a British team presents new spectral lines for methane with much higher resolution. Their experiments were conducted in a temperature range up to 1500 degrees Kelvin—with 9.8 billion transitions. For the same range, previous experiments had suggested only 340,000 transitions. For this project the researchers simulated the methane molecule in the COSMOS supercomputer. They also prove that the newly-calculated spectra correspond to reality. This shows that through our lack of knowledge the methane content of celestial bodies seems to have been systematically underestimated. This is not only relevant for searching out possible aliens, but also for our understanding of the structure and evolution of these bodies.

How do We Distinguish Inhabited Planets from Uninhabited Ones?

It was not long ago that the idea of identifying planets orbiting other suns was considered pure science fiction. But now, astronomers find hundreds of new planets every year. At the same time, they collect incredibly meticulous information about these alien worlds, analyze their surface temperatures, and try to determine the consistency of the surfaces. Just 50 years ago we knew less about Saturn's moon Titan than we know today about some exoplanets.

Of course scientists are most interested in whether a world is habitable. They don't shy away from a purely-human perspective, as we don't have another one, and they search for life as we know it. At least this has the advantage that the necessary conditions are well-researched.

Which of the exoplanets fulfill these conditions? This is determined by a kind of exclusion system. Based on the fact that water should exist in liquid form, the heat emitted by the mother star determines a maximum and a minimum distance for the planetary orbit. Yet that is not enough. Some stellar types, for example, emit above-average amounts of dangerous radiation, so that a planet in the habitable zone might become uninhabitable.

Previously, the fact that water vapor existed in the upper air layers—the stratosphere—was seen as a sure sign that the planet was no longer habitable. If a planet and its sun were in the right position, astronomers on Earth could receive the light of the star after it had passed through the planetary atmosphere. When the spectrum contained indications of water vapor, it was assumed that the ground was hotter than 66 degrees, and that the planet was an uninhabitable 'moist greenhouse.'

However, a new atmospheric model by NASA researchers shows this might not always be the case. Under certain conditions, such as in the case of a tidally locked planet, which always faces the same side toward its sun, clouds can form and function as an umbrella. What happens depends on the energy emission of the star in the near-infrared, and thus the type of star. Red dwarfs in particular emit a lot of their energy in near-infrared. Water vapor absorbs this infrared radiation very well. Researchers' calculations show that the planet should have a climate somewhat warmer than the tropics on Earth. Because most stars around which we have found planets are red dwarfs, NASA emphasizes that this significantly increases our chances during the search for life.

With Darwin into Space: How Alien Life Develops

The Milky Way contains about 100 billion planets. Between 20 and 40 percent of these orbit in the habitable zone of their stars. If only one-thousandth of one percent of these celestial bodies develops life, which is a very conservative estimate, there would still be 200,000 inhabited planets, or one planet in each cubic region of space with an edge length of 230 light-years.

What might this alien life look like? Researchers and science fiction authors love to speculate. Here's the problem: We only have one example, life on Earth, so we tend to use it as a measuring stick. Even the concept of a habitable zone is based on it. But who could say whether silicon-based life forms might not find a very different environment optimal? On Earth, an eye-like visual organ has developed independently more than 40 times—therefore astrobiologists assume that aliens also would have eyes.

A research team who published an article in the *International Journal of Astrobiology* considers this a mechanistic perspective. It is not necessarily wrong to make such assumptions, but this approach is severely limited by the fact that, so far, we only know one form of life. Therefore the authors suggest to also use theory-based predictions. There is one theory that has worked very well in explaining the wide variety of life on Earth—the theory of natural selection.

This is a fundamental element of Darwin's theory of evolution. As this is a theory verified multiple times, it should also apply on other planets, just as quantum physics is universally valid. So if we find life somewhere in space, it will owe its shape to natural selection, unless it is so primitive that it creates an exact copy during each reproduction.

But in all other cases the theory of evolution will apply. Over time it causes a rise in the complexity of life. This is particularly true when there was a major transition. A complex organism can only develop from individual, independent cells, if these cells exist without conflict, but dependent on each other, without being able to reproduce individually. The cells in your hand, for example, are dependent on the cells in your foot, and they are not in conflict. Quite the opposite, as they can only reproduce and pass on their genes communally. Nature has to offer certain conditions before such a state can be reached. This is also something that would apply to life in space. Major transitions, for instance, are provoked when certain resources, such as food and land, become scarce.

What do researches deduce from this as regards alien life forms? Three points:

•They will be individuals consisting of smaller units. There might still be variants of the sub-units living individually in the wild.

•There must be something to balance the interests of these sub-units so that they work for the common good.

•Some process must limit the growth of the population so that different interests can adapt to each other.

Good Living Conditions on Enceladus, the Moon of Saturn

Carboxydothermus hydrogenoformans is a bacterium, or more precisely the endospore of a bacterium that helps it survive bad times. For carboxydothermus hydrogenoformans, 'bad times' mean disgusting fresh air that contains not a bit of carbon monoxide, which is poisonous for humans, as well as what it considers icy temperatures, anything below 100 degrees Celsius. This bacterium grows and flourishes in hot springs on the Russian volcanic island Kunashir, where it was discovered in 1991. Carboxydothermus hydrogenoformans was never bothered by the fact that the conditions there seemed, at first sight, to be hostile to life—and it is a very fast-growing species of bacteria.

It secures its survival—which it seems to have been doing for millions, if not billions of years—with the aid of a process which is now very rarely used by lifeforms on Earth: Carboxydothermus hydrogenoformans gains energy from carbon monoxide (CO), which during the same process turns carbon monoxide into carbon dioxide (CO_2), as the organism breathes water (H_2O) and molecular hydrogen (H_2) is created. On Earth that is a narrow niche, as there is plenty of water but little carbon monoxide. This was not always the case, though. In the early period of our planet, life had to make do without oxygen. Back then there were more ways to secure one's daily bread, whether with the help of ammonia (bacterium Planctomycetes), or of sulfur (Thiobacillus denitrificans) or even iron (like Acidithiobacillus ferrooxidans). All these microorganisms still live on Earth, even though they probably feel discriminated against by us oxygen breathers.

On other worlds, we might be the aliens, because we don't yet know any other planet with an oxygen atmosphere. But what about the living conditions of these species leading a niche existence on Earth? Carboxydothermus hydrogenoformans might do quite well on the Saturn moon Enceladus, as scientists proved in a recent paper published in *Science*. The decisive clues come—once again—from the Cassini probe, which crashed into Saturn on September 15, 2017.

Cassini recorded the data a while ago, during its last close fly-by in 2015. At that time the probe flew as low as 49 kilometers over the so-called Tiger Stripes, through which gas from the ocean below the ice crust vents into space. The INMS, or Ion and Neutral Mass Spectrometer, measured the composition of the gas clouds. This is the exciting part: It recorded up to 1.4 percent molecular hydrogen H_2, which is exhaled by Carboxydothermus hydrogenoformans. Incidentally, there was also 0.8 percent CO_2, which is not quite as telling.

Of course this does not mean that there have to be life forms exhaling hydrogen in the Enceladus ocean. Perhaps the opposite is true: If there were bacteria like Cupriavidus metallidurans, which breathe hydrogen into water, then less hydrogen should escape. Researchers have wondered, though, where the H_2 comes from—and they exclude geological deposits. The hydrogen could not have been stored in the ice, for example. It seems clear that it must be generated at the bottom of the Enceladus ocean, in processes that provide enough energy to enable the existence of life. Energy is a decisive prerequisite for the development of life—if it is available, life will somehow find a way, as the exploration of hostile environments on Earth proves again and again.

Alien Watch: Which Alien Civilizations can See Us?

To discover exoplanets, astronomers generally use one of two methods: the radial velocity method or the transit method. When considering the rotation of the Earth around the sun, one often imagines as if the sun were stationary, pulling the Earth around it on a string, so to speak. This image is incorrect. In reality, both Earth and Sun, planet and star, move around a common center of gravity. So the star in the telescope also turns in circles, though small ones, when it is influenced by its planet. We cannot see this circular motion from the Earth. But we can see that the star observed in the telescope moves back and forth, away from us and toward us.

The speed with which this happens is called the 'radial velocity.' Via the Doppler effect, this slightly shifts the star's spectral lines. We can measure this shift with special instruments and then calculate how heavy the planet or planets pulling on this star must be—that is the so-called radial velocity method. If this technique alone is used, though, it yields a lower value for the planetary mass.

In order to calculate the exact mass, and thus the density, the planet would also have to be detected by the transit method. The transit method presupposes that the course of the planet moves directly across the axis between the Earth and the planet's star. This reduces the brightness of the star at specific intervals, which can be measured by telescopes.

If an alien civilization wanted to discover Earth as a terrestrial planet, it would need both of these methods to gain all necessary information. This means that, as viewed from the alien home world, Earth and the sun would have to be on one plane, as otherwise the Earth would not move in front of the sun and obscure it.

In an exciting research project, astronomers from such institutions as the Max Planck Institute for Extraterrestrial Physics in Garching, Germany, determined which alien worlds would fulfill this condition. Only a fraction of them do. In general, terrestrial worlds such as Mercury, Venus, Earth, and Mars are easier to discover than gas giants, in spite of their small size, since the closer a planet orbits to its star, the more frequently it obscures the sun. In addition, there is no place in space from which more than three planets of our solar system can be detected via the transit method. The average chance of finding at least one of the planets is 1 in 40, for 2 planets only 1 in 400 and for 3 planets just 1 in 4,000. Among the more than 3,600 known exoplanets there are 68 from which at least one of the planets in the solar system could be discovered. Nine of these planets have a direct view of Earth, but not one of the nine is in a habitable zone. Scientists estimate there might be ten as-yet-undiscovered worlds in space for which both are true: they could detect Earth, and they orbit in a habitable zone. That is not very many—and perhaps this is the reason we've never received a call from ET?

What is going to be the last life form on Earth?

People say cockroaches could survive any catastrophe. Yet, if a supernova in our vicinity bathed Earth with gamma rays, it would mean the end of virtually all lifeforms, including the local cockroach population. There would still be survivors, though, as astrobiologists described in a paper in *Scientific Reports*. They are less than one millimeter long and belong to the genus water bears, or tardigrades.

Tardigrades can live almost anywhere, both on land and in water. Biologists have known for a while that they can survive even in extreme situations. They make it through droughts, cold snaps, strong fluctuations in salinity, and lack of oxygen using clever strategies. In 2007 the ESA put some of these animals aboard the satellite Foton-M3 where they were exposed to vacuum, cold, and cosmic radiation—and they still survived. Temperatures down to -273 degrees Celsius and dehydration cannot kill them.

These are good preconditions for becoming the ultimate survivors on Earth. Researchers showed that neither a supernova nor a giant asteroid strike would extinguish the tardigrades. Only a dying sun, which in its red giant stage would enshroud Earth and its atmosphere, would completely sterilize our planet.

This shows, as scientists say, that life might be hard to extinguish once it develops, both here and elsewhere. That is a good sign for our efforts at finding life on Mars or in the oceans of icy moons.

Hin: Register at hard-sf.com/subscribe/ and you will be notified of any new Hard Science Fiction books that I will be publishing. Also, you will get a beautifully illustrated version of the Guided Tour to Alien Life.

Glossary of Acronyms

AI – Artificial Intelligence
COSMOS – Cluster Of Systems of Metadata for Official Statistics
DNA – DeoxyriboNucleic Acid
EEG – ElectroEncephaloGram
ESA – European Space Agency
ET – ExtraTerrestrial
GNA – Glycol Nucleic Acid
INMS – Ion and Neutral Mass Spectrometer
LUCA – Last Universal Cellular Ancestor
NASA – National Aeronautics and Space Administration
PLOS – Public Library Of Science
PNA – Peptide Nucleic Acid
RNA – RiboNucleic Acid
TNA – Threose Nucleic Acid

Metric to English Conversions

IT IS ASSUMED THAT BY THE TIME THE EVENTS OF THIS NOVEL take place, the United States will have joined the rest of the world and will be using the International System of Units, the modern form of the metric system.

Length:
centimeter = 0.39 inches
meter = 1.09 yards, or 3.28 feet
kilometer = 1093.61 yards, or 0.62 miles

Area:
square centimeter = 0.16 square inches
square meter = 1.20 square yards
square kilometer = 0.39 square miles

Weight:
gram = 0.04 ounces
kilogram = 35.27 ounces, or 2.20 pounds

Volume:
liter = 1.06 quarts, or 0.26 gallons
cubic meter = 35.31 cubic feet, or 1.31 cubic yards

Temperature:
To convert Celsius to Fahrenheit, multiply by 1.8 and then add 32
To convert Kelvin to Celsius, subtract 273.15

Brandon Q. Morris

--

www.hard-sf.com
brandon@hard-sf.com
Translator: Frank Dietz, Ph.D.
Editing: Marcia Kwiecinski, A.A.S., and Stephen Kwiecinski, B.S.

-- --

Dr. Ludwig Hellmann
Cover design: BJ Coverbookdesigns.com

Made in United States
Troutdale, OR
04/10/2025